THE GIRL CLOAKED IN SHADOW

THE CHRONICLES OF MAGGIE TRENT, BOOK THREE

MEGAN O'RUSSELL

Ink Worlds Press

For the ones out there who are still fighting for their dreams—you are stronger than the worst shadows.

I believe in you.

THE GIRL CLOAKED IN SHADOW

CHAPTER 1

The sun peered in through Maggie's window, casting light across her bed. Dust motes swirled through the air, caught in the breeze off the Endless Sea. The rhythmic splashing of the waves tried to lull her to sleep, but she kept her eyes open, watching the specks float aimlessly through the air.

A shadow flickered past the window as a bird landed on top of her stone home. The gull's *caw* set Maggie's teeth on edge.

"Shut up."

At her murmur, the shutters swung closed, blocking out the sunlight and muffling the bird's call.

She rolled onto her back, staring up at the dark ceiling.

The waves kept up their steady hushing, like the sea itself whispered in her ear.

Get up, Maggie. Life is waiting outside these walls. There are a thousand worlds you've yet to explore.

The words of the waves didn't pull her from her bed. She didn't move until the pangs of hunger grew too strong to be ignored.

She kicked aside her blanket and dug through the dark for her fishing net.

A chill damp clung to the ropes of the net as she shoved open the door. The afternoon sunlight bored into her eyes, sending sparks zapping through her vision.

The flat rock that supported her home reached only five feet out over the sea. Maggie walked over the edge and dropped into the water, not bothering to take a breath before the plunge.

The waves swayed her body, dragging her closer to the sea floor. She didn't fight the current. Her toes touched sand as she drifted away from the shore.

The burning in her lungs told her to kick up. Her legs didn't seem to care to try. A fish the size of her head swam a loop around her, pausing for a moment to take in Maggie's limp figure, before settling itself in her net.

The Siren's will will be done.

Maggie kicked off, breaking through the surface of the water with a gasp.

A whirring *chirp* sent the gull who had perched on her house flying with an indignant *screech.*

"Hi, Nic." Maggie swam toward the shore, letting the heavy net drag behind her.

The silver bot rolled to the edge of the ridge above her roof, clicking at her and giving a shrill whistle.

"I was just catching lunch." She stopped at the edge of the rock that was her porch, tossed her net up, and climbed the slope that dipped into the Endless Sea.

Nic gave a dull *clunk.*

"I know it's closer to dinner," Maggie said, "but this is when I'm eating, so deal."

She had never been able to understand the exact words the little robot said, but there was no mistaking the judgmental tone of his *hiss* and *beep.*

Nic stared at her with his singular eye as she pulled the fish from the net. The late afternoon sun glinted off his upside-down teardrop-shaped head, which balanced precariously on his teardrop-shaped body. A ruffle of metallic arms lay dormant around his neck.

Maggie dropped the fish next to a mound of stones, ignoring Nic's eye watching her. She knelt and blew a long breath into the center of the rock pile. Fire instantly crackled to life. A tingle itched Maggie's fingers as the Siren took her payment for the flames.

Nic tinked his spindly arms together.

"I didn't ask for your opinion." Maggie stepped into her house, ignoring the mess that took up the tiny space, and grabbed her knife from the wooden table.

A *scratch* and a *thunk* sounded from outside as Nic landed on the ledge.

Maggie leaned out the door, glaring at Nic's back as he rolled toward her fish.

"Did I invite you down?" Maggie asked.

Nic grabbed the fish, lifting the floppy mass to be level with his eye.

"What do you want with a fish anyway?" Maggie said. "It's not like you eat."

The metal arms around Nic's neck sprang to life, slashing and clawing at the fish.

"Hey! I just caught that."

Before Maggie could think of how to rescue her meal from the whirling arms, Nic tossed the fish onto the flames.

"What are you..." Maggie's anger simmered away as she looked down at her cleaned and prepared lunch.

Nic whistled.

"I could have done it myself." Maggie sank to the ground, letting the dancing flames dry her clothes as they cooked her meal.

Nic raised his arms in a way that nearly looked like a shrug.

"And helping me with a fish doesn't excuse you coming down here without asking. This is my home. You live with Alden and"—she couldn't bring herself to say Bertrand's name—"and there's no need for you to come and check on me."

Nic stared at her.

"Alden sent you, didn't he?"

Nic purred.

"Alden!" Maggie shouted.

A bird somewhere out of sight squawked its displeasure.

"Alden, are you hiding up there?" Maggie lay back on the rock, staring at the overhang that was the roof of her home.

"I'm not hiding." Alden stepped into view, twisting the cuff of his pale blue shirt. "I was simply enjoying the view while you and Nic had a little visit."

"You sent a robot—"

Nic hummed in indignation.

"—to make sure it was safe for you to come down?" Maggie shut her eyes tight, the undeniable sense that she shouldn't have gotten out of bed stealing her will to argue with Alden.

"It's not that at all." Alden spoke over the clacking of stones as he climbed down to Maggie's rock. "I didn't want to be rude by overwhelming you with visitors."

His shadow fell across Maggie.

"I've brought food," Alden said, his voice swinging up hopefully.

"I have a fish." Maggie pointed to the flames.

The scent of the charring meat cut through the tang of the sea air.

"You need to eat more than fish, Maggie." Alden took Maggie's wrists, pulling her to sit up. "It's not healthy. I know these things—"

"You're a healer." Maggie opened her eyes wide enough to glower at Alden.

"Exactly." Alden let go of Maggie's wrists.

Nic rolled up behind Maggie, blocking her from lying back down.

"Look at the wonderful things I've brought." Alden reached into his bag and pulled out a spiked purple fruit, holding it out to Maggie as though it were a prized treasure.

"No?" He said after a long moment. "That's all right, I have more."

He reached back into the bag, presenting a basket of bright red berries, a sweet roll, and a box of chocolates.

"I thought you were trying to take care of my health?" Maggie bit the insides of her cheeks, stamping down the instinct to smile as Alden presented a glass smooth truffle.

"There is more to health than diet." Alden took Maggie's hand, placing the truffle in her palm.

Nic rolled toward the house. A *bump* and a *clatter* sounded as soon as he disappeared through the door.

"Don't break anything," Maggie called after him.

"Eat, Maggie." Alden sank to the ground, taking a moment to arrange his gangly limbs. His dark hair puffed up with the wind, flying in a dozen different directions. "You'll like it."

Maggie nibbled on a corner of the truffle. Deep sweetness flooded her mouth. A tiny thread of the knotted anger that had settled in her chest weeks ago unraveled.

She placed the chocolate back in the box. "You don't have to bring me food, Alden. I can take care of myself."

Nic rolled back out of her home, carrying the two plates and forks she owned. She had gotten a second plate in case Bertrand ever…

Rage flared in her lungs. She snatched the truffle back up, tossing the whole thing into her mouth.

"I would never think you incapable of anything," Alden said. "But you're my friend. One of the very few I have in the Siren's Realm. There is no illness here for me to cure. There is no battle for me to fight. The Siren provides for everyone's needs. I am useless here. Let me at least do a tiny thing to take care of you."

Maggie watched as Nic reached into the fire and pulled the

fish free, placing a portion onto each of the plates before handing them to Maggie and Alden.

"Thanks, Nic," Maggie said.

Nic purred.

"Fine, you can worry about me." Maggie kept her eyes on her plate. "But only because it gives you something to do, and no wasting magic on me."

"You could never be a waste, Maggie."

"The magic you brought into the Siren's Realm is all the magic you've got." Maggie dug into her fish with her fork, watching the meat flake into pieces, like the fish was meant to be nothing more or less than tiny bites for a person to eat.

"I have plenty of magic," Alden said. "I spent a whole lifetime in Alondra not being able to use any of it, I have enough stored inside to be able to pay the Siren's price for a very long time."

"What about Nic?" Maggie set her plate down, unable to look at the ill-fated fish any longer.

"He's not drawing magic from me." Alden rubbed the flecks of gold embedded in his wrists. "I can feel it when I pay people for things in the Textile Town, or even when I pay for something I've asked the Siren for. A tingle as the magic is pulled away from me, and a microscopic void forming where the magic used to live. Nic never pulls magic from me."

"Then how are you still running, buddy?" Maggie looked to Nic.

Nic turned his eye up to the sky.

"It seems to me the most likely answer is he's feeding off the ambient magic in the air."

Maggie looked away as Alden took a bite of fish.

"The Siren's Realm is created by magic, consistently altered by magic, powered by magic. It's as though the air itself is breathing power into him."

"At least the Siren is helping someone," Maggie said.

Alden gave a tiny gasp and looked up to the sky. "Maggie, you shouldn't say such things."

"Because the Siren will hear me?" Maggie leapt to her feet, energy like she hadn't felt in days coursing through her body. "Because then the almighty Siren will know I think she's nothing more than a thieving, murdering, little—ow!"

Nic jabbed her in the shin with one of his many arms.

"I will kick you into the ocean." Maggie rubbed her shin.

Nic rolled to the far side of the flat rock.

"Maggie," Alden said, unfolding his limbs as he stood, "I know how upset you are."

"Upset?" Maggie growled. "Upset! The Siren decided to let a plague sweep through her perfect realm, and now my friend is dead."

"Losing someone you care for is a great—"

"And you." She pressed a finger to Alden's chest. "You're living with the traitor, which makes you no better than he is."

"You think I'm a traitor?" Alden tipped his head to the side, something between hurt and confusion filling his eyes.

"No." Maggie's chest deflated as the anger rushed out of her, leaving her even more exhausted than before. She sank down onto the rock. "But I don't know why you put up with him."

"I know you blame him," Alden said slowly. "For convincing you to leave the Siren's Realm when the blackness was taking people, for helping to free my people—"

"Don't." Maggie waved a hand at the fire, extinguishing the flames. "Just don't."

Alden picked at his fish, tearing it into tiny pieces. "Bertrand Wayland aside, you can't hide out here."

"I'm not hiding."

"When was the last time you left this rock?"

Nic cocked his head to the side.

"When I left the Siren's Realm." Maggie grabbed a chocolate from the box. "When we went to Alondra and found you."

"You haven't left at all since you've been back?" Alden's eyes widened.

She popped another truffle into her mouth and looked out over the sea. There was nothing new or interesting in the waves, but staring at their shimmering surface was better than seeing the worry in Alden's eyes.

"People die, Maggie," Alden whispered. "That doesn't mean you get to stop living."

"People die, but you still have to eat breakfast." A coarse laugh rattled the knot in Maggie's throat. "My mother taught me that a long time ago."

"Then let's go find breakfast." Alden grabbed Maggie under the arms and hoisted her to her feet. "Her shoes please, Nic."

"But it's dinnertime, and my clothes are wet."

Nic rolled into her home.

"Nic, don't. I've already eaten," Maggie said.

Nic tossed her boots through the door. They landed limply at her feet.

"You haven't eaten enough." Alden crossed his arms in a way he seemed to believe was intimidating. "I'm the healer here. A long walk and some good food, that's what you need."

Maggie glared between Nic and Alden, the urge to throw both of them into the Endless Sea ebbing the longer her friends stared at her.

"Fine." Maggie pulled on her gray leather boots. "I'll agree to go into town. But If I see Bertrand and decide to kill him, you agree to stay out of my way."

"Perfect." Alden beamed at her. "I've got an excellent adventure in mind, and there's no worry of running into Bertrand at all."

"Has he decided to lock himself in the dark as penance for all the damage he's done?" Maggie climbed up to the overhang, not needing to look to know where to place her hands.

"He's gone on one of his adventures," Alden said. "I haven't seen Bertrand in more than a week."

CHAPTER 2

The sounds of the Textile Town carried to the very edge of the beach. The chatter of voices and *clatter* of wheels set Maggie's teeth on edge.

She stopped with her toes still on the sand and looked toward the rocky mounds that took over the sleepy beach. If she ran full out, she could make it to the rocks. From there, it would be easy to outpace Alden and Nic. She'd be locked safely in her house before they could drop from the overhang and onto her stone porch.

And you'd have to do all this again tomorrow.

Maggie stepped from the sand onto the packed dirt road.

That's the trouble with having friends. They won't leave you alone.

"That wasn't so hard, was it?" Relief softened Alden's face.

Nic gave a crackling *whirr.*

"Thanks, Nic." Maggie didn't fight the tiny smile that curved her lips.

"This really is going to be a remarkable evening." Alden lifted Maggie's hand, looping it through his elbow. "At least, I hope it will be a remarkable evening. I'm not really sure what you're used to."

"Hiding in a stone house?" Maggie let Alden lead her down the lane.

Bare sea grass surrounded the first stretch of road, swaying gently with the evening breeze.

"I mean before your little rest from the world," Alden said. "Before I came to the Siren's Realm."

"Well, before I met you I was here," Maggie said, "living on a rock, selling fish for magic, being an idiot who thought there might be meaning to all this."

Nic whistled.

"Fine." Maggie rolled her eyes at Nic. "And before here, I was at home on Earth, living in an awful Academy that was basically a prison for kids nobody wanted to deal with."

Heat pressed on the corners of Maggie's eyes.

Alden gazed down at her, a crease forming between his eyebrows.

Tents cropped up on either side of the street, low and made of plain canvas with their flaps tied shut against the setting sun.

"I suppose," Alden said, "that means your bar for a fantastic evening is set remarkably low."

"I guess. Avoid blood and dying and you've pretty much got it in the bag."

"Excellent." Alden sped up his pace, his long legs covering so much ground Maggie had to trot to keep up. "I had been worried you wouldn't be impressed. From what the others I've met have told me, things of this sort weren't normal before the dark time, but if your world held such wonders, then you might not be interested at all."

"Interested in what?" Maggie asked.

Alden didn't answer as he hurried down the road. The tents surrounding them grew wider and grander as they neared the heart of the Textile Town.

Every jewel tone Maggie could imagine had been used in the wishes to the Siren that built this part of the city. Intricate patterns of everything from soaring birds to words in languages Maggie couldn't read had been stitched into the canvas.

"Has the city been redone?" Maggie asked. "The tents weren't so colorful before. I mean, there were colors, but not like this. Not so—"

"Bright and new? There has been quite a bit of new textile created throughout town." Alden turned onto a narrow side lane.

Pale pink wildflowers that matched the surrounding tents covered the ground.

Maggie hesitated, not wanting to crush the blooms, but Alden plowed forward. The flowers had a bounce in them that gave an involuntary spring to Maggie's step.

Nic growled as he rolled behind them, his three wheels fumbling on the flowers.

"You okay?" Maggie asked.

Nic glared.

"Sorry you hate the flowers," Maggie laughed. The shaking of her chest tensed foreign muscles, sending a pang into her lungs.

"Nic doesn't like anything that bothers his wheels, and the roads are becoming more and more interesting by the day. Everyone seems intent on having a welcoming and delightful home. From what I've been told, the massive renewal of the Textile Town began when the dark times ended. Whether in gratitude for being left alive or a desperate need to prove to the Siren they are good stewards of her realm, I don't really know."

"And the Siren's just letting people redecorate?"

They veered onto a wide road filled with people all moving in the same direction.

"I suppose she must be," Alden said. "It keeps happening, and all magic works by her will."

"By the Siren's will," Maggie whispered.

A tent four stories high came into view at the end of the road, in a place Maggie had been a hundred times before.

"That's the market square," Maggie said. "Why is there a giant tent in the market square?"

"They did work quite quickly. It wasn't there this morning." Alden steered her through the crowd, cutting around others who, like Maggie, gaped up at the enormous, violet tent.

"Is it going to be there forever?" Maggie asked.

"No idea. I suppose not. None of the market shops mentioned moving locations when I visited for breakfast."

"Then why did someone put up a giant tent?" Maggie squinted at the fabric.

Golden embroidery sparkled in the red glow of the setting sun. The stitches were laid out in a careful pattern, but she couldn't quite tell what they were meant to be.

"They put up the tent for the festivities," Alden said. "I really hope you'll enjoy the evening. I've got us box seats and everything."

"Box seats?"

As the sun faded, the embroidery grew brighter, sparkling in the twilight.

Dead ahead, where people were filing into the violet tent, a lion with the tale of a scorpion marked the canvas. A woman with wings stitched to her back flew on one side of the great beast, while a unicorn galloped on the other.

They reached the front of the queue of people waiting to enter the tent. Centaurs with gold and silver ribbons wound through their manes flanked the entrance, collecting tickets as people passed.

"Alden, what are we going to see?" Maggie asked.

"A fantastic assortment of wonders only visible in the Siren's Realm." Alden patted his pockets. "I've been looking forward to it for days. Ever since the notices were posted. I purchased seats for us straight off, but Nic thought it best I surprise you. Not give you a chance to overthink coming."

"Smart, Nic."

Thick golden ropes tied back the flaps of the tent, letting the light from the hundreds of lanterns that filled the space spill out onto the street.

"Meat fer sale!" The familiar call came from within the tent. "Don't want to watch the spectacle hungry. Get yer meat. Finest roasted leg in the realm."

"Gabriel!" Maggie shouted, pushing forward in the crowd.

A troll rounded on Maggie. "Wait your turn." If the troll's glare hadn't been enough to turn Maggie back, the stench would have done the job.

Alden took Maggie's hand, drawing her back to their place in line. "We'll happily wait." Alden sounded like he had a terrible head cold. "Won't we, Maggie?"

"Right." Maggie coughed.

"This way if you please." A woman in a thick veil took the troll's ticket, leading him away from the crowd.

The throng gave a collective gasp of relief as the stink of the troll subsided.

"I know the meat seller," Maggie said as Alden handed their tickets to a centaur. "His name is Gabriel. I need to see him."

"This way, please." A girl of no more than fourteen beckoned them forward. A long, red braid trailed down the girl's back. Her skin shimmered as she moved, as though someone had rubbed silver dust all over her.

How did you get here? What brought a child to the Siren's Realm?

The questions balanced on the tip of Maggie's tongue as the girl led them around the wide, open space at the center of the tent to a set of sweeping stands. Waist-high walls separated the area into private sections of individual chairs.

"Here you are." The girl bowed them into a box.

Two wingback chairs and an empty table waited behind the gate.

"Will this do?" The girl turned to Alden. "We have other seating arrangements."

With a clap of her hands, the two chairs disappeared, replaced by a sofa just wide enough for two.

"I really don't think—" Maggie began.

"There are also privacy options." The girl clapped again.

The three walls not facing the open center of the tent turned opaque. A fainting couch took the place of the love seat.

Nic gurgled a trill.

"We-we're fine with the chairs, thank you." Alden blushed to the roots of his hair.

The girl clapped, and the chairs reappeared.

"The Compère wishes only for his guests' enjoyment." The girl bowed and backed out of the booth.

"Thank you." Maggie clicked the gate shut behind the girl. "Who is the Compère?" Maggie whispered to Alden, her gaze sweeping the vast space.

The tent had been laid out in quarters. The portion that housed their booth held the most private seating options. Some guests sat in seats much like Maggie and Alden's. Others had turned their walls dark, shielding themselves from the crowd.

To either side of them were stands with benches laid out in rows. Along the front stood a line of centaurs, their heads barely lower than the seats behind them.

Behind a shimmering patch of air along the far wall, a pack of wide and strangely scattered chairs held an array of trolls. Tables had been laid out, filled with everything from sweets to barely-cooked meat, which the trolls ate with abandon.

"To keep the smell in." Alden followed Maggie's gaze. "It was quite the selling point, believe me."

"Wine?" A woman in red silks strode past their booth, holding a decanter in one hand and a glass in the other.

"Would you like some?" Alden asked.

"I just want to talk to Gabriel," Maggie said.

She scanned the other vendors moving throughout the seated

spectators. Some sold cakes and candies, others offered paper pamphlets.

"Excuse me." Alden opened the gate of their booth.

"Wine, sir?" The woman in red winked at Alden. Her gaze slid over Maggie, and a smile curved her lips. "Or perhaps some companionship?"

"Actually, I was hoping you might be willing to send over the meat seller," Alden said. "Gabriel is his name."

"Meat with no wine?" The woman pouted. "That doesn't seem right at all. Better not have him come this way."

"Fine." Alden held out his hand. "I'll buy the wine if you send over the meat seller."

"Excellent." A glass cyclone filled with wine, and two glasses swirled into existence on the table. "Gabriel will be with you directly."

"I could have just gone to look for him," Maggie said. "You didn't need to buy any wine."

"I like wine." Alden sat in one of the wingback chairs. "And besides, this is a night for commerce. I have magic to spend. The wine seller needs to earn. It's the way of things. Now, would you like some wine or not?"

"Fine." Maggie sank into a chair.

Alden picked up the decanter. The swirling of the wine didn't stop as it poured into the glass. The liquid spun ceaselessly, creating its own vortex like a storm caught in a cup.

"I didn't know we were going somewhere fancy." Maggie took the glass Alden offered. "You should have warned me."

"Why?" Alden held his nose to his glass before taking a sip. "Aren't you having fun?"

"The wine lady looked at me like I was homeless."

"You look perfect just as you are."

"I could have worn clean clothes, or, I don't know, brushed my hair." Maggie held her nose over her wine. Her mouth watered at the warm scent of honey, fruit, and oak.

"The Compère won't care if your clothes are still damp," Alden said. "We're here for a night of fun, and a few tangles in your hair won't interfere."

"Yeah, well…" Maggie studied the storm in her glass. "I feel so wrong drinking this."

"Would you rather a white?" Alden asked.

"No." Maggie shook her head. Her hair had grown, falling down past her shoulders. The tangles tickled her bare skin, and goose bumps prickled her arms. "Back home, my drinking this would be illegal. I'm too young."

"But you were in a battle to save your world from an evil wizard." Alden wrinkled his brow. "You nearly died fighting him. You thought you had died when you came here."

"Yeah." Maggie sipped the wine. A hearty sweetness flooded her mouth.

"So you were too young to have wine but not too young to fight an evil wizard?"

"I never said it made sense. It's just the way it works."

"If there is ever a chance," Alden said, "I would love to see your world. A place where there is so much magic, and the non-magical people haven't even noticed. What a wonderful world it must be!"

"Maybe." Maggie shrugged. "I never got to see all that much of it myself. And I don't know if I'd want to go back even if I could ever find the right path."

Nic cocked his head at Maggie with a whistle.

"Too much time will have passed," Maggie said. "Everyone I knew will be gone."

"That is both the blessing and the horror of the Siren's Realm, I suppose. You can leave and find a thousand magnificent places, but you can never return to any of them. Not as you knew them before. Once you've passed through a stitch, the opportunity to change your path within a world is utterly gone."

Maggie took Alden's hand. Her fingers closed around his without thought.

"Do you wish you had stayed?" Maggie asked, the weight of knowing she had asked Alden to come to the Siren's Realm pressing on her chest.

"No. There was nothing left for me in my world. Only I sometimes wish I had been born to a different world, where seeking the Siren would never have occurred to me."

As one, the lanterns in the tent dimmed. A rush of whispers fluttered around the stands as a bright light burst into being at the center of the space, beaming down on a figure shrouded in swirling red.

CHAPTER 3

"*W*elcome!" A man's voice boomed from the center of the ring. "Welcome to the night we have all been waiting for!"

He raised his arms, and the crowd roared.

The red mist masked the man's face, but there was something in the way the tendrils curled that made Maggie quite sure he was smiling.

The man dropped his arms, and the crowd fell silent.

"My fellows, we chanced the fall into the Siren's Realm for the promise of a land of plenty, wonder, and endless joy. Has the Siren provided?" The man held out his hand. A tiny light flashed on his palm before taking off toward the top of the massive tent.

As the light soared, it tore into two-dozen pieces, each slice growing brighter as it neared the canvas. Inches before the lights would have struck the tent, they exploded, showering the cheering guests in fireworks.

First, green lit the air in a pattern of a surging wave. Reds followed, bursting out like the end of an aging sun. A blue star drifted close to the crowd, bathing their amazed faces in a sapphire glow. The sparks landed on the ground as gold.

"Through the Siren's power, her realm is a beautiful place of magnificent bounty," the man said, "and it is by her power I present the wonders you will witness here tonight. The Siren has taught us through her magnificent wisdom that it is not enough to languish in her land. We were brought to a place unlike any other, and we will live lives that cannot be found in any other world!"

The crowd cheered again.

Maggie's hand shook as she held her wine. She placed the glass on the table and gripped the edge of her chair, her nails digging into the thick upholstery.

"I am but the humble Compère to our revelry," the man said. "I could not create our performance without the Siren any more than a man could sail to the land beyond the Endless Sea. Tonight, we take but one small step toward the true glory of the Siren's Realm. Toward a magnificent future beyond all our imaginings. The Siren's will will be done!"

The Compère clapped his hands. A bright green light burst around the tent before everything went black.

"Alden," Maggie whispered. "Alden, what's happening? Who was that man?"

"The Compère," Alden said. "He's the one who arranged the festivities."

"But why?"

"I believe..." Alden's words faded away as a faint light shimmered into being, sprinting through the darkness.

The figure stopped at the center of the space—a young girl, who rotated in a slow circle, allowing everyone in the tent to view her.

"She's the one who showed us to our seats." Maggie leaned forward, peering at the girl.

The silver that had been rubbed on her skin glowed like the moon. Her loose clothes shimmered a pale pink and her hair a deep red. Her eyes held no light, marking her face as two horrifying voids.

The girl reached her right arm up, grasping for some invisible thing.

"What is she doing?" Maggie whispered.

Other hushed voices floated through the darkness.

"I've no idea," Alden said.

Nic hummed, shining the light of his eye up toward the top of the tent.

A swirl of white light began high above, slithering down toward the girl. She waited, arm raised, as the undulating light solidified into a rope that wrapped itself around her wrist.

The girl kicked up, knotting her ankle in the rope so she hung upside down. Bending backward so her hair trailed along the ground, she swung in a slow circle.

Music began, emanating from every corner of the tent. Maggie wanted to search the shadows for the musicians but couldn't look away from the girl.

She swung herself up, climbing the rope hand over hand.

"There," Alden said.

High above, a platform of green haze expanded from all sides of the tent. Four centaurs armed with swords appeared in the mist, pawing the ground as though ready to run.

A gasp carried through the crowd, drawing Maggie's gaze back to the girl. She had wrapped the rope around her waist and, kicking against the air as though it were a solid thing, swung in a wide circle above the heads of the audience.

Horns blasted over the music as the tempo changed, racing to a frantic beat. The centaurs charged at each other, swords raised high.

Maggie moved to stand, but Alden placed a hand on her knee.

"It's only for show," Alden said.

"But—"

The centaurs swung their swords at each other, ducking and weaving in time with the music.

A woman across the darkness screamed as the girl dropped, flipping over and over as she unwound the rope around her waist.

Flames burst from the floor of the arena, threatening to devour the girl. Men ran out of the inferno, fire clinging to their forms like loincloths.

Blazing ropes dropped into the hands of the men.

"'Scuse me," a voice muttered from the darkness. "I was told there were some hungry folks here."

"Gabriel!" Maggie leapt to her feet, throwing open the gate.

"I thought you'd come out of hiding sooner or later." Gabriel clapped Maggie on the shoulder, jostling the tray of roasted meat he had suspended from a cord around his neck. "Didn't think you one for this type of show, but I suppose such a thing is hard to resist."

"The meat smells wonderful." Alden stepped up behind Maggie. "May I buy a leg?"

"Of course ya can." Gabrielle reached out and shook Alden's hand.

"How are you?" Maggie asked. "Is everyone from your camp all right?"

"We made it through the blackness just fine," Gabrielle said. "The Siren didn't see fit to bother those of us that have no magic of our own."

"You came to the Siren's Realm without magic of your own?" Alden asked. "I didn't know such a thing was possible."

"He's new." Maggie grabbed a leg of meat, passing it to Alden and shooing him to his seat.

A roaring round of applause shook the tent.

Maggie glanced up in time to see the mist high above slanting down at a steep pitch. The centaurs cantered toward the flaming ground.

"I thought you were hidin' from the blackness and didn't

know it was safe to come out." Gabriel shook his head. "Didn't think you'd have found a fella to occupy you."

"What Alden?" Maggie shook her head. "It's nothing like that."

Maggie's words carried over the silence as the music suddenly stopped. Heat rushed to her cheeks.

"Come in." Maggie took Gabriel's sleeve, pulling him through the gate.

"I don't belong in a box this fancy."

"Neither do I." Feeling rather foolish, Maggie clapped her hands.

A third wingback chair appeared.

"I should be sellin' my wares," Gabriel said. "An opportunity like this hasn't come for me before."

"Just for a minute," Maggie said. "Tell me what's been happening. Did you hide through the blackness?"

"One thing at a time," Gabriel chuckled. "I hid a bit when things started gettin' bad. People were too scared to buy food from me, so there wasn't a point in bein' on the streets anyway. The Siren took away the blackness, and everythin' went back to normal. Streets filled back up with people like nothin' ever happened."

"This isn't normal," Maggie said.

Deep drums rumbled around the tent. Maggie's heartbeat sped up, racing in time with their ominous tempo.

"People died in the Siren's Realm," Gabriel whispered. "It never happened before. Not in all my time here. Derelict could be swept away by the Siren's storms, but pure death—never. Now, people are thinkin' about their time differently."

A shadow appeared at the entrance of the tent. A great cat twenty feet tall prowled to the center of the ring. The beast swished its tale, flicking the seats of those in the front rows. Gasps and screams followed the movement.

"When we all had forever here, it was easy not to worry about nothin'," Gabriel said. "Now that folks know their time could end, they want to do more with what they've got, and please the Siren so she takes the person standing next to them instead of gettin' smacked down with blackness themselves."

Two of the flaming dancers dropped from the ceiling, landing on the cat's back. The beast gave a yowl, and the music burst back into being.

"Do you think the Siren will send the blackness again?" Sweat slicked Maggie's palms. She reached for her glass of wine, taking a sip as a centaur seized the cat's tail.

Gabriel wrinkled his weathered forehead. "I don't think so. The blackness came and shook everybody up. People who had been hordin' are spreadin' the wealth of magic around the realm. People are payin' attention to what's happenin' around them fer the first time since I've been here. I don't presume to know how the Siren thinks. But I can't see her bringin' the blackness back. Not with how things are goin'."

The cat ran around the ring, turning into nothing more than a black blur. The centaur holding onto its tail was lifted off his hooves, spinning through the air as though he weighed nothing.

"You think this is it then?" Maggie said. "This is the way the Siren's Realm is now, and we should just accept it and pretend nothing horrible ever happened?"

"Not at all," Gabriel said. "We're just in a clear patch between storms. There's no shore in sight, so the best we can do is make ourselves as ready as we can for when lightnin' reaches for our sails."

Maggie took another sip of her wine. The hearty sweetness did nothing to dislodge the fear from her throat.

"How do you always seem to be able to read her?" Maggie said. "More than—than anyone else I know, you always know how to riddle the Siren out."

"I lived my life on a ship before I got sucked through a storm and landed here." Gabriel pushed himself to his feet. "Storms and the Siren have more alike than you'd think."

White light radiated from the ceiling as the glowing girl dropped from above, landing on top of the cat's head.

"Best be goin'." Gabriel clicked open the gate. "There's more earnin' to be done."

"Gabriel, wait," Maggie said. "What do you know about the Compère?"

"Paid us extra for sellin' our wares here tonight, and splashes the magic he earns around so others get it as well." Gabriel gave a nod. "He'll be the wealthiest man in the Siren's Realm by mornin'."

"But who is he?" Maggie asked.

"Don't know," Gabriel said. "Only the Siren does, I expect. Man's smart enough to keep his face hidden."

"Be careful," Maggie said.

"I'm always careful," Gabriel laughed. "I'll be seein' you on the streets."

He shut the gate and climbed the steps to the higher boxes.

"This meat really is delicious," Alden said.

"Gabriel's the best." Maggie turned her attention back to the center of the ring.

The shape of the cat had shifted, allowing light to filter through its form.

High strings pitched over the banging of the drums as the flame dancers caught hold of ropes and began swinging as though on trapezes.

The cat stopped in the dead center of the tent. Silver light poured out of its stomach, devouring the form of the girl.

"Where did she go?" Maggie moved to stand, but Nic extended an arm, pressing Maggie back into her seat.

The light spread, radiating beyond where the cat had been, overpowering the flames that licked the ground. Maggie's eyes burned at the brightness, but she couldn't look away.

High above, more people on fire dropped into view, swinging and twisting from flaming ropes. Centaurs tore around the outside of the ring, raising their swords high. Sparks flew from the metal, showering the spectators in rainbows of fire.

The light that filled the circle changed, morphing from pure white to dazzling green.

Instinct told Maggie to run. To get as far from the green as her legs could carry her, but the beauty of the swirling light kept her in place.

She reached for Alden's hand, twining her fingers through his, holding on as though the light would snatch her away.

The flame dancers leapt from rope to rope as the tempo of the music accelerated. There was no way to know which rope each dancer would leap for, no way to tell if they would fall into the terrible light.

A rumbling shook the stands, but the performers didn't stop. The gleaming pool on the ground swirled. The air in the tent shifted as the light pulled it into the ever-growing storm.

"We should go." Maggie couldn't remember how to move as a shape emerged from the light.

A woman, both beautiful and terrifying, spiraled up toward the sky.

The armed centaurs beat their breasts, chanting something in a language Maggie didn't understand.

The flame dancers changed their patterns, swinging in and out of the circle.

"No!"

The cheers of the crowd covered Maggie's shout as the dancers let go of their ropes, diving as one into the thirty-foot tall woman.

Her chiseled features didn't change as the centaurs raced forward, charging into the hems of her skirt.

Horns blasted a long note as the woman tilted her chin to the sky.

With a *pop*, the tent around them vanished, and stars appeared above. Sparks flew from the woman's body as though challenging the strength of the night sky. With a *crack* and a flash of green, she disappeared, her light flying off into the darkness.

Maggie held onto Alden's hand as the crowd around them roared and clapped. The sound pounded into Maggie's chest, shaking her lungs.

She blinked against the darkness, searching for the fastest way out of the stands.

But a dim red light appeared at the center of the ring where the woman had vanished.

The light morphed and twisted, expanding into the form of the Compère.

"My dear fellows," the Compère spoke softly, without the flare and dramatics the Master of Ceremonies had employed before, "by the grace of the Siren, we entertain. For the glory of her land, we seek pleasure. By the goodness of her realm, we feel joy."

The sound of Maggie's own breath rattled in her ears.

"This is but the beginning of a new age of revelry."

The Compère's whisper tickled Maggie's neck.

"Go forth into her great night. For it is by her will the dawn comes."

A chord surged on the unseen instruments, and the stars disappeared from view as the tent sprang back into being.

CHAPTER 4

"*H*ow breathtaking," Alden said.

The lanterns around the space flickered slowly back to life. Murmurs and *rustles* of fabric floated around the tent, as though no one was quite ready to admit the evening had ended.

"How did they do it?" Maggie whispered.

"Magic," Alden said. "The Compère asked the Siren for everything he needed for the evening."

"But to ask the Siren for a tent this big, and a shadow cat, and to light people on fire and have them not be hurt?" Maggie's hands tingled at the mere thought of losing that much magic. "How did he start off with enough to pay for all this?"

"No idea."

The shimmer around the trolls disappeared. As if it had been rehearsed as part of the performance, those on the open spectator stands stood and surged for the exit.

"Shall we?" Alden downed the rest of his wine in one swallow.

Maggie opened her mouth to ask another question, but the stench of the trolls touched her tongue.

"Let's go." She played with her hair, pulling it toward her face where the scent of the sea could deaden the stink.

The trolls were the only ones who didn't seem inclined to line up for the exit. Their tables had been refilled with food, and dozens of them sat together, tearing into huge sides of meat and downing bucket-sized glasses of wine.

"Pardon." A centaur stepped in front of Maggie.

She barely had time to dodge the man's hooves.

"I've never seen everyone together like this." Tears streamed down Alden's cheeks, and he spoke as though his nose were badly stuffed. "It really is a remarkable thing to see so many magical people in one place."

"That's it, everyone out of the way!" A seven-foot tall man with a long, black braid down his back clapped his hands over his head. A horn appeared in his fist. "I said move!" He held the horn to his lips and let out a painful note.

Maggie clamped her hands over her ears as he blasted the horn again.

The people in front of him pushed to get out of his way, knocking each other over in their haste.

"Can't he just wait?" Bile surged into Maggie's throat as they drew level with the trolls.

The tall man blew the horn again as he reached the flap of the tent. The crowd outside had stopped moving forward. Music and torches filled the street beyond.

"An evening celebration, how wonderful!" Sweat dripped down Alden's brow.

"Keep moving!" the tall man bellowed before lifting his horn to his lips again.

"Leave it alone." A hand reached up and smacked the horn away from the tall man's mouth.

"You little slitch." The man reached down into the crowd, knocking the offending person aside.

The crowd around the pair pushed as far away as they could, shoving their fellows into the sides of the stands.

"Oh dear," Alden said. "We should stop them, shouldn't we?"

"Don't go pushing people around!" A stout woman stepped up behind the tall man, yanking hard on his black braid.

The man swung around, punching the woman in the face.

"You're ruining my meal!" A troll leapt off the stands and into the middle of the crowd.

"Nope. This is where we get the hell out of here." Maggie took Alden's hand and ran to the far side of the tent.

Nic squeaked as he trundled along the packed earth behind them.

"We'll just slip out and sneak home." Maggie knelt where the violet canvass met the ground. She ran her fingers along the bottom of the fabric, searching for a hold to lift the material.

There was no seam or gap for her fingers to grab. The canvas went into the ground itself.

Maggie dug into the dirt with her fingers.

"A little help, Nic."

Nic's arms sprang to life, scratching and digging at the dirt. Ten seconds passed before Nic's arms went still. A few tiny scratches were all the progress he had made.

"I don't believe the Siren made this tent to have more than one possible exit," Alden said.

"Dammit." Maggie pulled a string from her pocket, ignoring the moon and stars charm as she tied her hair back.

With a roar, a club appeared in the troll's hand. She swung at a woman, knocking her backward into the stands.

"Should I wish for a weapon of some kind?" Alden asked.

"Not unless you have to." Maggie eyed the chaos at the exit.

Everyone in view had joined the fight. Some with fists, others with weapons. The few who had escaped onto the street beyond had stopped to watch the brawl. Drink vendors moved among the spectators selling wine.

"Keep up." She ran toward the open stands to the left of the entrance, across the aisle from the trolls' section.

A centaur tore past her, a whip raised high. Maggie covered her head with both arms, preparing for a blow that didn't come.

Alden kept pace by her side, and the *rumble* of Nic's wheels stayed close behind.

Two men broke out of the fight as they reached the front of the stands. Both had blood on their faces, and though they postured with fists raised, neither seemed willing to move in close enough to hit the other.

"Excuse me." Maggie ducked between the men and ran up the stands, leaping from seat to seat.

"Nic!"

She spun around at Alden's cry.

Alden had been only a step behind her, but Nic hadn't made it past the front row.

"Maggie, keep going." Alden ran back toward Nic.

"Really?" Maggie chased after him.

The fight had spread out in the few seconds she'd had her back turned. Four men with swords took up the center of the space. With a *crack* that shook the ground, the trolls' stands collapsed.

"I've got you." Alden lifted Nic.

"Duck!" Maggie screamed as a club flew through the air toward Alden's head.

Alden threw himself and Nic into a gap between rows.

The troll who had thrown the club ran toward Alden.

I need a weapon. Give me a weapon.

The sting of vanishing magic prickled Maggie's hands as a gleaming sword appeared in her grip.

She leapt down in front of Alden and Nic, raising her sword to be level with the troll's throat.

The troll opened her mouth in a rotten tooth sneer.

"When was the last time you were in a real fight?" Maggie

swung her sword in a wide circle, letting the hilt rotate in her grip. "Don't test me, lady."

The troll growled but didn't move as Alden stood and scrambled up the stands with Nic.

"Wise choice." Maggie took off after Alden.

"How do we get out?" Alden froze on the top of the stands, Nic held tightly in his grip.

"Drop down and cut out to the side. I'll go first. You and Nic follow."

Maggie eyed the fall, the twenty feet down that had seemed so manageable from below, now looked far enough to break her ankles.

"Toss me the sword." Maggie pressed the hilt into Alden's free hand.

Sitting on the edge of the stands, she twisted to hold on with her hands. Pushing herself off the edge, she dangled for a moment before letting go and dropping to the ground. Pain shot through her legs as a fist swung for her face. She dodged to the side.

The glint of her falling sword caught her eye. She spun toward the blade, catching the hilt and brandishing the sword with a shout.

The man who'd swung at her staggered away from her blade, knocking into a woman who held a dagger in each hand.

A *thunk* and a *thump* sounded behind Maggie.

"You okay?" Maggie asked without looking back.

"Fine, thank you," Alden said.

"Stay cl—"

Nic's whistle cut through Maggie's words. He rolled toward the opening, every one of his metallic arms spinning and jabbing at anything that dared get in his way.

"That works, too." Maggie pushed Alden in front of her, her sword tipped toward the brawl.

"Maggie!" Alden yelled.

Pain seared through Maggie's arm. She doubled her grip on her sword as she looked down to find blood dripping from her arm.

Maggie searched the crowd for whatever had hurt her. There was no sword or whip near her.

"From above." Alden grabbed Maggie's arm, yanking her out of the way as an arrow flew past her face.

They followed the path Nic had cleared to the outside of the tent and cut left, keeping close to the violet fabric.

The brawl extended all the way down the street, but it hadn't stopped the musicians from playing or the wine sellers from peddling their wares.

"What the hell is going on?" Maggie ran after Nic and Alden, her sword still raised. "How did a tent show turn into a battle?"

"I believe it started with a man who had an aversion to troll stench."

They curved around the side of the tent, leaving the shouts of the crowd behind. Before they reached the next street, the lights of the entrance had faded from view. By the time they turned down a row of gray tents, the sounds of the fight had disappeared completely.

"Give me your arm." Alden ripped the sleeve off his pale blue shirt.

"Someone shot an arrow at me." Maggie blinked at the blood on her arm, her mind stuck somewhere between disgust and amazement. "Why did they shoot at me? And how did they get the bow and arrows? You aren't supposed to just be able to wish for a weapon in…" Her words trailed away as she held her own sword up to the moonlight.

The stars sparkling off the metal dimmed as the blade faded from view, dissipating like fog.

"Maybe weapons still aren't allowed?" Maggie said.

Alden lifted her wounded arm. "I'm sorry if this hurts."

"It doesn't hurt." Maggie took his ripped sleeve, wiping the blood off her arm. The skin beneath had no sign of damage. "What the hell is happening?"

Frightened voices came from behind them as others followed the path they'd found to escape.

"I think we should leave." Alden took Maggie's hand, leading her down the long line of gray tents. "We need to get inside. If the fighting spreads, I'd like to be somewhere safe."

He turned down a street wide enough for centaurs to walk four across.

"It just doesn't make sense." Maggie flexed her bloodstained arm. "I was hit with an arrow, I know I was."

"I saw it happen," Alden said. "If you had turned a little farther, the arrow could've caught you in the heart."

"I didn't ask the Siren to heal me," Maggie said. "Didn't even have the stray thought that I'd like her to knit my skin back together."

They turned onto a dark road. Stone buildings rose up in front of them.

"No." Maggie let go of Alden's hand and grabbed his elbow, pulling him back. "I'm not going to his house."

"Bertrand isn't here," Alden said. "His home is sturdy, and we need to get inside."

"My home is sturdy," Maggie said. "We can go there and figure this out."

Alden took Maggie's hands in his. "To get to the Endless Sea we would have to cross through the Textile Town. We're almost to the stone Fortress. We would be fools to turn our backs on a safe haven because of a personal dispute."

"Personal dispute?" Maggie coughed. "Are you kidding?"

"Maggie, please." A wrinkle of worry creased Alden's brow. "I don't want to see you hurt."

"Fine." Maggie shook free of Alden's hands and ran toward the stone streets. "But if he is home, I get to stab him to see if it will heal."

"I won't stand in your way."

The sounds of their footfalls changed as they reached the stone laid streets. Each step echoed between the buildings, announcing to the residents of the sturdy homes that someone moved through the darkness. Canals took the place of roads, leaving only narrow footpaths on either side. A moored boat bounced against the rocks in time with the gentle lapping of the waves.

Nic's wheels clinked along behind them.

"You're really sure he's gone?" Maggie asked as they turned onto the street where Bertrand Wayland lived.

"If he were back in the Siren's Realm, he would have come to the revelry tonight and been in the thick of that fight."

They stopped in the shadow of a tall stone house. A few dim candles flickered in the windows high above Maggie's head.

"You're really sure?" Maggie asked.

Alden stepped deeper into the shadows. A moment later, a *creak* sounded and light spilled onto the street.

Taking a deep breath, Maggie walked into the narrow entryway, shuddering as Alden shut the door behind them.

"We should have some tea by the fire." Alden locked the door to the street and hurried across the room to a much less battleworthy wooden door. "It always calms me, and we're quite safe now."

"Running to a lion's den for safety," Maggie muttered. "So smart."

She followed Alden up the steps into the hall, glancing out the barred windows as they passed. There was no horde charging through the Fortress, and the only sound in the house was the creaking of the worn wooden floor.

Maggie's hands longed for the comfort of a sword as they walked into the sitting room. Her heart flipped up into her throat.

Bertrand would be in his chair by the fire. He would stand up and say *Miss Trent, you have been remiss in your hand-to-hand combat lessons. I can't say I find it surprising you were bleeding, but please don't get any on the sofa.*

A fire crackled in the wide fireplace. The warm glow of the flames bounced off the painting that hung above the mantle.

A narrow stream squeezed between two rocks. Shadows darkened the water at the top and bottom of the painting, but in the center the stream shone with an untainted light.

"Here you are." Alden pressed a cup of tea into Maggie's hands.

"How long did you say Bertrand had been gone for?"

"A little while," Alden said. "A few weeks…maybe a bit longer."

"But you said—"

"I didn't want to upset you by telling you he'd left for so long without saying goodbye. I'm sure he'll be back soon enough. He told me not to worry. Just to mind the house and keep an eye out for you and Nic."

"That's it? That's all he said?" Maggie walked up to the painting, ignoring the heat of the fire roasting her knees.

"He said if you wanted, you could have everything in the cabinet. But not to press you as you'd likely burn anything of his I gave you. I'm not sure which cabinet he was referring to, but I'm sure you can ask him when he comes back."

Maggie turned away from the dazzling water and strode to the wall. She slipped her fingers into the crack at the base of the bookcase and pulled. A panel opened. Two swords waited, safely tucked in the velvet casing. A pile of worn books rested in the bottom of the cupboard.

"He's gone." Maggie picked up the top book.

On the Siren and Her Realm

"Bertrand's not coming back."

CHAPTER 5

*A*lden sat in a high-backed chair, staring into the fire, an open book balanced on his knees. Maggie sat on the floor next to the cupboard, surrounded by the books Bertrand had left for her.

> *The ways of the Siren are both unknowable and utterly consistent. I have no doubt every change we see in her realm is made in a deliberate manner for an incontrovertible reason.*
>
> *We are but mere mortals who have, by her grace, been granted access to her realm. For over 36,900 days, I have studied the Siren and her realm. There are few mysteries more indecipherable to mortal man than the ways of our immortal lady.*

"Over a hundred years." Maggie pinched the bridge of her nose. "The man who wrote this book had been in the Siren's Realm for more than a hundred years."

"I don't know which I should find more shocking," Alden said, "that he was in the Siren's Realm for a century, or that he kept count."

"Bertrand didn't say where he was going?" Maggie asked for

the dozenth time.

Nic glared at her from his place by the fire.

"He said he was going to explore," Alden said. "He didn't seem too fussed, and I know he's slipped from the Siren's Realm to other worlds many times before. I didn't think it was anything to worry about."

Maggie flipped open *Tides of Green* by Merant A. Bouru.

Finding myself in a world of glory, the likes of which I had never dreamed of, was both a blessing and a curse. Having chanced the fall into the Siren's Realm to escape a place of war and death, the ability to wish for food and have a full belly took months to grow accustomed to.

"How do you know there *is* anything to worry about?" Alden asked for the tenth time. "He could just want you to have his books as a peace offering. And he might only have been gone for so long because he found a world of wonders."

"You don't understand." Blood rushed to Maggie's numb feet as she stood to pace the room. "Time outside the Siren's Realm always moves more slowly than on the inside."

"But it didn't when you found me in Alondra," Alden said. "You were there with me for a few days. Bertrand said when you came back, you'd been gone for two weeks."

"Yes, but only because the Siren screwed with time." Maggie dragged her fingers through the tangles of her hair.

"So, either Bertrand has been in another world for a very long time, or the Siren has decided to extend Bertrand's absence from her realm." Alden closed the book on his lap. "I'm not sure which option to be more concerned about."

"It depends on if you want Bertrand to come back or not," Maggie said.

Nic tinked one of his metal arms against his chest.

"It's great you think Bertrand is amazing, but some of us know better." Maggie stopped in front of the mantle. "If

Bertrand's decided he doesn't want to live in the Siren's Realm anymore, that's his choice. He's not a prisoner here. Maybe he's found a life where he can stop messing with other peoples'."

"Do you really believe—"

"Scarier option," Maggie said, "there's something going on in the Siren's Realm she doesn't want Bertrand to be around for. Maybe everyone in the tent tonight caught a new plague and she wanted to make sure he didn't get it. Maybe she knew if there was a fight after the revelry he'd be in the middle of it and she doesn't want him getting hurt."

"Does she really care so much about his safety?"

"We've spent two hours thumbing through these books. I've read bits of them before. None of the authors ever slipped in and out of the Siren's Realm. None of them had the, I don't know, connection he has with her."

"Even if she does care for him beyond her usual citizens"—Alden stood, knocking the book from his lap—"that might not mean anything particularly dire is coming."

Nic picked up the fallen book, replacing it in the cabinet.

"Dire things are already happening. Or did you miss the weapon-filled brawl we escaped?" Maggie paced again.

"There were a lot of people and quite a bit of wine. Surely, this isn't the first fight in the Siren's Realm."

"Weapons aren't allowed. No one should have been able to ask the Siren for a club, much less a bow and arrows."

Nic buzzed and knocked one of his arms into the cabinet, pointing at the two shining swords.

"Those are different," Maggie said. "Bertrand had to ask for those very carefully, and they cost a ton of magic."

"But they're still weapons."

"Nic, toss me a sword." Maggie held out her hand.

Nic pulled one of the blades free from the folds of velvet and threw it to Maggie.

"Bertrand asked for the swords so he could practice for

worlds where hand-to-hand is more useful than magic." Maggie hoisted open one of the heavy windows. "One of the bargains he made with the Siren is that the weapons can't leave the house."

She poked the tip of the sword through the thick iron bars that crisscrossed the window.

As soon as the blade passed the bars, it disappeared, shimmering away into nothing.

"See?" Maggie said. "No weapons allowed."

Alden took the hilt from her and pushed the blade farther out into the night. "How magnificent!" As he pulled the blade back into the sitting room, the metal reappeared as though nothing had happened.

"The sword I wished for disappeared when we got out of the market square," Maggie said. "What if she made the square like this house, where it's okay to ask for weapons?"

"And no one's ever noticed?" Alden began pacing the worn path Maggie had trod only moments before.

"Impossible. Someone would have gotten into a fight and wished for a weapon before. The moment someone had a sword, everyone would have noticed and tons of people would have asked for weapons of their own."

"Then why did she change the rules tonight? Did the Compère make the request?"

"That his patrons try and kill each other?" Maggie laughed. "That doesn't seem like a great business model."

"Could people have died?" Alden's face paled. "Would the Siren have allowed death to take them?"

"I don't know." Maggie took the sword from Alden and, gritting her teeth, ran the blade across her palm.

"Maggie!"

Pain came with the cut, and blood pooled on her palm. By the time she reached for Alden's discarded shirt sleeve the ache had vanished. When she wiped the blood away, there was no trace of any wound at all.

"The Siren can heal when she chooses," Maggie said. "If people died tonight, it means she wanted to pare down the population even more than she managed to with the blackness."

"How far will she let it go?" Alden stared at the blood-covered scrap that had been his sleeve. "Will the market square always be dangerous? Could people attack each other on the streets at will?"

"No idea." Maggie sank into the high-backed chair.

I wish Bertrand were here.

The thought pressed hot rage into her throat. Visions of his smug face flitted through her mind. He'd think about what the Siren might be doing for a few minutes, then race off to solve the mystery and protect everyone in the Siren's Realm.

Or he'd get a few thousand people killed.

"Maggie?" Alden asked.

"We should rest." Maggie stared up at the white-painted ceiling. "We can't go out there again tonight. In the morning, we'll head to the market square and see what we can find out. It should be easy to see if people are still trying to murder each other. And if anyone did die, someone there will know."

And then what?

"What about Bertrand?" Alden asked. "If he's been trapped outside the Siren's Realm, we can't simply abandon him."

"Bertrand Wayland can take care of himself." Maggie pushed herself to her feet.

"I'm sure." Alden stared at the sword in his hand. "I only, well, he would never leave one of us. So, it does feel a little terrible of us to not be worrying about where he is."

A thread of fear tugged at Maggie's chest.

"Bertrand has visited a lot of worlds on his own," Maggie said. "If he's gotten into trouble, he'll weasel his way out. If he's been named king, he'll still weasel his way out."

"Of course." Alden nodded. "You're completely right."

The worried lines on his brow didn't disappear as he bowed Maggie toward the hall.

"There are plenty of rooms upstairs. If we're to wait until morning before doing anything else, we might as well get a bit of rest." He followed the path of grooved wood all the way down the hall.

Maggie had never been beyond the door that led to the outside before. She'd come to Bertrand's home to train, and learn, and plot their next adventure dozens of times. But she had never been upstairs.

Narrow wooden steps curved up and out of sight.

Maggie stopped at the bottom of the stairs. "I can just sleep on the couch."

"Don't be silly. There are plenty of comfortable beds."

"But I don't mind."

Nic jabbed her in the calf, urging her forward.

"Fine, I'll go." Maggie shot Nic a scathing look before following Alden up the steps.

There were no candles along the stairs. By the time they'd reached the middle of the flight, the lights from below had disappeared, leaving only a faint glow up ahead to guide them.

"This way." Alden reached the top of the steps and beckoned her down the hall.

Windows took up one wall and doors the other. He stopped at the third door.

"This should do." Alden opened the carved wooden door.

With a glance from Alden, flames burst to life in the fireplace.

A four-poster bed stood in the middle of the room, with a heavy blue quilt and a dozen fluffy pillows waiting to be used.

"There's a tub through there." Alden pointed to a narrow door in the back corner.

"Thanks."

The floor of the room was smooth under Maggie's feet. The

blue quilt held the softness of silk and showed no signs of having been used before.

"Does anyone ever sleep in here?" Maggie asked.

"I don't know." Alden said. "I suppose someone must have at some point, but not since I've been here."

"Right." Maggie nodded. "Good night then."

"Good night, Maggie." Alden gave a smile and backed out the door, shutting it behind him.

Maggie trailed her fingers along the pillows. She'd never slept on anything so soft. Not in her time in the Siren's Realm, and certainly not in her years at the Academy.

She ran her fingers through her hair, catching them on the snarls, feeling the grit of the salt that clung to the strands from swimming in the Endless Sea.

Untying the string that held her hair back, she walked toward the narrow door in the corner of the room.

Holding her breath, she paused with her hand on the knob.

"Bertrand is not waiting behind a door to jump out at you, you stupid girl."

She opened the door and stepped into the bathroom.

A clawfoot tub longer than her whole body waited in the marble lined room. A basket filled with soaps of every color sat next to a pile of crisp white towels. A small table in the corner held a hand mirror and comb.

"Not too bad." Maggie turned the bronze taps. Steaming water poured into the tub. "Maybe living in the Fortress does come with a few perks."

aggie lay in bed, watching the sun creep through the heavy curtains. She hadn't slept, not really. There was something in the wide bed that left her feeling vulnerable. Like she was a child abandoned in the dark with monsters hiding all around. Or an imposter masquerading as a princess.

There was no scenario she could imagine in which she belonged in the big bed in the stone house, but the sheets were soft against her bare skin. Their comfort kept her pinned to the bed as the sun climbed ever higher.

As soon as she left the comforting weight of the quilt, she would have to go find Alden and Nic. Then they would have to go to the market square to try and figure out what had happened after the revelry. Questions would have to be asked, and decisions would need to be made.

I can't do it.

Maggie pulled the blankets tight around her shoulders.

I'm not the solver of mysteries and fixer of problems.

I'm only Maggie.

She tossed the covers back, letting them flop to the floor.

"No one is going to save you, Maggie Trent. Qualified or not, you're all you've got."

She climbed out of bed, letting the cold of the wooden floor shock her into alertness.

Her clothes lay in a pile on the floor by the fireplace. The caked white lines of salt from the Endless Sea were visible even from a few feet away.

"Dammit, Maggie." She went into the bathroom, snatching up the comb and tearing it through her hair.

The length of her hair, the mere fact that it touched her shoulders, sent anger bubbling in her stomach.

"Siren"—Maggie spoke to the empty room—"I'd like my hair cut back to the way it was when I first arrived here."

A faint flutter circled her shoulders, like a butterfly searching for a place to land.

She picked up the hand mirror, taking a deep breath before looking at her reflection. Her hair was exactly the same as when she had been dragged into the Siren's Realm. Brown and cut to barely below her chin. She had more freckles on her tanned face than she'd ever had at the Academy, but she looked like herself. Maggie Trent, the clanless witch from Virginia who'd grown up in a school made of gray concrete walls. The girl who'd been stolen from a battle and tossed into a new world.

The leather string with the moon and three stars charm waited on the table. Maggie tied the cord around her wrist.

"My name is Maggie Trent. I come from Earth, and I may never find my way back. But I will not let Bertrand, or the Siren, or living in her realm for a hundred years make me forget who I am. I've fought and killed, and almost died, and I've survived it all. I don't need Bertrand to hold my hand so I can find out what the Siren has planned. I've made it through Hell before, and I'll make it through whatever the Siren has up her sleeve."

Maggie tipped her chin up to the ceiling. "I'd like a clean set of clothes. Something I can travel in. And I want the pants to have pockets. Nice, big pockets."

The tingle of magic leaving her body dragged through her fingers as she walked back into the bedroom. A pair of black pants and a maroon top waited for her.

"Thanks," Maggie muttered.

The shirt flowed gently around her and left her arms bare. The pants were loose enough to allow her to climb the rocks to her home, and had four good-sized pockets hidden throughout their folds.

She pulled on her gray boots and rolled her old clothes into a bundle.

"Waste not, want not."

A tap sounded on her door.

"Maggie, are you awake?" Alden said. "I've made breakfast."

"I'm up." Maggie opened her door.

Alden stood in the hall, a cup of tea in one hand and a plate with a biscuit in the other.

"Maggie you've…" Alden mouthed wordlessly as his gaze drifted from her hair to her new clothes. "I see you've been up for a while."

"Yeah."

"And cut your hair." Alden's lips twisted into a frown.

"You don't like it?" Maggie crossed her arms as Alden's frown grew.

"I do like it." Alden's hands shook as he passed her the cup and plate. "You look quite lovely. You always look lovely, of course. But this suits you a bit more. You seem more like Maggie. Not that that makes any sense." He picked at the cuff of his sleeve.

"It makes sense." Maggie sipped her tea. "I feel more like Maggie."

"Good." Alden nodded.

"And the best part, the pants have pockets." She squeezed around Alden and out into the hall. "Now come on, we've got a mystery to solve."

"Of course." Alden hurried after her.

Nic waited in the hall at the bottom of the stairs. He buzzed and tipped his head as he caught sight of Maggie.

"Yes, Nic, I made an attempt at looking like an actual person. Congratulate me later, we've got things to do." She downed the last of her tea and abandoned the cup and plate on the windowsill.

"There's more food in the kitchen if you like," Alden said.

"No time." Maggie marched down the steps to the small room that led to the outside. "We're going to go and figure out all sorts of things."

"I don't know how she cut her hair," Alden murmured to Nic.

Maggie bit back her smile as Nic whistled.

"I don't know if the Siren could fix my hair, and I don't care to ask," Alden said.

A bright, clear morning greeted them on the streets of the Fortress.

A boat bobbed down the canal. The man working the oars hummed to himself as he passed. The song held a hint of hope in it that grew the bubble of delight that had taken up residence in Maggie's chest.

She took a deep breath, letting the distant tang of ocean air fill her lungs.

"Are you quite all right?" Alden picked at the sleeve of his new blue shirt.

"I'm fine." Maggie lifted his hand from his cuff, dragging him down the street. "I'm better than fine. We have something we have to do, and we're going to do it, because it's important. Which means we have purpose, and that feels really good right now."

Alden quickened his pace to walk by Maggie's side. "That is excellent."

"Yeah, well, someone smart pointed out that I can't hide on my rock forever." Maggie rolled her eyes at Alden.

She didn't slow her pace as they left the stone streets for the dirt lanes.

Centaurs milled about in front of their wide tents, the canvas marked with words Maggie had never been able to understand.

There was no fear in their early morning chatter as Maggie passed. No urgent tone to their conversation.

"I think a trip into the woods is the thing today," a dappled centaur said.

A black Arabian tilted his chin up to the sky. "I'm going to run with the breezes today. The shadows call for the pounding of my hooves."

"Doesn't sound like the Siren's Realm is breaking apart to me," Alden whispered as they turned onto a lane lined with bright yellow tents.

Identically colored flowers had been planted down the whole street. The blooms had the petals of a sunflower, but their centers shimmered with glittering gold. Their sweet scent tickled Maggie's nose.

"We should still be careful," Maggie said. "The end of the world to one person is after breakfast entertainment to another."

Maggie didn't let go of Alden's hand as they weaved their way closer to the market square. There was something in having his palm pressed against hers that brought comfort. Not in a way of being protected by him or feeling safer in his company. There was a thrilling sense of calm in holding his hand, though she had no need for him to hold hers.

"We're nearly there." Alden slowed his pace.

The road in front of them widened. The tents here had their flaps tied open, inviting customers to enter. One stall had displays of fine silk dresses for sale. Another was filled with tiny tables where people drank out of small, silver cups.

Nic rolled in front of Maggie, leading the way into the square proper.

The violet tent had vanished, replaced by the normal array of stalls. A man selling pastries hovered in front of his goods, ready to shake hands and take payment for his treats.

Wide tables set out in front of the wine seller were already filled. Illial, the gray-speckled centaur, stood in his usual spot on the outskirts of the square, blue smoke surrounding his head as he puffed on his pipe.

Maggie's heart gave a painful lurch as her gaze found the corner where Mathilda's shop had been. There was no white mobcap fluttering through the shadows as Mathilda prepared fish to sell. A different woman in long, multicolored robes had taken over the space.

The woman weaved between canvases, instructing her patrons, whose faces were all twisted with various states of confusion and frustration as they tried to paint a picture of a tree.

"Maggie?" Alden squeezed her hand. "Are you all right?"

"Yeah." She blinked back the burning in the corners of her eyes. "I'm fine."

She weaved her way through the crowd toward Illial. The centaur made no movement of greeting or even acknowledged her with a smile as she approached.

"Good morning, Illial." Maggie stopped just outside the cloud of blue smoke. "How are you this morning?"

"Surprised. I didn't think I would see you again outside the land of shadows," Illial said.

"The blackness didn't get me." Maggie's hair tickled her cheeks as she shook her head. "I just stayed hidden for a bit longer than I needed to."

Illial nodded slowly.

"Do you know anything about what happened here last night?" Maggie asked.

"The revelry?" Illial said. "I will not attend a thing where centaurs are expected to perform as horses in a circus."

Alden tightened his grip on Maggie's hand.

"Fair enough," Maggie said. "But what about what happened afterward? All the fighting? If anyone would know if there were bodies left in the market square this morning, it would be you."

Illial stared at Maggie for a long moment before nodding.

"There were bodies left behind?" Alden asked.

Illial kept his gaze focused on Maggie, ignoring Alden completely. "I do know of the ending of the skirmish. There were no bodies."

Alden let out a long breath.

"Some were left bleeding on the ground in the square, but the Siren, in her goodness, healed them all," Illial said. "I arrived after dawn to see the last of them crawling home."

"Okay." Maggie nodded, her mind racing. "That's good."

"There is nothing to fear in the Siren's Realm," Illial said. "Our only duty is to enjoy the sparkling of the Endless Sea. The Siren's will will see to the rest."

"You should go and watch the Endless Sea sparkle for yourself, Illial." Maggie smiled. "Who knows what wonders you could learn from watching the patterns of the Siren's waves?"

"When I have nothing more to learn from the patterns of her people as they move through her streets, perhaps I will try the Endless Sea as a thing to watch." Illial gave a little bow.

"Then I'll expect to see you by the water tomorrow." Maggie returned the bow, knowing full well Illial would not be visiting the Endless Sea in the next hundred sunrises.

"Maggie," Alden whispered in Maggie's ear as they cut back through the square, "have you tried asking for a weapon?"

I want a sword in my hand right now. Maggie thought the wish as loudly as she could. She looked down at her free hand, waiting for the rush of magic to pour from her fingers and a blade to appear in her grasp.

Nothing happened.

"I couldn't ask the Siren for one either," Alden said.

"She only lifted the ban for one night." Maggie chewed the

inside of her lip.

"Maggie, I'm quite new to the Siren's Realm, and I'm not wholly sure how these matters work…"

"But?" Maggie stopped in front of a tiny, brown tent selling leather-bound books.

"Is it possible the Compère wished for weapons to be allowed in the square?" Alden peered over Maggie's shoulder, his gaze darting around the square. "Could he have made a bargain with the Siren as Bertrand made with the swords in his house?"

Maggie's pulse quickened, thumping through her racing thoughts. "Why would he do that? Prepare a grand spectacle, then stage a fight?"

"It does seem odd," Alden said. "I'm sure it's a foolish notion."

"Not necessarily." Maggie led Alden down one of the small alleys that twisted away from the square. "We don't know who this Compère is. If he's bent enough on hiding his identity to cover his face in mist, he could be up to all sorts of things. Maybe the brawl was the point of getting everyone together."

"I don't suppose there's some loophole in the Siren's Decree that allows us to ask her if anyone is intentionally causing trouble in her realm?" Alden asked.

"Try it if you like." Maggie turned down a narrow lane of waist-high tents.

"Dear Siren, if it please your will, tell us who caused the trouble in your realm last night. If it was caused by a mortal. We seek only to preserve the peace in your great land."

Maggie held her breath for a moment as the foolish fear of a voice speaking from the sky pressed down her sense of reason.

No voice spoke from above.

"I suppose it doesn't work then," Alden said.

"There's someone who might know without asking the Siren." Maggie squeezed between two tents. "Lena from the palace knows all sorts of things."

"The palace?" Alden stopped dead, all color draining from his face. "You mean the big tent. With the minotaur, and the…"

"Yeah, that one." Maggie yanked on Alden's arm. "People talk in there, so we should be able to figure out something. Don't worry. I won't let any of the women eat you alive."

Maggie squeezed through the last bit of the passage between tents and onto the street beyond.

"Here we are." Maggie pointed to what should have been the towering green tent with a line of people waiting out front.

There was no tent or even street for that matter. They'd stepped out of the alley and onto a patch of wildflowers next to the forest.

"What?" Maggie spun back to the tents.

"We were meant to be at the palace? I think you must have made a wrong turn."

"I didn't." Maggie pulled Alden back onto the narrow strip of tramped down earth between the tents. "I've been this way dozens of times, and the palace should be there. It can't have moved, right?"

"The palace was where I've always known it to be yesterday."

Maggie stopped dead, hitting her face against the canvas as she rounded on Alden. "What were you going to the palace for?"

"I wasn't"—Alden blushed red—"I mean, I didn't… I would never frequent such a location for physical pleasure."

"So…" Maggie narrowed her eyes.

"It's a good marker for the city. I've been trying to learn my way through the warren of streets, and the market square, fountain square, and the palace are the best landmarks. There is also a fine wine vendor not far from the palace."

"If you did go for the ladies, or gentlemen, it really wouldn't be any of my business." Maggie sidled through the gap between tents.

"Of course. But Maggie, I would…"

Alden's words faded as they stepped out from between the tents and onto the same patch of wild flowers next to the forest.

CHAPTER 7

"*N*o," Maggie growled, shoving Alden through the alley in the other direction.

They burst out from between the tents back onto the patch of flowers bordering the forest.

"Maggie," Alden whispered, "I think there might be something strange going on."

"Think?" Maggie squeezed her eyes shut. "Stay here, okay?"

She didn't wait for Alden to speak before running back through the alley.

"Please let this work." Maggie burst out from between the tents.

"What did you find on the other side?" Alden asked.

"This is the other side." Maggie stared back at the gap between the tents.

"Oh dear. This isn't the path to the palace at all, is it?"

"No." Maggie shook her shoulders. "Okay. So we're stuck out here. That's okay."

"Is it? Perhaps we could cut around the side?"

Nic gave a growl and rumbled along the side of the tent.

"Nic, I don't think—"

A tinkling *hum* filled air, and Nic rolled back three feet as though shoved by an invisible hand.

"Are you all right?" Alden knelt in front of Nic.

Nic gave an indignant whistle.

Maggie turned in the opposite direction of where Nic had rolled, holding her hands out in front of her. She made it five steps before the *hum* sounded. Vibrations shook her fingers. Her shoes scraped against the flowers, tearing them up, as an unseen force pushed her backward.

"This is the Siren's doing?" Alden asked.

"I hope so," Maggie said. "I guess. Better that than someone managing to wish us trapped."

She spun in a slow circle, studying the tents, the flowers, and the woods beyond.

"This way." Maggie walked toward the trees, holding one hand out in front while reaching behind for Alden with the other.

Her jaw tensed as she waited for a hum to shove them backward. A fallen branch cracked under her foot as she stepped into the trees. Maggie's heart throttled into her throat.

Nic gave a low whistle.

"I don't know why we're supposed to go this way," Maggie said, "but we don't seem to have a choice, so we might as well go."

Sunlight broke through the leaves, bathing the forest floor in a speckled pattern of light. Birds sang up above, fluttering from branch to branch.

"You know," Alden said when they'd been walking for a few minutes, "if we weren't being herded, this would be a rather lovely walk."

He changed his grip on Maggie's hand, moving up to walk by her side.

"Once we've figured out why the Siren is allowing her people to attack each other and if the Compère has a nefarious plan, perhaps"—Alden paused—"perhaps we could bring a picnic out this way. Enjoy the quiet. I've met an excellent cheese vendor."

"I'm not actually a woods person."

"Of course." Pink crept up Alden's cheeks. "I understand."

"Maybe you could bring the cheese to the beach. There's a section of pure white sand. It's so soft, it feels like flour between your fingers."

"What a wonder that would be! I'll look forward to our afternoon."

Maggie opened her mouth to speak, but the sound of flowing water drove all other thoughts from her mind.

A brook wound through the trees straight ahead of them. Rocks cut through the water, sending the current leaping as it cascaded downstream. Trees gave shade to the brook, as though luring every random passerby to sit along the banks and dangle their feet in the cool water. A gap in the trees shed sunshine on the center of the stream, bathing the water in bright light.

"You've got to be kidding," Maggie said.

"I've seen this before." Alden dragged Maggie to the very edge of the stream. "On the painting in Bertrand's home."

Nic swiveled his head, searching the clearing.

"I don't know, Nic. I suppose there could be some sort of clue as to where he's gone." Alden let go of Maggie's hand. He walked to the nearest tree, trailing his fingers along the bark.

Maggie stared down at the light in the stream.

"Perhaps the Siren led us here to find answers about the Compère," Alden said.

The bright swath of water seemed both too narrow and too deep to be allowed, as though the creek weren't merely reflecting the sun, but drawing a light from a depth far out of reach to radiate into the Siren's Realm.

"I don't think this has anything to do with the Compère." Maggie leapt out onto one of the rocks that broke through the middle of the stream.

Nic dipped one of his many arms into the water, reaching for the rocky bottom.

"Nic, don't," Maggie said.

With a grumble, Nic backed away.

"Do you smell it?" Maggie leaned over the stream, taking a deep breath.

"Smell what?" Alden gingerly sniffed from the bank.

Maggie squinted down into the light. "Magic. Like perfume on the wind, but there's something alive in it."

"We are in the Siren's Realm. We're surrounded by magic."

"This is foreign magic." Maggie's voice trembled, and her pulse raced. "This is a stitch to another world. This is where Bertrand went."

She lifted her foot to leap to shore, but the edge of the bank moved, pushing Alden and Nic back ten feet.

"Maggie, are you all right?" Alden reached for her across the water.

"I'm fine." She lifted her other foot to jump to the far bank.

Without even so much as a *swish* of rushing water, the bank surged away, as though the Siren herself had simply stretched out the painting above Bertrand's mantle.

"I'm not afraid of getting my feet wet." She reached her toes toward the water. The gentle stream became a rushing torrent.

"Maggie!" Alden called over the *roar* of the water. He had a heavy rope in his hand. With a wide swing, he tossed one end to her.

A wave leapt up, batting the lifeline aside.

"I'll come to you!" As he stepped toward the bank, the water became wider still.

"Stay where you are," Maggie said. "She doesn't want you to come with me."

"Come with you where?"

"To Bertrand. She wants me to find him."

"Why?" Alden tore his hands through his fluffy hair.

"No idea." Maggie leaned over the bright patch of water. "Find the palace. Ask Lena what she knows about the Compère. If you need help, go to Gabrielle, he's a good friend. He'll do what he can. Stay away from anywhere people manage to ask for weapons, and guard your magic. If things get bad, you'll need every ounce you have. And the Derelict aren't above stealing it all."

"Don't do this. We'll find a way to get you back across the water."

"My way across the water is down." She crept her toes out to the very edge of the rock.

"What if you can't find Bertrand?" The water raged over Alden's shout. "What if you can't find your way back?"

"I'll be fine." Maggie gave Alden one final smile. "Promise you'll stay safe until I come home?"

Alden nodded and placed his hand over his heart.

Maggie did the same, willing her pulse to calm. She took a breath and jumped into the light.

Her boots flooded with chill water, and, for an instant, she thought her feet would meet the bottom of the river. The raging water would suck her under and carry her downstream.

But the brightness closed in around her, stealing her breath and robbing her of movement as she tumbled from light into pure dark.

No air rushed past her as she fell through the void. The panic that thumped in her heart flipped over and over, turning into something more like excitement. A flash of green danced before her eyes as her feet struck solid ground.

"*Oof*." Her hands hit hard stone as she tipped forward, landing on her knees. "Ouch."

She checked her palms for blood before looking around.

The sunlight that had filled the woods in the Siren's Realm had disappeared. Shadows shrouded the square where she'd landed. Wide, drooping trees burrowed up through the earth, and shoulder-high brick walls blocked everything beyond from view.

As Maggie pushed herself to stand, her fingers found texture on the stone slab where she'd landed.

"*Inexuro.*" At Maggie's muttered spell, a ball of flames burst into being in her palm.

She held the light close to the ground where weathered words had been carved into the stone.

Ezibell Lawrence ~ Taken by the shadows in the Year of the Storm.

Maggie held the ball of fire high over her head.

All around the bricked-in square, stone slabs were set into the ground.

"I've landed in a graveyard."

CHAPTER 8

A tickle of wind kissed the back of Maggie's neck. "Do not freak out, Maggie Trent. You've been around plenty of death before. Just because these corpses are older doesn't mean they should scare you."

Standing with her light held high, she could see what lay beyond the brick wall. Roads lined with houses branched out in every direction. Street lamps had been lit, though their light did nothing to make the night any friendlier.

"Okay." Maggie nodded. "Find Bertrand. That's all I've got to do. Find Bertrand and tell him the Siren's decided to use me as her personal messenger, and I've been sent to summon him home. And if I don't murder him, maybe I'll toss in the bits about the Compère and market square brawl."

The soft soil gave under her feet as she made her way to the wall, carefully avoiding the stone slabs in the ground.

"Am I going to have to climb the wall?" Maggie murmured.

There was no break in the barrier on this side of the square. She followed the wall, trailing the fingers of her left hand along the bricks and holding her light high with the right.

The trees in the square held the promise of new blooms on

their branches. White and pink had just begun to peek out through the tips of the green buds. The scent of flowers and moist soil sailed on the slight breeze.

A sharp *clatter* of wooden wheels on a stone street came from the far side of the graveyard.

Maggie took off at a run, charging toward the sound. Before she'd made it to the far wall, her fingers left the brick and smacked hard into a set of wrought iron bars.

"Dammit." Maggie shook her bruised fingers before reaching out for the bars.

An intricate pattern of swirls melded together to form a gate wide enough for a horse and cart to travel through. Words had been etched into each of the swirls.

Maggie held her light up to the lettering on the peak of the gate.

In the Year of the Flood, and season of drowned blood, this cemetery was consecrated by order of General Wisham.

Maggie traced her fingers along the writing under the dedication. These words she could not read.

Invate unburom livse…

The letters continued on and on, twisting their way down the gate.

"Why can't I read you?" Maggie squinted at the words.

A heavy latch on the outside of the gate kept it tightly shut.

Maggie squeezed her arms through the swirls, twisting her wrist toward the latch. Her fingers grazed the edge of the handle.

"Come on." Maggie pressed her arm farther between the bars, feeling bruises forming where the metal bit into her skin.

Leaning all her weight against the gate, she grabbed the latch between two fingers, pressing it down. With a heavy *thunk* the lock clicked open. The gate swung away from the wall, taking Maggie with it.

She stumbled onto the street beyond the cemetery, her toes

catching on the uneven brickwork. Her feet flew out from under her, but her arm wedged in the gate kept her upright.

"Ow, ow, ow," Maggie groaned as she finally pulled her arm free from the bars. Red scrapes covered her forearm. She closed the gate with a *clang*. "Stupid lock. At least you made it—"

A piercing *wail* cut across her words, radiating from the graveyard she'd just left. The sound drove into her ears, setting her teeth on edge. No sooner had instinct kicked in, telling her in no uncertain terms to run from the sound, than the door of the nearest house flung open.

Maggie squinted against the bright light pouring from the doorway.

"Stay inside, Deana," a man shouted. He slammed the door behind him, but the light didn't disappear. It glowed with exorbitant brightness from a lantern gripped in his hand.

Maggie stepped forward to speak to the man, but more doors opened on the street, each pouring light into the darkness. The sounds of panicked voices grew louder as all the people who had emerged from their homes moved toward Maggie, holding their lights high.

"Who's there?" a voice boomed over the crowd.

"Maggie"—she swallowed the bile that tickled her throat—"Maggie Trent. Can anyone make that noise stop?"

"Did the shadows bid you touch the gates?" An older man with a white beard that hung down to his waist stopped ten feet in front of Maggie, holding his light up to her face.

"What?" Waves shifted through Maggie's vision as the *wail* pounded into her brain. "I was stuck inside the cemetery, and I tried to get out."

The *wail* stopped.

Silence rang in Maggie's ears.

"Thank you."

"You were in the graveyard?" The bearded man squinted at Maggie.

"Yes." Maggie scanned the faces of those surrounding her.

At least fifty people had come out of their homes at the noise, all holding their lights toward Maggie. A mixture of confusion and fear filled each of their faces.

"I'm sorry." Maggie gave a little bow. "I didn't mean to trespass. I sort of—"

"Flung from the shadows?" The bearded man nodded.

"Actually, yeah," Maggie said.

A woman with bright red hair gasped, clasping a hand over her mouth.

"It is possible?" A man in a white nightshirt grabbed the redhead's arm, as though afraid she might faint.

"I never thought to witness such mercy." The bearded man lowered his light, holding out a withered hand toward Maggie. "Come into the light, child."

"Okay." Keeping her own flame held high, she stepped onto the street.

The lantern people surrounded her. Even with dozens of lights pressing their glow against her, Maggie's skin held no heat.

A rush of whispers raced through the crowd.

"She's shed the shadows."

"Another shadow stalker freed."

"How long was she trapped?"

"I'm sorry," Maggie said, "but I think you have me—"

"How long were you cloaked in shadow?" The bearded man squinted at Maggie's face.

"I—what?"

"What year did you disappear in your hunt?" he asked.

"I really don't know what you're talking about." Maggie shook her head.

"She's been gone too long." A woman with a shock of bright white hair twisted into a bun laid her hand on the old man's shoulder. "Don't push too hard. She's barely more than a child, Elver."

"Too true." Elver nodded, his beard swaying with the movement. He reached out and took Maggie's hand. "Come with me. We'll see you safely to rest. There will be time for answers when your mind clears."

The crowd parted, lighting a path up the road.

"I'm sorry, but I still don't understand." Maggie didn't fight as Elver guided her up the street. "I think you might have me mistaken for someone else."

"No need to worry about who you were," Elver said. "After the battle you've survived, no one faults you. The blessed light allowed you to return, that's enough to be grateful for."

"Right."

Tell them you've come from the Siren's Realm. Ask them to help you find Bertrand and be done with this place.

She stayed silent as the crowd ushered her up the row of houses. A park waited at the end of the street. Wide trees dripping moss from their branches gave shelter to low bushes with white flowers blooming in the dark.

The pack led her down another street. The road rose and fell every few feet, as though someone had deflated parts of the ground. Still, the houses on either side stood strong, with no cracks or faults marring their foundations.

"Are you sure they'll take her at night?" a woman whispered to Elver as though Maggie wouldn't be able to hear.

"She's been returned from the shadows. They'd take her on Saint Lucas day and be happy about if they know what's good for them," Elver grumbled.

Knots formed in Maggie's shoulders as she fought the urge to run with every step.

The houses they passed were well manicured. The three and four story homes had been built right next to each other, leaving no alley for Maggie to dodge through. Shutters had been left open to the night, but breaking into a person's home for a chance at escape held no appeal.

"I really think I'll be all right on my own," Maggie said. "There's no need for an escort."

"The shadows have tasted your scent," Elver said. "It would be no less than murder for us to leave you in the dark with only a fire spell for protection. I'll not have murder on my soul when the day comes for my end."

"Of course. Thank you." Maggie nodded. "Silly me."

They turned down another street. Here, the road was made of well-worn cobblestone with none of the dips and grooves that marred the other streets.

A bright light shimmered up ahead, bathing the road in a luminous glow, as though dawn had come and chosen only one building to shine upon.

Maggie bit back the dozen questions she wanted to ask as Elver led her to the front of the light-bathed building.

The bright beams were coming, not from lanterns as Elver and the others held, but from the building itself. The white columns gracing the façade glowed brilliantly. The stairs shone with a light so radiant it seemed impossible that anyone could step on them without having their feet burned off.

"You'll be safe here."

Maggie let Elver step onto the first stair before following him up.

He stopped in front of a door that shone with a pale golden gleam. "Put out your fire. The brethren don't like outside magic in their home."

"Right." Maggie closed her hand, extinguishing the ball of flames.

Giving Maggie a nod, Elver raised his fist to pound on the door.

A hollow *thud* resonated through the wood, vibrating the light the surface emanated.

"If they don't answer," the white-haired woman said, "we

should have them brought up for dereliction. Shouldn't be us responding to alarms at any rate."

"Hush, woman," Elver warned.

Maggie's pulse quickened as seconds ticked past. "I really think I'll be okay on my own. I could just sleep out here until morning and then figure things out."

"Not a person with a soul would leave you out here." Elver pounded on the door again. "Get out here, you lot! We've been woken up in the middle of the night by an alarm and found a shadow stalker returned from the darkness. If this girl can fight her way out of the black, and we can brave the shadows to fetch her, you brethren can at least get out of bed to claim her."

"Oh, Elver," the old woman said.

A moment later, the golden door swung open. A middle-aged man peered out into the night. He wore nothing but a loose robe that covered him from shoulders to thigh. His black hair sparkled with a glittering light, and his skin glowed like the young girl's from the Compère's festivities.

The memory of the girl being swallowed by shadows drove all other thoughts from Maggie's mind.

"Why have you come to the sanctuary?" The man spoke, not with the booming voice Maggie had somehow expected, but with a soft tone.

"The siren sounded in the West Worth Graveyard," Elver said.

Lines formed on the glowing man's forehead.

"We found this girl as she made her way out of the gate," Elver pressed on. "She fell from the shadows and has no memory of how she got there."

The glowing man tucked his hands behind his back and leaned in toward Maggie. "You fought your way from the shadows?"

"I'm very confused about a lot of things," Maggie said. "I was just trying to get out of the graveyard. I'm looking for someone, he might have ended up falling out of the shadows like me."

"Poor child." The glowing man shook his head.

"Actually, it's Maggie." She held her hand out. "Maggie Trent."

The man stared at her.

"I prefer my name to *child.*" Maggie waited for a moment, her hand extended.

"She has lost much to the shadows," the glowing man said. "We will keep her from losing more."

"Thank you." Elver bowed.

"It's late for you all to be traveling in the darkness." The glowing man reached behind the door toward something Maggie couldn't see. A bright bell rang from within the shimmering sanctuary.

Better than the wailing alarm.

"Brethren will see you all safely home." The glowing man bowed. "Thank you for venturing out to save this child."

"Maggie," Maggie murmured.

"Hold on to your name, Maggie." Elver clapped her on the shoulder. "It may not seem like much to remember, but it's far better than nothing when the time comes to find yourself."

"Thank you, Elver," Maggie said.

Six shimmering people filed out the door. The crowd parted, giving the new arrivals a wide berth. As soon as the first from the sanctuary made it to the front of the group, everyone turned to follow her back the way they'd come.

"Thank you." Elver bowed to the glowing man and started after the crowd, his lantern held high against the darkness.

CHAPTER 9

"Come, child." The glowing man opened the golden door wide, gesturing for Maggie to enter.

Maggie looked after the disappearing group for one moment more before stepping inside the shining building.

"Wow." The word tumbled from her lips.

Every surface in sight glowed with the same shimmering brightness that covered the man. From the chandelier that hung from the ceiling, to the table and vase that stood in the center of the entryway. Even the pale purple flowers in the vase radiated a strange light.

"This way." The man skirted the table and opened another glowing door.

In this room, as in the entryway, every surface gleamed.

Here, three rows of tiered benches faced the open center of the room. High windows peered into the night, but the darkness outside didn't penetrate the inside of the sanctuary.

"We'll find you a place to rest." The man turned toward a door halfway down the long room. "I promise no darkness will touch you in sleep."

"What's your name?" Maggie asked.

"Fellow Serber." Serber turned to Maggie, giving her another bow.

Maggie bowed back. "Thank you for taking me in for the night."

"You are welcome in the sanctuary for as long as you need. It is our honor to host one of the returned." Serber led Maggie into a long hallway.

On one side, a bright golden gate blocked the way to a pool. The water in the enormous marble basin swirled in a twisting pattern, as though stirred by the hand of an unseen giant.

Across from the pool, a set of wide double doors opened into a library stacked to the ceiling with shelves of books and lit with dozens of torches. The glittering spines of the books seemed to call for Maggie to caress every volume.

Would I even be able to read the words?

She stared at the library for so long she had to run for a moment to catch up to Serber.

"If it's all right to ask"—Maggie gave a little bow—"what is this place?"

Serber stopped and turned to Maggie.

Her muscles tensed, ready to be hit.

But Serber didn't shout or raise his hand. Rather, his shoulders rounded, and a crease formed between his brows.

"You must have been with the shadows for a very long time to have forgotten so much. We will do everything in our power to guide you back into the light."

"Thank you," Maggie said. "So…"

"The sanctuary is the home of the brethren." Serber continued down the long hallway.

"Right," Maggie said. "How could I have forgotten that?"

"We are the light that stands between the shadows and the living of Sarana." Serber turned down a narrow hall lined with doors.

Maggie shoved her hands into her pockets to hide their shaking.

He stopped at a door near the end of the hall. "Rest in peace, Maggie."

A skip of fear jumped in Maggie's heart as Serber opened the door.

There was no monster waiting to take her to her eternal rest in the tiny room beyond. A narrow bed, a desk, and a chair took up most of the space, leaving barely enough room on the shining floor for the mosaic of two men facing each other.

One of the men had been made of silver tiles and one of deep gray. Both reached toward the other, their fingers barely separated by a thin strand of pure white.

"Someone will come to collect you when the shadows fall." Serber held the door open for her, waiting to close her in.

A thousand questions raced through Maggie's mind, but fatigue and fear muddled them all up too much to seem worth asking.

"Thank you, Fellow Serber." She stepped into the chamber, carefully avoiding stepping on the tiles that formed the two men.

The door clicked shut behind her.

A wave of panic crashed into Maggie's chest.

"Dammit, dammit, dammit. What the hell have I gotten myself into?"

She reached for the doorknob, half expecting the polished metal to shock her. Her fingers closed around the knob, which twisted without trouble.

"Not being locked in is good," she whispered to herself. "Good start, Maggie. Fall into a world and end up in a sanctuary. Could be worse, right?"

She bit her lips together as she searched the room. There was no window to the outside for her to climb through. No switch to turn off the light that emanated from every surface. No way to lock the door from the inside. And no hint of what sort of person usually occupied the room.

"Option one—run. Get through the door and bolt for the exit. Getting out of here would be great, but people with lanterns might decide to rescue you again. Or figure out you're not someone who's returned from the shadows and decide to kill you."

She ran her fingers over the surface of the shimmering desk. Her skin didn't steal any of the wood's light.

"Option two—stay here and let them think you're a shadow stalker and see where that gets you."

Maggie sat and pulled off her boots. She carefully loosened the laces before setting them next to the bed, ankles open and ready to be slipped on at a moment's notice.

The sole blanket on the bed weighed barely more than a normal sheet. The fabric shimmered as she climbed beneath it.

"Bertrand Wayland, if I ever find you, you are going to owe me so badly."

She clamped her eyes shut against the brightness.

"Is there any way to shut off the lights?" Maggie asked the wall.

There was no reply.

A strange twinge tugged at Maggie's chest.

There was no Siren to answer her. No omniscience to hear her every word. No one to ask for a thicker blanket. No guide to give answers.

"You are pathetic." Maggie swung both legs out of bed.

The wooden chair didn't weigh much as she carried it to the door and jammed it under the handle.

She jumped back beneath the sheet, as though a monster hiding under the bed might bite her.

But there were no shadows under the bed. No shadows anywhere in the room.

Maggie held up her hand near the wall. The light from the wall itself prevented her shadow from forming.

The underside of the desk glowed, lighting the patch of floor under its top.

"Shadows." Maggie peeked under the covers.

The glowing of the sheets kept shadows from forming around her.

"They're afraid of their shadows, and they think I used to stalk shadows, and escaped from shadows, and..."

Her voice trailed away.

She dug her fists into her eyes until white dots danced through her vision.

"And it still doesn't make sense. What did you figure out, Bertrand? How long until you understood what was going on here?"

She draped her arms over her face, trying to block out some of the light.

One deep breath, then another.

Her breath was the only sound, rumbling rhythmically through her chest.

~

Waves lapped against her rock on the edge of the Endless Sea. A whale's fluke cut through the water in the distance.

Maggie laughed as the whale spun lazily in the sea.

"There are such pleasures to be found in the Siren's Realm," Bertrand said.

"Bertrand!" Maggie hadn't known he stood beside her until she heard his voice.

"It really is a wonder all the populations of every known world have not found her realm or died in the attempt to seek her." Bertrand didn't look at Maggie as he spoke. His gaze stayed fixed over the waves.

Maggie blinked several times, trying to focus on his face.

It was the same face she'd always known, but a bright glow radiated from his skin. His dark hair, though still pulled back in its customary ponytail, glistened in the sun. His normal dark tailcoat and silver buckled shoes had disappeared, leaving him with only a robe as Fellow Serber wore.

"Bertrand," Maggie said, "I've been looking for you. You need to come back to the Siren's Realm. She made me come after you, and I need to get back. There's something—"

"There is nothing but light and shadow. There is no in between. Only light and shadow."

"That's great. But the Siren—"

"In the end, there can be only shadow and peace. Rest in peace, Miss Trent."

His gaze shifted to her face. His eyes turned inky black.

"We have to get you out of here." Maggie reached for Bertrand's hand.

The black poured from his eyes, staining his cheeks.

"No!" Maggie swiped at the black that covered Bertrand's face. "Get off of him!"

The black wouldn't come off. The color stained Maggie's hands and grew, creeping its way up her arms.

"No!" She tore at her own skin, desperate to free herself from the black.

A low laugh carried from over Maggie's shoulder. She spun toward the sound but couldn't look away from the black consuming her hands.

"Bertrand, help me."

The darkness crawled up her arms.

"Get off of me!" She took two longs strides and plummeted off the edge of the rock into the Endless Sea waiting below.

Water closed in around her.

≈

a gasp punched air into her lungs.

"No!" Maggie screamed. The sound bounced off the wall a few inches in front of her face.

She pushed against the glowing wall, struggling to break free from the sheet that bound her limbs.

With a *squeal*, she fell out of bed, cracking her shoulder on the floor.

A person yelped behind her.

"Stay away from me." Maggie kicked free from the sheets and rolled to face the door.

"I won't touch you." A boy stood by the door, back plastered to the wall. "Just please stop flinging your limbs about."

"Flinging my limbs about?" Maggie tossed the sheet onto the bed and leapt to her feet.

"You need to be more deliberate with your movements," the boy said. "I've only come to bring you to breakfast."

Maggie yanked on her boots. "I had a chair against the door. How did you get in here?"

"Very carefully." A faint smile played at the corners of the boy's mouth. "I knocked, but you didn't answer. When I heard you screaming, I thought it best to enter." He held up the doorknob. "I had no intention of invading your privacy."

"So you pulled the knob off my door?"

"I was worried." The boy shrugged.

Maggie considered the boy as she tied her boots.

He seemed to be only a year or two older than she was, and barely an inch taller. His hair would have been dark brown if it didn't have a glittering glow mixed within its strands. He wore only shoes and the same loose robe as Serber.

"You're a fellow?" Maggie asked.

"An acolyte." The boy dipped his head. "I am still only Diven at the moment."

"Diven." Maggie nodded, wrinkling her forehead in what she

hoped looked like a knowing way. She held out her hand to Diven. "I'm Maggie."

Diven stared down at her hand. "I've already been bathed, Maggie. I'm afraid my time for touching has passed."

"Right." Maggie forced out a laugh. "Silly me. Who would want to touch someone after being bathed?"

"None who wish to remain in the sanctuary. They'd warned me your time in the shadows had stolen a part of your memory, but I never imagined it would have taken more than the memories of yourself."

"I don't remember anything but my name, so any tips you've got for not getting kicked out of the sanctuary would be great."

Diven's chest shook as he laughed. "Don't touch the bathed, don't run in the bright hall, and don't invite the shadows in. That's really all you need to know. The brethren are kind. They'll help you in your journey back to the light."

"Thank you. I'm very grateful to have been found by such good people after fighting my way out of the shadows."

"You are a noble warrior." Diven nodded solemnly.

"Right." Not sure what else to do, Maggie plastered a smile on her face.

Bertrand would know what questions to ask.

"Which way to breakfast?" Maggie said after a long moment.

"Follow me." Diven led Maggie out into the hall and back the way Serber had brought her the night before.

"How many people live here?" Maggie asked.

"There are twenty-two thousand living in the light in the city of Sarana," Diven said. "If you add the shadows who walk among us, the estimate runs from fifty to one hundred and thirty thousand."

"I—" Maggie mouthed wordlessly for a moment. "I meant in the sanctuary."

"Oh," Diven laughed, like the thought of thousands upon thousands of shadows living in the city shouldn't be shocking.

"There are seventy brethren and acolytes living in the sanctuary at the moment. Imagine thousands of people trying to live in these walls. We'd never fit."

"Right..."

At the end of the corridor, Diven opened a door that looked identical to the rest in the hall. Rather than a small bedroom, another hallway greeted them. This corridor had no doors. Instead, portraits lined the space. Some were no bigger than Maggie's palm, others were larger than life.

"Who are all these people?" Maggie asked.

"The shadows were cruel to you." Diven shook his head. "I'm sorry for what you've lost."

"I'll be fine, but who are the people in the paintings?"

"The best of the shadow stalkers. The practice began years ago to help those who returned as you have. To have a record of their faces if the shadows stole everything else from them. To have a likeness on these walls is a great honor some hunters never achieve."

The hall ended in an open doorway. Dozens of voices carried from the room beyond. The scent of something like coffee and fresh baked bread wafted down the corridor.

"Everyone will be thrilled to meet you," Diven said. "It's been a few years since a shadow stalker has returned to the light."

A bell clanged up ahead.

Diven quickened his pace, jogging toward the open door. "It's time for prayers."

Maggie stopped, her legs unable to match his stride, her mind unable to process anything beyond the portrait of Bertrand Wayland scowling down at her.

CHAPTER 10

"*Y*ou have got to be kidding me." Maggie reached for the painting.

There was no mistaking the lines of the face or the faint look of disdain at being told to sit still long enough for a portrait to be drawn.

A tiny plaque had been set into the sparkling wood of the frame.

Bertrand Wayland ~ Shadow Stalker First Order

"How long have you been here, Bertrand?" Maggie whispered.

"Maggie." Diven popped his head back into the hall. "It's time for prayers."

"Diven, how long does someone have to work as a shadow stalker to get their portrait on the wall?" Maggie jogged down the hallway.

"Some work their entire lives and never achieve the honor. Some of the best are taken by the shadows before they're sought for recording."

Maggie's head swam, blurring the portraits she passed.

Diven's face paled as he examined Maggie. "Are you all right?" He clasped his hands behind his back.

"There's someone on the wall I recognize. An old friend of mine."

"You're starting to remember on your own?" Diven's face brightened.

He looks like a cherub. Shining and smiling.

A coarse laugh rattled Maggie's throat.

"We should get you some food." Diven waved Maggie into the kitchen. "A first meal in years, that would perk anyone up."

As Maggie stepped into the kitchen, everyone present turned to stare at her.

"Hi." Maggie gave a little wave.

No one spoke.

"Thank you so much for your hospitality." She gave a slow nod.

Why am I nodding to sparkly fairy people?

"We are honored to have you," Serber said. "What good would a sanctuary be if we could not offer safe harbor to those who fight for freedom from the darkness?"

"We've saved you a seat." A young girl with dazzling blond hair pulled a chair out from the long table.

"Thanks." Maggie searched the faces of the brethren as she walked to her place.

A woman who seemed to be in her nineties sat at the far end of the table, her eyes closed as though in prayer or sleep. A few near Maggie's age sat along the middle of the table. There were empty chairs at odd intervals that had been left pushed in with no plates set in front of them. There was no sign of Bertrand in the crowd.

"If you please." The girl gestured to Maggie's seat and took a step back.

"Thanks." Maggie sat and scooted in toward the table, wincing at the sound of her wooden chair scraping on the marble floor.

Serber stood in front of his seat and raised both hands. The room fell silent as everyone turned to face him.

"May the light protect our hearts and minds. May the shadows be merciful in their pursuit. May the hunters find those who are lost. May those who lead us be ever shielded from darkness. And may the ground remain strong under our feet."

"For the light," the fellows murmured.

A moment of silence followed before the clattering of plates being passed.

"Bread?" The blond girl placed a silver tray of bread on the table next to Maggie. Though the tray sparkled with the same light that coated the rest of the sanctuary, the bread was a normal brown.

"Thank you." Maggie took a slice and passed the tray toward Diven. "Did you want some?"

"Yes." Diven stared at the tray.

Maggie held the tray closer to him.

"You"— Diven glanced around the table—"you have put it down."

"Right." Maggie set the tray on the table. "Sorry."

"It's all right," Diven said. "You'll remember soon enough."

"Fruit?" The girl placed a multicolored assortment next to Maggie.

"Thanks." She chose a pink sphere. "So, the people who have their portraits in the hall, is there a list of where to find them?"

"Of course," Diven said. "We have an index of living and lost shadow stalkers in the library. When we've finished eating, we can go to the library and search for you. There's a chance some of your descendants are still living."

"Descendants?" Maggie choked on the pink fruit.

"Don't get her hopes up, Diven." The blond leaned back in her chair, whispering behind Maggie. "Her family could all be in the shadows by now."

Diven shot the blond a glare before looking to Maggie. "I'm sorry if I spoke out of turn."

"It's fine," Maggie said. "I want to find my friend. The one from the hall. Bertrand Wayland."

The blond's fork clattered to the floor. "You know Bertrand Wayland?" Her pale blue eyes widened.

"Yes," Maggie said, "and I need to find him."

"Then you couldn't have been taken very long ago," Diven said. "You might only have been in the shadows for a little while."

"What's he like in person?" The blond leaned toward Maggie.

"A bit of a jerk," Maggie said then turned back to Diven. "So Bertrand is still alive and in the city?"

"Of course he is," the blond said. "He's everywhere, every night. Bertrand Wayland is a legend."

"Of course he is." Maggie's eyelids twitched as she fought the temptation to roll her eyes. "So, you can get me to him?"

"I would be honored to lead you to Hunter Wayland," Diven said, "but we need to visit the library, find out who you are."

"I'm sure *Hunter Wayland* will have no problem telling me who I'm supposed to be," Maggie said. "How long has he been here working as a shadow stalker?"

"You don't know?" The blond clapped her hand to her mouth.

"She was in the shadows, Stilla," Serber said. "Be kind."

"Sorry." Stilla bowed her head. "I didn't know you were listening, Fellow Serber."

"You should speak all the more kindly when there is no one listening to admonish you," Serber said.

"Yes, Fellow Serber." Stilla kept her chin low as she turned back to her plate.

"Bertrand Wayland has been fighting the shadows since he arrived in Sarana four years ago," Serber said.

"Four years." The air rushed from Maggie's lungs.

"He's a legend," Diven said. "He's ventured further into the world of shadows than any other has ever dared."

"You said arrived," Maggie said. "Where did he arrive from?"

"The land across the water," Serber said. "Not many whose

ancestors don't rest under the streets of the city would venture into the shadows at all, let alone devote their lives to the light."

"Wait, what?" Maggie pressed her thumbs to her temples. "There are people under the streets?"

Serber tented his fingers beneath his chin as he considered Maggie.

The whole kitchen had fallen horribly silent.

"She should be purged." The old woman at the end of the table leaned forward. "For the shadows to have pulled so much from her mind in such a short time, there is darkness lurking within her."

"I'm really fine." Maggie pushed away from the table. "It's coming back to me in bits. The shadows were super shocking, that's all."

As Maggie stood, so did all the brethren.

"You know what?" Maggie's bright voice bounced off the walls. "I think I remember coming from across the water like Bertrand. A place with no shadows, and I followed him here, and got sucked into the shadows, then they spit me out, and you brought me here. So really, all I need to do is find Bertrand and everything will be just fine."

"They would never let a woman travel from the land across the water," Serber said.

"Really?" Maggie said. "A little sexist, don't you think?"

"The shadows are playing tricks on your mind," Serber said. "The light carries truth. Let us help you, Maggie."

Maggie walked backward, feeling for the opening that led to the hall.

"I really don't want help." Her fingers found the edge of the kitchen wall. "I'm just going to go."

"Maggie!" Diven shouted as she turned and sprinted down the corridor.

"Help the child." Serber's voice carried after her.

Maggie glanced behind as the *rumble* of footfalls followed her.

The brethren ran single file as they chased her, keeping a careful distance between them.

"Amateurs." She flung open the door to the main corridor and ran toward the hall of light.

She chanced a glance through the open library doors and the gate that led to the bright, shimmering pool. There was no one lurking in the light to snatch her.

Flinging open the door to the hall of light, she charged across the center of the room. A set of circles shone on the floor where she hadn't noticed them the night before. The circles throbbed with a bright glow, their span growing with every pulse. Maggie sprinted through the middle of the light, hands ready to push through the glittering door beyond.

A weightlessness grabbed her feet, stopping them mid-stride. Before she could scream, the unseen force flipped her onto her back and lifted her body three feet into the air. The more she fought to free herself, the lighter her limbs became. After a few seconds, her body held no weight at all. There was no sense her body even existed.

"Let me go!" Her scream wavered as her mouth fought to form the words. "Let me out of here."

"Let the light carry you." Serber appeared over her shoulder. "The light will wash away the darkness."

"I don't want washing."

The fellows surrounded her on all sides. As one, they lifted their hands. Maggie's body rose with their movement.

"Bertund." Maggie's words muddied in her mouth. "Brig me to Bertund."

A shining light began at the center of her eyes, swallowing her vision.

Bertrand. Her mouth didn't move.

The light held shapes and infinite color. And the color had meaning just beyond the reaches of Maggie's mind.

People coming from across the sea and landing in a great

storm. The storm calming and the land allowing people safe harbor. A town being built stone by stone. Sickness spreading, the dead outnumbering the living. Burying the dead in vast fields. The sickness leaving, the city spreading. A battle, more death, more graves. Peace. More building. Building on top of the dead. The dead themselves anchoring the houses. The storm returning, the waters rising. Shadows being pushed out of their graves.

A scream broke through the swirling light.

But the colors hadn't finished painting their horrible picture.

The shadows grew stronger, waking up more of the dead. Drawing the living into their fold.

The screaming didn't stop.

People bathed in light entered the darkness, their shine making them immune to the shadows. Pushing the shadows back with the pure brilliance of their glow.

Suddenly, Maggie found she had form. Arms and legs the shadows fought to touch.

The shining people surrounded her, blocking the shadows from violating her flesh.

The screaming ebbed away.

The colors around her lost their brilliance. The light meant more.

The shining eternal glow held the only true meaning. Peace and safety. A comfort that could not be bought or broken.

Fear dissipated in a single gasp.

The light dampened. Not disappearing into nothing, but merging with her flesh, becoming armor under her skin.

A shouting voice echoed through the blissful peace.

Words that made sense in some far corner of Maggie's mind. Knowledge she should have understood tickled her thoughts, bringing more awareness.

"I demand you cease the ceremony at once," the voice echoed, bouncing off walls Maggie couldn't see.

The want to see the walls forced her eyes open. She lay hovering in the air, facing the shimmering ceiling.

"We're nearly done," a new voice spoke softly. "Her memories were tangled up in darkness. We are freeing her mind with the light."

"The only freeing Miss Trent needs is from your spell."

"Bertrand." Maggie kicked against the air to no avail. "Bertrand!"

"Back away from her." Bertrand's voice came closer. "The help Miss Trent needs cannot be provided by the brethren."

"What's that supposed to mean?" Maggie squirmed, her shoulders gaining purchase against the magic, allowing her the tiniest bit of movement.

"Let her go," Bertrand said.

With a *smack*, Maggie hit the floor.

"Ow." She rolled onto her side and found herself facing a worn pair of buckled shoes.

"Miss Trent"—Bertrand knelt beside her—"what in all the shadows brought you here?"

CHAPTER 11

"*B*ertrand." Maggie pushed herself up, her arms shaking. Lines of worry, which hadn't existed the last time she'd seen him, marked his brow. Gone were his usual dark coat and billowing white shirt. He wore a suit of gray with a high button collar.

"Bertrand," Maggie whispered, "what are you still doing here?"

"Hunter Wayland"—Serber loomed over them—"I cannot allow you to interrupt a brethren ceremony."

"And I cannot allow you to perform a resurrection of light on this girl." Bertrand stood. "While I appreciate your help in sheltering Miss Trent, I will take full charge of her."

"There are shadows lurking in her mind," Serber said. "They will draw her back into darkness. We cannot allow her to become a danger to herself or others."

"There are no more shadows invading Miss Trent's mind than there are yours or mine," Bertrand said. "Come, Miss Trent."

"She was taken by the shadows." Diven stepped up behind Serber, blocking their path to the door. "She fought her way free and still can't remember—"

"Miss Trent is my apprentice." Bertrand weaved past Serber and Diven.

Maggie followed close on his heels, the foolish feeling she was snaking between cacti rather than people pinking her cheeks.

"I know precisely where I left her and precisely where she's come from. I give you my word as a shadow stalker your rituals will be of no benefit to her." Bertrand stopped in front of the shining door.

"Hunter Wayland," Serber said, "while the brethren and all Sarana are grateful for your service, you have no power in the Sanctuary."

"Which is precisely why we are leaving." Bertrand flung open the door, sending the nearby brethren scattering. "Come, Miss Trent. We have urgent matters to attend to."

Maggie stayed close behind Bertrand, the remembered sensation of terrible weightlessness still sending tremors through her limbs.

Bertrand cut around the table with the glistening flowers and out onto the street.

The sun had come out, but gray clouds filled the sky. The day held a dank feeling, and the muted colors of the homes gave evidence of the clouds winning the daily battle for a very long time.

"Bertrand." Maggie chased after him.

"We are very short on time, Miss Trent." Bertrand didn't slow his pace.

"For what? How did you find me? What did they just do to me? How long have you been here?"

"None of those answers hold any real relevance."

"Yes, they do."

As they turned off the street that housed the sanctuary, the day became grayer still. The oppressive dimness weighed on Maggie's chest.

"Where are we going?" Maggie said.

"*We* are going nowhere, Miss Trent. You are going back to the Siren's Realm."

"I'm sorry, what?" Maggie grabbed Bertrand's sleeve.

He looked down at her hand on his arm for a moment before sliding his gaze to her face.

"As shocked and honored as I am that you came to find me after I was quite sure you were done with me forever, this world is no place for you, and I cannot leave it. You are going home, Miss Trent."

"First of all"—Maggie spoke through gritted teeth—"I *am* done with you, Bertrand Wayland. In fact, the Siren's Realm was pretty damn peaceful without you. Second, I didn't choose to come looking for you. The Siren trapped me by the stitch and forced me through. So, I sincerely doubt she'll let me back in if I don't have you with me.

"Maybe she's dumb enough to miss your smug, self-satisfying attitude polluting her realm. Maybe she wants you to get rid of the red mist-cloaked guy who's decided he's the new dick in town. I don't know. Last, but very much not least, you have no right to tell me where I do and do not belong."

"How long have I been gone?" Bertrand strode down the street, leaving Maggie jogging to keep up.

"In Siren's time, about a month," Maggie said. "How long have you been here?"

"Four years by local counting," Bertrand said.

"And you were just going to hang out in shadowland forever?"

"You made me see, in no uncertain terms, that my former way of life was detrimental to everyone I touched. I made a choice. Sarana is my home now."

They ran down a wobbling street past a park filled with drooping trees.

"Why are we going back to the cemetery?" Maggie said. "I've told you, the Siren sent me to get you. She's not going to let me back in."

Bertrand ignored her as they arrived at the West Worth Graveyard.

"The alarm will go off," Maggie warned as Bertrand flipped the latch.

Bertrand glanced over his shoulder, one eyebrow raised, before pulling the gate open.

Maggie's heart forgot to beat as she waited for the horrible wail to begin.

"This way, Miss Trent." Bertrand held the gate wide.

"There was an awful alarm last night, okay?" Maggie followed him into the graveyard.

"I am acutely aware of how the shadow alarms work," Bertrand said. "But the sun is out—"

"Sort of."

"—and there is no need to fear shadows coming up from the ground at the moment."

"Shadows coming up from the ground?" Maggie scanned the dirt for fingers clawing their way to the surface. "You're kidding, right?"

"It is a complex problem there is no need for you to understand, Miss Trent."

Bertrand stopped next to the headstone Maggie had landed on several hours before.

"There's not going to be a way out." Maggie leaned against a tree.

"The Siren has no business demanding my return."

"The Siren had no business dragging me out of my world mid-battle, but…"

Bertrand ran his fingers along the drooping limbs of the tree.

"Why do you do the tree groping thing?" Maggie asked.

"A tree of this size has been alive longer than any living resident of this city," Bertrand whispered. "It has seen more storms and felt the workings of more magic. The life of a tree is written like braille upon its bark."

"What's it say?" Maggie asked, careful to keep the curiosity from her voice.

"Here." Bertrand ran to the far side of the graveyard where the earth dipped in a shallow basin. He tipped his chin up, taking a deep breath. "This is the place."

"There's nowhere to go." Maggie walked to the center of the basin.

"Miss Trent," Bertrand warned.

"No stitch to slip through." She jumped up and down.

"There's got to be a way." Bertrand crawled around the scant grass surrounding the divot, running his fingers along the ground. "Unless you go up?"

He tipped his head back, examining the cloud-strewn sky.

"Or this is where the stitch was but she's only going to let me through if you go too," Maggie said. "So come on, jump up and down right here with me and see if the Siren sucks us into her realm."

Bertrand stood and backed away from the basin. "I cannot return to the Siren's Realm, Miss Trent."

"Well, then I cannot go back, Mister Wayland." Maggie stomped on the ground. "The Siren doesn't want me without you, so let's go."

"I'm afraid that is quite impossible, Miss Trent. As much as I wish to return you safely to the Siren's Realm, I cannot leave Sarana."

"Why?" Maggie climbed out of the divot. "You've built a life here you can't possibly leave?"

Bertrand's face was unreadable.

"Oh, good God you have," Maggie laughed. "Do you have, like, a wife and two kids hidden in some brick house in the suburbs of shadowville?"

"Don't be absurd, Miss Trent." Bertrand turned back toward the gate, walking away while Maggie continued laughing.

"Then what?" Maggie chased him. "You have a dog you don't think the Siren will accept?"

"I have a duty and responsibilities. I made a vow I cannot break."

"What vow?" Maggie planted herself in front of the gate.

"There is a darkness hunting in this city."

"I gathered as much."

"It goes beyond shadows stalking the night," Bertrand said. "The dangers of the city are buried deeper than even the brethren have discovered. Leaving Sarana would be condemning her people to death."

"Death?" Maggie dug her knuckles into her eyes. "So if you hadn't slipped from the Siren's Realm into this particular world at this particular time, everyone here would have died?"

"The Siren's connections to the many magical worlds are a mystery."

"Fine. Let's say you did discover some darkness no one else has been clever enough to find. We can go back to the sanctuary, tell them what you've found out, make sure they understand, and then leave."

"You don't understand, Miss Trent," Bertrand said with the tone of one explaining the dangers of a fire spell to a small child. "The brethren are not capable of freeing Sarana."

"You know what? That's your problem." Maggie spread her arms wide, shouting to the sky. "Bertrand Wayland, savior of magic! He alone knows what's best for the worlds he randomly drops into. Only he can save everyone. Worlds can't exist without his interference."

"This one can't. I have made many mistakes in my long life. I will not make the error of abandoning this world."

"It's not abandoning a world if you put its own people in charge of its fate."

"You don't understand the gravity—"

"Then explain it to me. Stop acting like there couldn't possibly be anyone as clever as you. If you've really been here for four years trying to stop an evil no one from this world can defeat, explain it to me. Because if you're that bad off after trying for so long, you clearly need some help."

"I will explain all, Miss Trent." Bertrand stepped around Maggie to the gate. "I only hope when I'm done you will see why you need to leave this world without me."

"Trust me, if leaving you were an option, I would jump back to Alden in a second."

Bertrand turned left, skirting the perimeter of the cemetery.

"Is Alden adjusting well to the Siren's Realm?" Bertrand asked.

"You mean is he enjoying the house you abandoned him in that he really thought you were coming back to?"

"I worked for many years to build my home," Bertrand said. "I would hate to have it fall into the hands of anyone I do not consider a friend. After all Alden suffered in his world, is it so wrong to wish him a life of ease?"

The stone of anger that had lodged itself in the middle of Maggie's chest wiggled a little, lessening its pressure against her lungs.

"Alden was doing fine," Maggie said. "Then the Compère with his swirly red mist decided to throw a circus in the market square with a weapon-filled brawl as a grand finale."

"Weapons in the Siren's Realm?" Bertrand quickened his pace.

They turned onto a narrow cobblestone street, which seemed to have been shaken apart by an earthquake.

"I don't know where the weapons came from," Maggie said. "Unfortunately, I'm not like you. I don't know why the Siren decided to let someone shoot me with an arrow."

"You were shot?" Bertrand stopped dead in his tracks.

"Only in the arm, but yeah."

"Miss Trent, I am so horribly sorry." A line creased the center of Bertrand's brow.

"My arm is the smallest thing you should be worrying about apologizing for."

Her words hung in the air.

A woman burst out her front door with four children trailing behind her. She held a glowing rope in her hand, and each of the children clung to the tether.

"Hunter Wayland." The woman blushed as she passed.

The youngest of the children stared openmouthed at Bertrand until his mother led him around the corner.

"You really are famous?" Maggie asked.

"Venturing into the shadows to rescue a shade has never been attempted by any other." Bertrand continued down the street, not glancing back to be sure Maggie would follow.

Maggie planted her feet and crossed her arms. "Why would anyone try and rescue a shadow from a shadow?"

Bertrand stopped fifty feet in front of her. "Not all shadows are made of the same darkness." He spoke with his back to Maggie.

"What is that supposed to mean?" She stayed resolutely in place.

"A shade is not the same being as a spirit, and only specters seek darkness."

"That makes no sense. You've got to know that makes no sense."

"The details would be easier to explain in my home." Bertrand bowed. "If you would be so kind as to follow me?"

"Now that you've asked so nicely." Maggie arched one eyebrow in her best Bertrand impression as she slowly sauntered toward him. "But a good explanation does not sanity make."

"Well said." Bertrand again started down the street, careful to keep to a speed that didn't require Maggie to jog beside him.

"It took me two years to discover why shadows behave so differently from one another," Bertrand said. "At first, I thought it merely a reflection of how the deceased behaved in life."

"So shadows are ghosts?" Maggie said. "The brethren thought I'd been dead and fought my way back to life?"

"Roughly. But the consistency of the shadows proved we were dealing with very different types of beings."

"Meaning?"

"The city is contaminated with the spirits of the dead." Bertrand spoke in a hushed tone. "Those whose bodies have been taken over by the growth of the city and suffer to live again in darkness."

A shiver shook Maggie's spine.

"The shades are living dragged into the darkness by specters." Bertrand turned down another, even narrower street.

"I'm sorry, *who* is dragging the living into the darkness?" Maggie leapt over the decaying carcass of a rat.

"That is just the question, Miss Trent. I know *what* they are, but the *who* still eludes me. Until I know who the specters are and where they are coming from, I have no hope of stopping their growing mass. If their numbers continue to swell, there will be no living left in Sarana come the rains of next year."

Bertrand stopped in front of a house barely three times wider than its front door. The bricks were aging and crumbling at the corners where they met the well-tended homes on either side. The only thing distinguishing the house as a place where Bertrand Wayland might wish to reside was the turret crowned in a circle of brightly glowing metal, which towered above all the other houses in sight.

"This way, Miss Trent."

The front door opened with a nerve-tingling *squeal*.

"The day is brief when death and shadows wait with the sunset."

CHAPTER 12

The inside of the house had been as neglected as the outside. Tears ripped through the tiny red flower pattern on the wallpaper, white threads were all that remained of the carpet in places, and the wooden bannister of the staircase that took up most of the hall had no shine of polish left at all.

"This way, Miss Trent." Bertrand started up the stairs. "It's such a subtle difference to explain to one who has not faced the shadows themselves."

Newspaper clippings had been tacked to the wall along the steps. Maggie glanced at the articles as she passed.

Tragic news of Shiver's transition in the shadows...

A flock of shadows found moving through the sea lanes has driven commerce from the docks...

The Rulc family disappeared from their home last night...

"How old are these clippings?" Maggie asked.

They turned off the stairs and into a hallway only wide enough for one person to walk through at a time. One door waited at either end of the hall. Every bit of wall from waist to head height had been plastered in clippings.

"Bertrand?" Maggie prompted.

"The oldest is from six months before my arrival." Bertrand climbed the next set of stairs. "It took months to hunt down the documentation. I've been keeping track of every sighting since."

"There have been this many sightings in four years?" Maggie ran up the steps behind him.

"These are only those the papers have seen fit to print."

They entered another corridor identical to the first and climbed another set of stairs.

"It is a truth I have never seen vary in all the worlds I have visited," Bertrand said. "Tragedies that affect only the poor and have no impact on commerce are rarely seen as news."

"So, the city is literally swarming with shadows at night?"

At the top of the last flight, a wooden ladder led to an open trapdoor in the ceiling.

"I was out last night," Maggie said. "I didn't see a single shadow thing."

Bertrand spun to face her, leaning back against the ladder, his fingers tented under his chin.

"You landed in the graveyard, correct?" Bertrand asked.

Maggie nodded.

"You left the graveyard to be welcomed by the wail?"

"Thought I'd never be able to hear again."

"I would assume at that point you were greeted by the local watch and their lights?"

"They all came out of their houses when they heard the alarm."

"Then you were brought to the sanctuary." Bertrand started up the ladder. "The only time a shadow could have approached you was in the spilt second between when you opened the gate and when the wail began."

"How? I was in the graveyard for a while." Maggie followed Bertrand. The wood of the rungs had been worn smooth on top by countless trips through the trapdoor.

"It is possible you could have met a shadow in the graveyard.

Though the dead lucky enough to reside in the gated yards are rarely known to rise and wander as spirits. And other forms of shadows tend to avoid solemn ground."

Maggie pushed herself through the trapdoor and into a conical room.

Shimmering metal coated the edges of the three windows. The rest of the walls were again covered in newspaper clippings.

"But I was stuck in the dark with the wail for—"

"The wail exists to drive off the shadows," Bertrand said. "The noise is designed to simulate the keening of the grief-stricken. There is nothing the shadows hate so badly as one freshly dead."

"Tell me you didn't invent that horrible sound."

Bertrand raised an eyebrow and pointed under the table to a crooked horn that looked something like the top of a gramophone.

"Of course you did."

Bertrand strode to his desk, which was crammed in between a table filled with beakers and an armchair.

Maggie warily eyed the threadbare couch, which blocked the path to the sagging cot behind it.

The couch groaned as she sat. "Bertrand, are you sleeping up here?"

"Occasionally, one has a moment of weakness during which rest is required." Bertrand pulled a paper from his pocket, carefully clipping the edges before pressing the article to the wall.

With a sound like a flock of birds taking flight, all the papers on the wall shuddered and shifted to the left.

The unlucky article with no space to shift to fluttered down through the open trapdoor. The sound of rustling paper carried up from below.

"Whoa." Maggie sprang to her feet, leaning over the trapdoor in time to see the oldest article from the floor below flutter down to the second level.

"It took me quite a while to train them to stay in chronological order." Bertrand stirred the black pot that perched between beakers on the table. Its contents glowed, shooting rays of light beneath Bertrand's chin.

Maggie wiggled into the gap next to the desk to peer at the article.

A shadow stalker returned from the darkness last night, finding her salvation in the West Worth Graveyard. The girl, claiming her name to be Maggie Trent, has been taken to the sanctuary for her own, and others', protection. Any descendants should contact the brethren to welcome their hero home.

"And here I thought you had some sixth sense about a stitch opening and decided to scour this world to save me," Maggie said.

"Never doubt I would scour a world to save you, Miss Trent. The newspaper simply deemed such action unnecessary."

Maggie pinched the bridge of her nose, hiding the tiny smile that curled her lips. "You'd think people with such a speedy news system would have figured out what was going on in their city."

"Spreading news is rarely helpful if the news cannot be relied upon to be true," Bertrand said. "Read the next article."

A new shadow, believed to be the late Kayle Newel, daughter of the late Barrister Newel, has been found circling the street in front of the Public Offices of Sarana where her father worked. It is said Kayle used to play every day on the street as she waited for her father to be finished with his daily labor. Kayle was taken into the shadows in the Year of the Wilted Roses. Her place of burial lies under what are now the homes of East Herrin St. Kayle's shadow has been deemed loving of the light by the brethren and should not be considered harmful.

"They built houses on top of a little girl's grave?" Maggie blinked at the article. "Are these people crazy?"

"Crazy is a very broad, generally useless term." Bertrand thumped his spoon against the side of the pot, knocking free the few stray specks of light. "However, yes, the people of Sarana are in the habit of building on top of the dead."

"And no one stopped to think that would be a bad idea?" Maggie perched on the edge of Bertrand's desk.

"Sarana is more or less a tiny island of dry land surrounded by swamp. Land for burial and building are both at a premium."

"And they never considered cremation as an option?"

"No." Bertrand pulled a bell from between the beakers and gave it a long ring. "To Saranans, it would be the worst thing to do to a loved one—forcing the deceased's soul to burn forever."

"Got it, burning bad."

"The practice of building a home on top of the bones of your loved ones began quite reasonably. The poor had already bought a portion of land to bury their dead. They had no money to buy a plot for their home, so they consolidated their needs. Should more family members die, it was only a simple matter of pulling up a section of the floorboards, digging a new grave, and lowering the coffin in."

"I think I'm going to be sick." Maggie swallowed the bile that crept into her throat.

"It keeps the dead and the living linked. One line of family. Only the very richest are buried in graveyards in Sarana."

"And when shadows started climbing out of their graves, no one thought *hey, maybe let's not bury grandma under the dining room table?*"

"The shadows didn't come until the practice was very well established." Bertrand pulled a hollowed out ring, like a large, narrow Bundt cake pan, out from under the table. "The year the floods began, the shadows emerged. The moisture in the ground washed the dead up from their graves. A skull blocked a drainage hole. A femur was found on a front door step. Ribs were carried home by proud pups."

"I really might puke."

"That is when the spirits began to emerge. The dead who had been pulled from their rest by the rising of the water. Every year when the floods come, more spirits rise from the eternal darkness to walk the streets of Sarana. At first, all the shadows found in the city seemed peaceful or, at the very least, harmless. Capable of entering a house, but not of injuring its inhabitants. A few years later, things began to change. This is, I believe, where the brethren went astray."

Bertrand paused as he tipped the glowing contents of the pot into the Bundt cake tin.

"The nature of some shadows changed, gaining the ability to cause catastrophe. To knock over a candle and burn down a home, to tip poison into the stew, and, in some very horrible cases, to grab the living and drag them into the darkness, creating a new shadow, and leaving the surviving kin with no body to bury and no way to mourn.

"The brethren believe those shadows who are so violent are the same as the rest, but, rather than gently accepting they've been woken from death, are horribly angry with those who have failed to protect their graves. The brethren try to appease the spirits and protect the graves of those yet to rise. They give light to the houses to protect the residents from the entry of violent shadows."

"But…" Maggie pressed.

"The shadows that are so bent on causing harm to the living are not like the spirits who have died and are now doomed to walk the city again. They are specters, who were never alive at all. The living who are drawn into the shadows are not dead. They are shades, living cloaked in darkness, trapped in a black place just beyond this world, where the specters have dragged them. The spirits are dead. There is nothing we can do for them. The shades can be saved if one is only brave enough to try."

"And you won't go back into the Siren's Realm until you've figured out a way to stop the big bad specters," Maggie finished for him. "Okay, assuming you haven't completely lost your mind, which based on your lovely clipping collection it's sincerely possible you have, I get why you want to stop the specters from stealing people. But how are you supposed to know which shadows are what?"

"There are subtle ways to tell the difference." Bertrand flipped over the Bundt pan, shaking the beakers as he banged it hard against the table. "But the easiest way to start is by looking for undeniable facts."

"Such as?"

Bertrand pointed to the article Maggie had read only minutes before.

"Kayle Newel, daughter of Barrister Newel, who now happily haunts the streets," Bertrand said. "I've checked the census, combed through Newel's papers. The Barrister never had a daughter."

"But then why would they print that?" Maggie ran her finger along the clipping. The paper trembled at her touch.

"The speed at which the paper can print is far more important to terrified people than the reliability of the information." Bertrand banged harder on the back of the pan. "There is a painting hanging in the office of a man and a little girl sitting on the steps of a fine house. However, the man in the painting is not Barrister Newel, but rather the man who, upon his death, donated the funds to build the public office. His was predeceased by his daughter who never would have had any cause to visit the office at all."

"So then, who is the girl playing on the street?" A chill tickled Maggie's skin.

"That is precisely what we are going to find out." After one final *thump*, Bertrand lifted the pan, leaving a glowing circle on the table. "It should fit well enough."

"Bertrand."

Maggie tipped off the edge of the desk, crashing to the floor as a woman's voice called up the ladder.

"Bertrand, you're massively late," the voice chided.

"Who is that?" Maggie whispered.

"Nilla." Bertrand didn't look up as a tea tray floated through the trapdoor. "Nilla, I'm frightfully busy at the moment. Just move the tray to the desk if you please."

Maggie rolled out of the way as the tray zoomed to the corner of the desk she had occupied only moments before.

"Bertrand"—the sounds of someone climbing the ladder carried through the trapdoor—"if I left you alone every time you were *frightfully busy*, I would never see you, and it's absolutely wrong to let me get so *frightfully* lonely."

A woman with flowing, jet-black hair climbed into the attic. She brushed off her deep green dress, carefully removing a speck of dust from her plunging bodice before looking up.

"I've missed you this morning." Her bright green eyes looked to Bertrand before her gaze sank down to Maggie kneeling on the floor. "What in the world is that?"

CHAPTER 13

"*N*illa"—Bertrand didn't look up from the glowing ring—"this is Miss Trent, my apprentice from across the sea come to help in my work. Miss Trent, this is Nilla. She makes an excellent cup of tea."

"Huh." Nilla tossed her dark hair over her shoulder. "Well, if tea is all you value me for, I guess I'll go back to my room."

"Bring Miss Trent a proper meal, if you would." Bertrand grabbed a magnifying glass from under the table and peered down at the ring.

"Miss Trent needs a meal?" Nilla sauntered over to the tea tray where two purple patterned tea cups waited. Nilla snapped her fingers, conjuring a third, brown mug. "Will Miss Trent be staying in the house?"

"For as long as she remains in Sarana," Bertrand said.

"And how long will that be?" Nilla poured tea into the three cups.

"For as short a time as possible," Maggie said. "I'm really just here to bring Bertrand home."

"Bertrand," Nilla laughed. "You allow your apprentice to call you *Bertrand?*"

"It's how she began, and I didn't see the use in arguing." Bertrand poked the ring, wincing as the light touched his skin.

"If she's going to drag you home, I just assume she does it now," Nilla said. "The neighbors are complaining about the house again. It doesn't do to be so peculiar, Bertrand."

"The neighbors don't complain when I delve into the shadows for their protection. They can make do with the state of the house." Bertrand opened the desk drawer and pulled out a spool of thick wire and a set of heavy clippers.

"Fine then." Nilla fluffed her skirts. "Be the horror of the street. After all, it's not *my* house."

"You're correct. It isn't," Bertrand said. "Now, do as I ask and find food for Miss Trent."

"Yes, Bertrand." Nilla lifted the spool and clippers from Bertrand's hands. "Of course, Bertrand."

She leaned in, pressing her lips to his.

Maggie looked down to her bracelet, fiddling with the leather cord and resisting the urge to hum.

"Here." Nilla sloshed the brown mug in Maggie's direction. "Wouldn't do for the apprentice to get thirsty."

With a last wink at Bertrand, Nilla disappeared down the ladder.

"You're sleeping with your housekeeper?" Maggie whispered as Nilla's footsteps sounded on the stairs below. "Isn't that just a little weird?"

"Nilla isn't the housekeeper." Bertrand unwound a long piece of wire.

"She's your girlfriend, who lives with you, and you order her to make tea?" Maggie stood. "I don't know if that's any better."

"The fact that my paramour brews tea and fixes meals hardly has anything to do with the darkness. Honestly, the first time I asked I thought she would hate me forever and leave. But being angry at being asked to tend to tea makes her so happy I don't know if I'll ever get rid of her."

"I knew it." Maggie smacked Bertrand on the shoulder. "You fell in love. That's why you don't want to come back to the Siren's Realm."

"What I feel for Nilla has no bearing on my decision to stay in Sarana. Affection is dangerous where survival is concerned. I have learned that caring for those who count on you for protection ends badly. I allow Nilla to stay because I pulled her from the shadows, and there are none left who will claim her. I can't ask her to leave, as she has nowhere to go."

"And the whole cleavage and kissing thing? Part of the rescue package?"

"Even a wizard is only human at times, Miss Trent."

"Eww." Maggie sipped her tea as Bertrand attached the wires to the glowing ring.

"The tea is pretty good," Maggie said. "You still lose points for chauvinism."

"I didn't believe I had any merit left to lose." Bertrand laced the wires together, crafting something like an ugly headband. "Besides, I asked Alden to make the tea in the Siren's Realm. If someone is going to be underfoot, they might as well be useful in feeding me."

"You're a real gem. No wonder Nilla just can't leave you."

A tray floated up through the hatch, landing on the floor with a loud *thunk*.

"She is a rather good cook." Bertrand flipped the ring over, holding it by the base he had built as though testing his creation for balance.

"How does magic work here anyway?" Maggie knelt by the tray. An unspilled bowl of soup awaited her.

"Magic is nothing more than a dance between light and darkness with an avid sprinkle of unpredictability." Bertrand pulled a large leather satchel from under the table.

"What have you hoarded under there?" Maggie asked.

"Everything one could need to fight the shadows." Bertrand

pulled out another glowing ring, placing it into the bag with the first.

"And you just asked the light and darkness to make a magical hiding spot for you under the table?" Maggie sipped her soup. The creamy mix held a hint of the sea and a touch of spice.

"I asked the shadows to make a bit of extra room for me." Bertrand pulled out a long, glowing chain and a glass pipe that ended with a rubber ball.

"And Nilla asked the light to bring a tray up and dump it on the floor?" Maggie watched as Bertrand slid the eighteen inch glass pipe into the nine inch deep bag.

"She asked for the tiny space between the darkness and the light to do her bidding." Bertrand pointed toward the tray. "*Reseum mellor.*" The tray lifted itself off the ground and zoomed over to the desk. "The spell language is a bit unpredictable, but the channeling of magic is rather elementary."

"Any chance you have a—"

Bertrand tossed a small leather notebook to her. "I no longer need my notes. But I will ask you leave them with me when you return to the Siren's Realm."

"Not going to get to go back unless you come along."

Maggie thumbed through the pages as Bertrand loaded more strange things into his bag.

Illusios therma ~ For seeking life among the lost

Melivious varax ~ A violent ray of bursting light

"How did you figure all this out?" Maggie flipped to *Nessusium ~ For defense against a specter.* "Really focused on the cheery."

"I asked, Miss Trent." Bertrand took a final sip of his tea and carried his satchel toward the trapdoor. "And I have no need for spells to please the eye. There is rarely a use for pretty magic."

"Somehow I forgot how cheerful you are."

He let go of the bag's handle, leaving the leather case to float down the ladder. "Come along, Miss Trent. We have much to do and very little time before the sun sets."

"You're going out again?" Nilla called up.

Bertrand leapt to the floor a story below.

"We have to visit the Barrister to gain the keys to the vaults, then—"

"You're going to see the Barrister?" Nilla interrupted.

Maggie tucked the notebook into her pocket and started down the ladder.

"As I've said, we need keys," Bertrand said.

"Then I should come with you." Nilla crossed her arms over her large bust. "You know what the Barrister is like. I'll fare better than the apprentice."

"What's that supposed to mean?" Maggie said.

"I'm coming with you, Bertrand." Nilla clapped her hands. Her green garments vanished, and a pale pink dress spun into being around her form. "I'm more useful than you give me credit for. I was a shadow stalker before you were even born."

Maggie coughed a laugh.

"Are you going to let her tramp about town dressed as she is?" Nilla cast Maggie a sideways glare.

"Of course." Bertrand snatched his bag from the air and started down the stairs. "Her apparel is perfectly fitted to the task at hand, and the color suits her."

"Thanks." Maggie grinned at Nilla and followed Bertrand. "And the pants have pockets."

"I do appreciate your practicality," Bertrand said.

Nilla's skirts swished along behind Maggie.

The front door opened as Bertrand stepped off the last flight of stairs. Wind blew in from the street, sending the newspaper clippings rustling in a disgruntled way.

The air had changed in the brief time they'd been inside the house. A damp chill carried in with the sea breeze.

"Bertrand, we should go back in the house." Nilla skirted around Maggie to walk by Bertrand's side. "There's nothing you're going to accomplish today that can't be done tomorrow."

"Of course," Bertrand said. "The only reason one would consider moving quickly in the matter of defending the city against the shadows is the lives that could be lost on any given night we rest. There are too many things that haunt me, I will not allow resting while the innocent suffer to be another stain on my hands."

A pain punched through Maggie's chest.

"You want to save the city, and you go about it recklessly," Nilla said. "If you are taken by the shadows, you won't be able to help anyone at all. Have you ever once considered that it is better to wait and live to fight another day?"

"Never," Maggie said. "The only thing Bertrand sees is the problem in front of him. Things like death and consequences don't really occur to him."

The tendons on the sides of Bertrand's neck tensed. Maggie balled her hands into fists, waiting for him to shout.

He said nothing as he turned down a wide street filled with people. Horse-drawn carts moved in either direction. Shops lined the street with wooden signs hanging out front. A butcher sat between a bookseller and a bakery.

This should be a nice place.

But even in the daylight, a hint of fear tinged everything. Giant, glowing orbs hung from the front of every building. The shoppers' faces were drawn, and their eyes scanned the street around them even as they spoke to their fellows.

"Shadows don't come out during the daylight?" Maggie asked.

"Shadows can be wherever shadows are," Bertrand said. "It's only easier to avoid the darkness during the day."

"Did you explain nothing to the apprentice before you brought her from across the sea?" Nilla laughed. "Did you only want to feed her to the specters?"

"I wouldn't recommend underestimating Miss Trent," Bertrand said. "I fear it wouldn't end well for you, and I'm not sure I would be useful in your protection."

Bertrand stopped in front of a wide stone building. Like the rest of the city, the façade had the feel of something that had been left in damp darkness for too long, though the occupants of this building had at least taken care to scrub the gray stone clean. Seven glowing tubes rested over the seven windows, their radiance noticeable even in the daylight. Large letters had been carved into the front of the building.

Public Offices of Sarana.

"Try to be polite, Miss Trent," Bertrand said. "We need that key, and I would much rather have it given willingly."

"I am capable of being nice," Maggie said.

With one eyebrow raised, Bertrand opened the door to the public offices.

A tinkling bell greeted them as they entered the well-lit lobby. Four desks stacked high with papers blocked the path to the hall beyond. The surfaces here didn't glow as everything had in the sanctuary, but the pale painted walls and many lights overhead kept the space bright.

"Hunter Wayland." A man jumped up from his desk, simultaneously bowing and straightening his glasses. "How may I help you this afternoon?"

The three other people seated at their desks looked up.

"I've come to see the Barrister," Bertrand said. "I've no appointment, but it is a matter of some urgency."

"Of course." The man gave another bow, his glasses nearly slipping off his nose. "We've been hoping you would come, but I hadn't imagined you'd have gotten the message yet."

"I'm afraid I've received no message," Bertrand said. "But I am, as always, at the Barrister's service."

"Thank you, Hunter Wayland." The man stepped aside.

With a faint *click*, his desk swiveled, clearing a path to the corridor beyond.

"Come, Miss Trent." Bertrand walked down the hall.

"Thanks." Maggie gave a little bow to the man and followed Bertrand.

Nilla's shoes clacked on the floor behind her.

"*Come, Miss Trent,*" Nilla said. "I suppose you think I should wait on the street."

"Of course not." Bertrand stopped in front of a white painted door. "I assumed you would follow. I cannot make that presumption of Miss Trent."

Bertrand knocked lightly on the door.

"Careful, Bertrand," Nilla said. "I might not follow you someday."

"And you would be all the wiser for your choice," Bertrand said.

Maggie took a step back, clearing Nilla's line of sight as she glared daggers at Bertrand.

The door swung open, revealing a man as broad as the doorframe.

"Hunter Wayland." The Barrister's face reddened as he shook Bertrand's hand. "I requested they summon you, but I never know if those oafs will do a thing I ask them to."

He left the door ajar as he moved back to his wide, wooden desk.

"My apologies, Barrister. But I'm afraid I never received your message. It's merely by chance I needed to see you today."

As Bertrand entered the room, three chairs detached themselves from the wall and floated down to face the desk.

"Who have you brought with you?" The Barrister's chair creaked as he sat.

"Would you ever be displeased to see me?" Nilla simpered as she sauntered into the office.

"Nilla." The Barrister heaved himself to his feet. "It is always a great honor to see a returned shadow stalker."

"And the battle is all the more worthwhile knowing a man as renowned as yourself appreciates my sacrifice," Nilla said.

Maggie swallowed a laugh.

"This is my apprentice Miss Trent."

The Barrister eyed Maggie. "It's a pity to bring one so young into the fight, but with the trouble I have today, I am glad for the extra assistance."

"And what trouble worries the illustrious Barrister?" Nilla sat in the center chair, fluffing her pink dress around her.

The Barrister leaned forward, straining the buttons of his coat. "A shadow has found its way into the building."

CHAPTER 14

*M*aggie glanced around the corners of the room, searching for spindly fingers reaching from the darkness to seize her.

"Where has the shadow appeared?" Bertrand paced in front of the door.

"It was found wandering the hall," the Barrister whispered. "We managed to lure it into the closet and set lights around the door to keep it in."

"A wise precaution," Bertrand said.

"Imagine the embarrassment if word got out." The Barrister pulled a handkerchief from his pocket and dabbed at his forehead. "Having the shadow of a child circling the front of the office at night is bad enough. If people knew one had gotten into the building...Hunter Wayland, I would be the laughing stock of the city. My place is to be the warrior of Sarana. To protect all its people. How will they believe in me if they know there's a shadow hiding in the closet?"

"You poor thing," Nilla said. "Such a trial for a man who already does so much for the city."

"Has the shadow done anything in its time in the building?"

Bertrand asked. "Does the being display any intent or interaction?"

"Intent or interaction?" The Barrister fluttered his handkerchief in the air. "I had the staff back the thing into a closet and block the door."

"If you'd show me to the shadow," Bertrand said, "Miss Trent and I would be more than happy to assist."

"And I would be more than happy to stay by your side." Nilla winked at the Barrister. "Perhaps a game of cards while we let them play with their toys?"

"Charming of course." The Barrister pulled a deck of black and purple cards from a drawer in his desk. "Closet at the very end of the hall, if you will."

With a look to Maggie, Bertrand left the room.

She opened her mouth to say, she didn't quite know what, to the Barrister, but he had already started dealing and had eyes for nothing but Nilla.

Resisting the urge to shake her head, she slipped into the hall after Bertrand.

"I hadn't planned on solving a shadow problem this morning"—Bertrand spoke in a hushed tone—"but I'm sure gaining the key will be all the easier once we've rid him of his guest."

"Sure," Maggie whispered. "Just do his job for him and he'll lend you a piece of metal. Do people really think he's the protector of the city?"

"He sits behind his desk and says reassuring things. That is all most people expect of politicians."

Just when Maggie was about to ask how they were to know which door hid the shadow, they met a corner and turned right. A door surrounded by lights of every shape waited at the end of the corridor.

Bertrand gave a heavy sigh. "I suppose I should be grateful they were thorough."

Spheres of light had been hung from the ceiling down the last ten feet of the hall. Table lamps had been placed on either side of the doorframe. Tubes of light had been glued to the plaster around the door.

Bertrand ducked under the hanging lights, shaking his head.

Maggie reached up, gently grazing one of the orbs with her fingers. The light held no heat, but there was something in it that shocked her skin, telling her to pull away from the glow.

"Bertrand, what's in these lights?" Maggie weaved between the spheres toward the door.

"Magic," Bertrand said. "Flames can hold back the shadows for a moment or two, but the pure light of magic is best."

He set his black case on the floor and opened the latch. Maggie had expected a jumbled mass of squished-in objects, but all the bag seemed to contain was a constant glow.

"The Barrister gave us very little usable information on what his clerks might have locked in this closet." He pulled out one of the glowing rings, passing it to Maggie. "Stay behind me and do exactly as I say."

"That's it?" Maggie said. "No more information, just stay behind you?"

"Put the light on." Bertrand pulled the second glowing ring from his bag. He set the curved wires on his head like a headband, leaving the ring hovering over him like a halo.

"Okay?" Maggie laughed and slipped her own halo on.

"Make sure it's tight," Bertrand said. "That light is the only true protection I can offer you."

Maggie's laughter faded and she squeezed the wire tighter around her head.

With a wiggle of his fingers, Bertrand reached for the doorknob.

"What if it's a spirit?" Maggie whispered.

"Then we guide it gently from this place." Bertrand turned the knob.

"But what if—"

112 | MEGAN O'RUSSELL

Bertrand opened the door before she could finish her question.

Mops and brooms had been stacked inside the closet. A chair with a broken leg hung from the wall.

There's nothing here.

Maggie took a deep breath, brushing away the tension she hadn't noticed seizing her shoulders.

Then she saw it.

A flicker of movement in the very corner where the lights of the hall couldn't quite reach. An inky blackness that twisted and swirled but kept the unmistakable shape of a person.

The thing reached up, touching its face with its fingers as though drying invisible tears.

"Hello," Bertrand said in a low voice. "I'm sorry to startle you. You've been trapped in a very tight place. I think you'd be much happier if you had a bit more room to roam."

The shadow pulled into itself, growing three feet in height like stretched out taffy.

"Is there a place you'd like to go?" Bertrand reached into his bag, not looking away from the shadow. "Is there a home you belong in? I would be happy to help you find your family."

The swirling of the shadow stopped. The shape shifted, jittering around like an image stuck on an old film.

"Is that so?" Bertrand said.

"Is what so?" Maggie whispered.

"Watch carefully," Bertrand said. "I'm going to remove you from the Barrister's offices and take you home."

The shadow twitched again. An opening formed where its mouth should have been as though the being were screaming in protest.

"It doesn't want to leave," Maggie whispered.

"More than that," Bertrand murmured. "It has a very strong opinion on the matter."

"Where do you want to go?" Maggie asked.

The shadow shrunk back to the height of a normal person.

"What does that mean?" Maggie said as the swirling of the shadow continued.

"It means we're here to help." Bertrand kept his eyes locked on the shadow as he pulled a wooden box from his case. One side of the box hinged up. "It's nice and dark in here." Bertrand opened the little door and slid the box forward. "Think how happy you'll be when I take you away from here."

The shadow tilted his head as though considering the box.

"Go on," Bertrand said. "It will be so peaceful if only you let me help you."

With a *whoosh* the shadow grew, its head extending up onto the ceiling.

"I cannot give you a choice." He pulled a pipe from his pocket. A shining crystal had been set into the end of the silver metal, creating a bright beam of light.

Bertrand directed the beam at the shadow's face.

The shadow shrunk, dodging the brightness.

Bertrand lowered the light, pressing the shadow closer and closer to the floor.

"It's working," Maggie said.

"Yes, Miss Trent." Bertrand stepped into the closet. The glow from his halo bathed the space in light.

The thing hissed and dodged into its sole remaining refuge, the tiny shadow left by the box Bertrand had placed on the floor.

"In you get." Bertrand swept the beam toward the box.

Cowering away from the light, the shadow swirled into the safety of the darkness.

Bertrand reached down to push the door closed. A whip of darkness lashed out of the box, striking the shade of Bertrand's palm.

He slammed the door shut and flipped the latch.

"*In summon me battoo. In orther estravis.*"

The wood of the box began to glow.

"Estravis mahoon, tradis bathis."

The box shook, rattling against the stone floor.

"Tendisay marensay e un noot!"

A *shriek* shook the hall, bouncing off the walls and pummeling Maggie's ears.

With a final scream, the box went still.

"Bertrand," Maggie whispered.

"It's done." Bertrand sagged against the wall.

"Is everything all right?" The clerk with the glasses peeked around the corner.

"Fine," Bertrand said. "No cause for alarm, I assure you."

"Excellent." The clerk bowed and ducked out of sight.

"What just happened?" Maggie knelt next to the box. "Did you trap the shadow in there?"

"Had it been a spirit, I would have. That was a specter. Its immediate dissolution was necessary." Bertrand sank to the ground.

"Are you okay?" Maggie crawled to Bertrand.

"Certainly." Bertrand wheezed. "But I would appreciate your passing over my bag."

Maggie seized the satchel and slid it toward Bertrand.

"Most kind."

Holding his right hand to his chest, Bertrand searched through the bag with his left. The sound of clinking metal resonated from inside the bag.

"Damn." Bertrand leaned over the case. His right hand fell into his lap. Black covered his palm and reached toward his fingers in thin lines that squirmed over his flesh.

"What the hell is that?" Maggie squeaked.

"That was a specter," Bertrand panted. "The being's only goal is to bring more into the darkness. This is how the process begins."

He pulled the glass pipe that ended in a rubber ball from his bag. He fumbled the instrument, trying to press the open end to his blackened palm.

"Let me help."

He didn't look at Maggie or even seem to notice she had spoken. He held the tube steady and squeezed the ball. The tube suctioned to his skin and pulled the black back from his fingers. He squeezed again. A tendril of black mist broke free from his flesh and swirled to the back of the tube.

"Be a good shadow." Bertrand squeezed the ball once again and winced as the black stain tore free from his skin.

"The light please." He nodded toward the crystal.

Maggie passed him the light.

Carefully balancing the tube on his palm, he snaked the crystal into the glass.

A tiny *wail* bounced from the tube as the shadow dissolved.

"What did you just do?" Maggie leaned against the wall.

"This is a suction system to pull away the shadows, and a crystal stick." Bertrand squinted at his palm.

"On Earth we called those flashlights." Maggie gave a tired laugh.

"How apt." He began reloading his bag.

"Is this how dealing with specters always goes?" Maggie pulled off her halo.

"Oh no," Bertrand said. "That was quite tame. An enclosed environment in a well-lit area. Quite a simple trapping, actually."

"But you got bit," Maggie said. "That specter could have made you a shadow."

"That is nowhere near as close to becoming a shade as I have come, Miss Trent," Bertrand said. "Though I do appreciate your concern."

"What was that thing doing in here?" Maggie asked as Bertrand shoved the box back into his bag.

"My best guess is the Master of the specters set the creature here to take the Barrister into the darkness." Bertrand stood, brushing invisible dirt from his coat.

"You just stopped an assassination attempt?" Maggie glanced down the hall. "We have to warn the Barrister. He needs to know if someone is trying to kill him."

"We will tell him nothing but that the shadow is no longer his concern."

"But—"

"As with most in Sarana, the Barrister is of the impression that all shadows are ancestors to be cherished," Bertrand said. "He does not believe in the existence of specters, the means with which I dispose of them, or the danger the city faces."

"Great." Maggie stood. "That's really great."

"Come," Bertrand said. "We have happy news to present to the Barrister. His office is now free from shame."

"You should have just left it in the closet," Maggie said. "Let everybody find out how useless he is."

"But we gained much from a few minutes' work," Bertrand said.

"What did we gain from you almost turning into a shade?"

"The Barrister's favor and some valuable information." Bertrand raised a hand before Maggie could speak. "Whoever is creating the specters very specifically targeted this building. The more we know about what the Master wants done, the closer we'll be to finding him."

They rounded the corner. All the clerks had stopped working and were staring down the hall.

"Full success," Bertrand said cheerfully, holding his bag in the air.

"So quickly?" Nilla called from the Barrister's office. "We were only beginning to have a bit of fun."

She had moved to sit at the corner of the Barrister's desk. A fan of cards lay in front of her.

"She hasn't had time to win yet," the Barrister chuckled.

"It was a simple matter." Bertrand stood behind the chairs. "The shadow will no longer be a bother to the offices."

"Wonderful." The Barrister leaned on his desk and wiggled out of his seat. "I am so grateful for your help, Hunter Wayland. Elections will be coming as the sun fades, and one must avoid scandal."

"Of course," Bertrand said.

Maggie bit the insides of her cheeks as Bertrand gave a sanctimonious little nod.

"I was hoping we might now speak of the matter for which I originally came," Bertrand said.

"Of course." The Barrister fluttered his hands. "I always seek to help the shadow stalkers."

"I need a key to the vaults," Bertrand said.

The Barrister's smile faded. "Hunter Wayland, those keys are for the brethren and city officials only."

"I understand," Bertrand said. "However, as the brethren have made no use of the knowledge the vaults might hold, and no city official dares enter the darkness, I believe the time has come to extend access."

"It's just not possible. I'm sorry, Hunter Wayland, but it cannot be allowed." The Barrister sat with a *creak*. "If there is a more reasonable request you would like to make, I would be happy to oblige in view of your service. The clerks could make you tea on your way out."

"Are you serious?" Maggie said. "He just got rid of a shadow for you, and you're offering him a cup of tea?"

"Miss Trent," Bertrand warned.

"If you're supposed to be the defender of the city, then maybe you should take care of the next shadow yourself." The words rushed from Maggie. "There's a problem in this city, and you're just sitting behind your shiny desk, playing cards while people are in danger. This is your city, not his. It shouldn't be his job to save you. So get off your ass and do something."

The Barrister's face flushed bright red. "You insolent child."

"I am not a child," Maggie growled.

"Out. Both of you get out." The Barrister pounded on his desk.

"There will come a time when you can no longer deny the dangers of the darkness," Bertrand said. "When that day comes, I will be at your service."

The Barrister's face darkened to maroon. "Out!"

"Come, Miss Trent." Bertrand strode into the hall and toward the clerk's desk.

"That girl is simply dreadful," Nilla said.

Maggie shot her a glare and ran after Bertrand. "I didn't mean to lose it, but he can't just sit there and pretend to be helping."

"Very true," Bertrand said. "That man's lack of action has caused the loss of many innocent lives."

"Yeah, but now we have no key," Maggie said. "Where is the key to anyway?"

"The vaults." Bertrand nodded to the spectacled clerk. "If you please."

The clerk swung his desk aside to let them pass.

"*The vaults* isn't very descriptive," Maggie said.

They stepped back out onto the street. A chill mist set goose bumps on Maggie's arms.

"The vaults are where the darkness meets the light, both figuratively and literally," Bertrand said. "I have spent years roaming the night, exploring under the floorboards of shadow-laden homes, venturing to the docks where the herds of shadows roam, and still I'm missing something. There is a link to this riddle I cannot solve, and the only place I have not looked is the vaults. If the answer does not lie there, I have nowhere left to look."

"And I just lost you your shot at the key." Maggie dragged her fingers through her hair. "I'll go back in and apologize, see if that helps."

"The Barrister is hardly a forgiving man." Nilla stepped onto the street. She scowled at the mist falling from the sky and clapped her hands. An umbrella materialized in her grip.

"Well, we have to do something," Maggie said.

Nilla looped her arm through Bertrand's. "There is nothing to be done, *Miss Trent*."

The two of them strolled down the street.

"But Bertrand needs to get into the vaults." Maggie stepped up to walk on Bertrand's other side.

"And so we shall," Bertrand said. "Nilla has the key."

Nilla pulled a glistening key from between her breasts.

"He gave it to you?" Maggie gasped.

"Of course not," Bertrand said. "Nilla had the key before we ever came back from the closet."

"Dolt should have watched his desk drawer instead of staring at me like a letch."

CHAPTER 15

*T*he lights under the bridge burned brightly. Maggie glared up at the spheres, wishing they would produce some heat. Bertrand stood just under the overhang, watching the few people who ventured out into the rain. Nilla had tucked herself in the corner and spent the last hour twisting her hair into an elaborate crown of braids.

Maggie pulled the little notebook from her pocket. The blue cover had worn at the corners, but the ink stayed crisp.

He probably put a spell on it.

She glanced at Bertrand's back before skimming the first page. Even though he had placed the notes in her care, it still seemed like an intrusion to be reading spells written out in his hand.

Iltsavor mortis ~ For the occupation of the dead.

Lissam ~ For the purification of light

"Are you finding my writings of interest?" Bertrand asked.

Maggie looked up. Bertrand still stared at the street.

"Sort of," Maggie said. "Not really sure how any of it will be useful, but you haven't been wasting your time here."

"I meant to be a scholar in the beginning," Bertrand said. "I thought to study the ways of this land and become a teacher of some sort. But the shadows could not be ignored. From my second night in this place, I knew my plan for a peaceful life would be hard won."

"What happened?" Maggie asked.

"I had found lodging at an inn," Bertrand said. "The owner warned me of a spirit that wandered the halls. A woman who had taken her own life after her lover died. I thought the innkeeper was superstitious."

"Obviously," Maggie said.

"I heard a *creak* in the middle of the night," Bertrand said. "I left my bed to see if I could find the source of the noise. The shadow of a woman walked the hall, trailing her dark fingers along the walls."

"Was she not a spirit?" Maggie asked.

"She was," Bertrand said. "But upon seeing her, I knew I had to see more. So I ventured out onto the streets. I had made it barely ten minutes walking the city before I met my first specter."

"How did you get away?" Maggie stepped closer to Bertrand, wincing as a loose stone clattered under her foot.

"The specter wasn't interested in me." Bertrand examined his palm, touching the place where the blackness had marked him only hours before. "The beast had already found its victim. A drunkard caught stumbling through the darkness. I watched the specter wrap its tendrils around the man, marking him with black. Within a few moments, the man was gone, replaced by nothing more than a shadow."

"What did the shade do?" Maggie whispered.

"Stared at me. It was as though he were asking why I hadn't helped him. Both of the shadows came toward me. I had no more magic available than to light the street on fire in my wake. With fames trailing behind me, I ran back to the inn.

"When the rest of the house woke the next morning, I told them what I had seen, tried to find out how to save the man.

They thought it had been no more than a nightmare. I found news of the man's death in the paper the next day. They acknowledged his demise, but not the means of his execution."

"So what do they think happens to people who are taken by specters?" Maggie asked.

"They died," Nilla said. "Frightened to death in the middle of the street and immediately accepted into the shadows' fold. Or a heart attack, or a missed step and a fall. None of them can ignore the instinct that screams to their flesh that not all shadows are harmless. But they won't look beyond what they've always known to save themselves. It's been this way for ages.

"I became a shadow stalker nearly eighty years ago, when the shadows were no longer easily identifiable as the dead. I remember the black wrapping around my wrists, and decades of horrible figments in the rushing of the dark, then Bertrand rescuing me. I tried to tell them all. I hadn't been killed by an accident in my pursuit of ill-tempered shadows and brought back to life by a miracle of the light. I was taken by something else. They all thought I was mad. Bertrand is the only one who's ever believed me."

"They must think a ton of their ancestors were really horrible people." Maggie rubbed her hands over her arms.

"It's nice to think your generation is better and kinder than the last." Nilla clapped her hands.

Warmth tugged on Maggie's arms, and her hands were suddenly no longer touching her skin. A warm black sweater had appeared on her body.

"Thanks," Maggie said. "But I'm really fine."

"The last thing I want is you sneezing all over me." Nilla waved Maggie's words away. "Just be careful with it. I like that sweater."

They all stood in silence for a long while, listening to the patter of the rain against the cobblestones.

"It's been a long time since I've seen rain like this," Maggie said. "It doesn't do this in the—"

"The rain across the water is quite different," Bertrand cut in. "Either constant sun or a terrible deluge. Never the blissfully numbing patter Sarana enjoys."

"Enjoys?" Nilla gave a low laugh. "I don't think most Saranans enjoy it."

Ask him. Ask him why she doesn't know.

It's none of your business.

"If we wait much longer we won't be back out before dark," Nilla said.

"We need only wait a few more minutes," Bertrand said. "Once the brethren know we have a key, our path through the gates will become much more difficult."

As though summoned by Bertrand's words, a dozen shimmering people walked down the street in a widely spaced line.

"Aren't they worried the light will wash off?" Maggie asked.

"Water doesn't have that sort of power. Shall we?" Bertrand stepped out into the rain.

The sweater kept most of the chill from Maggie's skin, but her neck still prickled as though shadows would reach out and grab her. She kept close behind Bertrand as he turned onto a long road by the sea.

In the distance, ships with tall sails waited at the docks. Warehouses lined the road with workers bustling in and out as they hurried to finish their daily tasks.

He turned between two buildings whose wooden exteriors had been tinged gray by the sea air.

A stone embankment blocked the warehouses from the rest of the city. High archways had been carved into the stone, leading to tunnels that cut below the belly of Sarana.

Wagons rattled in and out of most as goods were carried from the ships to the city's merchants.

Bertrand kept moving past the wide tunnels to a gate too low for a horse and only wide enough for two people to walk side by side.

"I never thought I would see the day." Nilla clapped. Her pink dress disappeared, and with a swirl of gray, tight pants and a trim high-collar coat materialized around her frame.

She pulled the glowing key from her pocket and pressed it into Bertrand's hand.

"You may do the honors if you wish," Bertrand said.

"I'd rather not," Nilla said. "Stealing a forbidden key is one thing. Being the one to open a sacred place is quite another."

"As you wish," Bertrand said.

Maggie held her breath as Bertrand slipped the key into the lock. A wave of light undulated across the gate.

"May the light bathe us," Nilla whispered.

Bertrand turned the key.

There was no wail. No alarm shouting to all of Sarana that invaders had arrived.

Maggie let herself exhale.

"Stay close, Miss Trent," Bertrand said. "I have only a vague idea of what might await us below the city."

"Great," Maggie whispered.

Bertrand went first into the tunnel, Maggie keeping close on his heels.

"Ancestors forgive me." Nilla shut the gate behind them.

The bricks forming the walls and floor were time-worn but shimmered with the same glow that filled the sanctuary. Water had gathered on the floor, forming deep puddles that reached from wall to wall. Clammy cold seeped into the sides of Maggie's boots.

What are we looking for, Bertrand?

Maggie swallowed her question.

There was something beyond the sloshing of their shoes that kept her quiet. A rustling that bounced off the bricks.

Bertrand led them deeper into the tunnel, stopping every now and then to touch the walls and dip his fingers into the water around their feet as though testing the temperature.

Maggie shivered as the dank cold cut through her sweater.

She looked back to Nilla, glancing down at her borrowed sweater before giving a nod.

Nilla winked.

The rustling grew stronger.

Like bats without the rubbery sound of their wings.

Maggie took two quick steps. Bertrand looked back before she could tap on his shoulder.

She pointed to her ear.

Bertrand gave a quick nod before looking up to examine the ceiling.

Maggie followed his gaze.

The ceiling looked the same as the walls, but someone had taken extra care to fill in the cracks within the mortar, leaving not a trace of darkness where the water dripped in from above.

Bertrand beckoned them onward.

How big is the city? How long could this tunnel go on for?

She should have asked before they'd opened the gate. Should have questioned what Bertrand and Nilla hoped to find down here. But she had only followed, trusting Bertrand would know what to look for and what to do.

He's always kept you safe before.

Maggie hated the little voice in her mind.

A second gate blocked the tunnel up ahead.

Bertrand looked back at Nilla.

Nilla shook her head and shrugged.

The path sloped down toward the gate.

Bertrand ran his hands over the metal. A keyhole waited just like on the outer gate. He pulled the key back out of his pocket.

The gate hummed as metal met metal, but the key turned easily.

The rustling filled the air as Bertrand pushed open the gate.

Maggie peered around Bertrand's shoulder, her heart thudding in her chest.

A staircase cut deeper into the earth.

Bertrand started down the stairs without looking back.

This is dumb, Bertrand. This is really, really stupid. We're going deeper underground in a city that floods.

Nilla tapped Maggie on the shoulder.

She turned to find Nilla holding a gleaming knife in front of her face.

Nilla flipped the blade, presenting Maggie with the hilt.

Nodding, Maggie took the weapon. The weight of the knife in her hand brought comfort. She didn't know if the blade could cut through a specter, or if shadows waited for them in the depths. But having any sort of weapon made her feel less foolish as she followed Bertrand down the steps.

The staircase spiraled down, cutting farther into the earth.

Just as the circling began to make Maggie's head spin, a room came into view.

The place was built of the same marble that adorned the sanctuary. Shelves of books lined one wall. A giant cauldron sat in the center of the room, flames dancing under its base. A long table set with scrolls and beakers stood behind the bubbling pot.

There should be someone here.

But the absence of brethren wasn't what set goose bumps on Maggie's arms. It was the two sidewalls.

Glowing doors with eyelevel slats took up the left and right-hand walls of the room. The rustling that had called to them from above seemed to come from both sides at once. Maggie stepped around Bertrand, moving toward the nearest door.

The movement grew more frantic the closer she got to the door, like a thousand whispered words with none fighting to rise above the rest.

Maggie ran her hands along the glowing wood. The fluttering resonated through the surface, shaking her palms.

She trailed her fingers up toward the eyelevel flap. A tiny latch was all that kept the metal in place.

Bertrand placed his hand on hers, moving her fingers away.

He tapped his own chest. Setting his satchel on the ground, he pulled out a disk that had been curved into a small shield. The front shone bright, contrasting with the tinted black of the back.

Maggie shook her head, but Bertrand ignored her, stepping up to the flap.

Bright side of the shield pointing toward the metal, he let the flap fall.

The rusting behind the door grew to a frenzied pitch.

In one swift motion, Bertrand flipped the shield, forming a tiny shadow over the opening. A tendril of black emerged, swirling into the form of a hand as it reached for Bertrand's flesh.

Maggie lunged forward, slashing with her knife and slicing through the shadow's wrist.

With a faint *wail*, the shadow's hand dissolved.

But the wrist remained, pushing out more blackness to form another set of fingers.

Maggie pressed her blade to the black, shoving the shadow back through the opening.

Bertrand swung the flap shut, locking it in place.

The shadows rustled their anger.

"Well"—Maggie leaned against the wall—"at least I know the knife works."

CHAPTER 16

"The brethren are insane." Maggie sat on the table, rubbing her temples in a failed attempt to stop the pounding in her head. "How many hundreds of shadows have they locked down here?"

"Thousands." Nilla thumbed through a wide book at the back of the room. "If these ledgers are even half right, there are thousands of shadows locked down here."

"I think the more troubling figure would be the sorts of shadows they've locked in," Bertrand said.

"What do you mean?" Maggie asked.

"The brethren don't deal with the normal spirits that wander the halls of homes, or walk by the sea at night," Bertrand said. "The brethren are called to take care of the shadows Saranans find troublesome. The ones that do damage, cause mischief."

"Shades and specters." Nilla closed the book, her face pale. "They've trapped people who have been wrapped in darkness in the same cells as the very creatures that unleashed the horrible torment upon them."

"Nilla, no," Bertrand said.

Nilla walked to the door, ignoring Bertrand's warning.

"We have to help them, Bertrand," Nilla said. "Some of these shades might have been trapped as long as I was. We can't allow them to continue in such agony."

"We cannot open these doors, Nilla." Bertrand planted himself between her and the shadows. "The moment we give any of them a path back into darkness we would be overwhelmed by specters. We'd never make it out, none of the lost souls in these vaults would be saved."

"We have to do something," Nilla growled.

"We will find a way to help them." Bertrand took Nilla's shoulders. "But we can't be hasty. To move on compassionate impulse could cause massive amounts of harm."

"Promise me we won't leave them trapped," Nilla said.

"I swear." Bertrand turned her away from the doors. "We need to find the source of the specters. If we can stop more of the dark creatures from being made, we stand a chance at turning the tide."

"What are we even looking for?" Maggie asked. "We know now why they're called the vaults. The brethren locked a bomb's worth of shadows away. The sparkle dust stops working, and the whole city could be swarmed and taken. But we knew they weren't destroying specters. What are we supposed to learn?"

"What the books can tell us," Bertrand said.

"You don't already know everything?" Maggie slid off the table and headed over to the bookshelf.

"I never presume to know everything, Miss Trent," Bertrand said. "The brethren hold their knowledge close to their chest. I even considered joining them to gain access to their secrets."

"Why didn't you?" Maggie asked. "The sparkle bath too much for you?"

"There are some rules of the brethren by which I could not survive." Bertrand pulled a book down from the top shelf.

"I, for one, am glad you didn't join." Nilla stretched out a scroll on the table.

Maggie knelt by the bottom shelf, carefully pulling out a large gray volume. "What would the brethren hide in their books?"

"I don't know." Bertrand quickly scanned each page of his text. "And that's exactly what bothers me."

"The brethren didn't exist until the flood," Nilla said. "When the first shadows rose, the group formed to investigate what had happened. Honestly, they spent most of their time trying to return bones to the right graves in hopes of luring the spirits back to their rest."

"But that didn't work?" Maggie flipped open the book. Illustrations of bones being pushed up from graves by rising water greeted her.

"Not at all," Nilla said. "Once the group knew returning the bones to their rightful place wouldn't help, they went about comforting the city the only way they knew how. Bathing themselves in light so the shadows couldn't approach them, they became the captors of the dead. But of course one can't say such things. So instead they are *shepherds* and *protectors*."

"And in all this time they never figured it out?" Maggie asked. "Never realized someone was making monsters and setting them loose in the city?"

"No." Bertrand said at the same moment Nilla said, "Yes."

"What do you mean?" Bertrand was at Nilla's side in two quick strides.

"It's all right here," Nilla said. "Their peace and light is nothing more than a sparkling sideshow."

Maggie joined the other two to stare down at the table.

A chart had been drawn out.

Malicious – Ancestor – Taken

Below each title someone had written the attributes of each type.

"Same problem, different names," Nilla said. "They know and they're still locking them down here like rats. They deserve to be shoved in with the shadows."

"The Barrister has a key to get in down here," Maggie said.

"Well, he did." Nilla said.

"Does he know, too?" Maggie said. "Does he know there are shadows that can eat people and he's just pretending not to?"

"It would seem so." Bertrand tented his fingers under his chin. "I had hoped in coming here I would find a clue as to where the specters began to appear. A hint of where in the city the trouble had started. Instead, we find the people we believed to live in ignorance indeed know of the problem and have done nothing about it."

"Done nothing because they can't figure out what to do, or done nothing because they believe the spread of the shadows is best for Sarana?" Nilla asked.

"I wish I were naïve enough to fully believe the former." Bertrand unrolled another scroll.

"If the Barrister knows about specters or malicious shadows or whatever you want to call them," Maggie said, "he knew he wasn't sending you to get a misplaced spirit out of the closet."

"From ignorance to attempted murder so quickly," Nilla said. "I'm going to need something stronger than tea when we get home."

"The question then becomes did he send me to the closet assuming I would succeed but willing to sacrifice me to save himself—" Bertrand began.

"Or did he plant a specter and hope you'd get devoured by the darkness?" Maggie finished.

Bertrand moved on to another scroll.

"If they know about the specters, maybe they know where they're coming from," Nilla said. "I say we break into the Barrister's house, pin him down, and make him tell us exactly what he knows."

"It's not a terrible plan," Maggie said.

Bertrand moved back to the shelf, mumbling to himself as he ran his fingers along the spines of the books.

"We could also go to the brethren," Maggie said. "Serber seems like a reasonable man. If we tell him we want to help, maybe he'll talk."

"Or he could decide we're dangerous heretics." Nilla unrolled the last scroll on the table.

"What do they do to heretics?" Maggie asked.

"No idea," Nilla said. "We never hear of them after they're taken."

"And no one has a problem with that?" Maggie said.

"A few did," Nilla said. "But after they were declared heretics as well, everyone decided they didn't so much care."

"This place is really screwed up." Maggie dug her fingers through her hair.

"Bertrand, look at this," Nilla said.

Bertrand came back from the shelf, a book with a red cover clutched in his hands.

Nilla spread her arms, opening a scroll displaying a map of the city drawn in minute detail.

Streets reached from the seaside, which bordered half the city, to the swamp that surrounded the rest. Each house had been carefully sketched, and every business labeled with the type of trade offered.

"What are those?" Maggie pointed to the thousands of little gray rectangles under the buildings and streets.

"Graves," Bertrand said.

"They laid streets over the graves?" Maggie said. "I mean, houses are bad enough, but streets?"

"Why do think the streets curve like waves?" Nilla said. "The graves have collapsed."

"That's just sick." Maggie shook her head. "Not to sound harsh, but it kind of feels like this city was begging for the haunting from Hell."

"I do believe you've both overlooked the most interesting aspect of the map." Bertrand tapped the parchment.

The tunnels that led under the city had been traced in faint blue, including the chamber where they now stood. Another corridor led from the back of the chamber off toward the swamps.

"Oh." Maggie turned toward the bookcase. "What would they want to hide back here?"

"That is indeed the question," Bertrand said.

Nilla squinted at the bookshelf. "Come, Bertrand." She took him by the sleeve, leading him to the center of the case. "Lift me."

At her order, Bertrand made a step with his hands.

Maggie grabbed her knife as Nilla stepped up onto Bertrand's palms, peering at the top of the bookcase.

"I don't see a hinge," Nilla said, "and I doubt the whole thing would swing. It would knock the table over."

"Perhaps they used a bit of magic to conceal the entrance," Bertrand said. "It would be the wise thing to do."

"Do you believe the brethren to be wise?" Nilla jumped out of Bertrand's hands.

"I believe they were clever enough to keep me from this place for four years," Bertrand said. "Making a place seem forbidden and yet unappealing requires a kind of talent I have seldom seen."

"You only didn't want to come here because you hate their rhetoric and didn't want to be pulled in," Nilla said.

Maggie tucked her chin, unable to keep from smiling as Bertrand bristled at Nilla's words.

A tiny chip marked the floor, breaking the perfect gleam of the room.

"Exactly my point," Bertrand said. "They played me for years, and I had not thought such a thing possible."

If Maggie squinted at the chip just right, lines of brighter light cut away from the spot at a right angle.

"Bertrand," Maggie said.

"If everyone in the world knew how easy it was to dissuade the great Hunter Wayland—"

"I think I found the tunnel." Maggie knelt by the chip, running her fingers along the brighter paths of light.

"Well done, Miss Trent." Bertrand knelt beside her.

"A trapdoor?" Nilla said. "I was so hoping for a tunnel hidden behind a bookcase. I've never gotten to break through one of those."

Maggie ran her nails along the edge, searching for purchase. "If trapdoors are so boring, why don't you open it?"

"How mundane." Nilla shooed Bertrand and Maggie back.

Steadying her stance, Nilla raised one hand, circling her palm over the trapdoor.

After a few moments passed with nothing changing but the deepening wrinkles on Nilla's brow, Maggie glanced to Bertrand.

He squinted at the center of the trapdoor as though watching something.

Maggie followed his gaze, trying to see past the constant shimmer of light.

At the very corner of the door, the shine seemed to be pulling away, leaving a border of darkness. As the light receded farther, it swirled up, twisting toward Nilla's palm, marking her skin as the blackness had swallowed Bertrand's.

Is this how the brethren glow? They siphon the light off of everything around them?

The glow left more quickly now, swirling up in a great spiral to coat Nilla's arm. With a faint *pop*, the last drop of light disappeared, leaving nothing but a gray stone slab on the floor. A rusted iron handle waited in the center.

"We'll have to repaint with some *lish* if we don't want them to notice." Nilla grabbed the metal ring, hoisting the stone slab away.

Maggie blinked at the hatch, her mouth drifting farther open with each moment.

"What have they been hiding?" Bertrand leaned over the void.

Hands shaking on the ground, Maggie joined him.

A rush of water carried up from far below. But the water itself could not be seen.

One line of light cut down into the darkness. The edges were muddied and fading as though some unseen force ate away at the magic.

"We can't go down there," Nilla said.

"I don't think we've a choice." Bertrand opened his satchel, pulling out his flashlight.

Its beam found a rope ladder but couldn't reach all the way to where the ladder led.

"Bertrand, listen to me," Nilla said. "I've been taken as a shade before—it is a fate I wouldn't wish on anyone, least of all you. It's too dark down there, you won't come out untaken."

"We have waited years to know where the darkness comes from." Bertrand pulled his halo from his bag. "I will not turn back now. There are too many innocent lives that could still be lost."

"Does your life have no value?" Nilla asked.

He fitted his halo onto his head.

"It's nearly dark," Nilla said. "We need to get home."

"I wander in the dark every night." Bertrand took Nilla's hand in his. "I never ask you to come with me, and I don't ask you to join me now."

"Give me the other halo," Maggie said.

"Miss Trent, I don't expect—"

"I don't get to go home without you." Maggie held out her hand. "Besides, I've seen worse than darkness."

"Be careful, Miss Trent." Bertrand pulled her halo from his bag.

"So I should just wait here and see how long it takes to hear the wails of your being consumed?" Nilla asked.

"Keep the way out lit." Bertrand swung his legs over the darkness, twisting to perch on the rope ladder.

"Come, Miss Trent. The burden of knowledge awaits."

CHAPTER 17

The rope ladder swung every time she or Bertrand took a step. Maggie clutched the hilt of her knife in one hand, leaving herself only two fingers to cling to the rungs. The sound of rushing water drifted up from below.

"Think we'll find solid ground or just watery death down there?" Maggie's voice echoed through the black.

"Solid ground I would assume," Bertrand called back.

The sound of him speaking loud and clear brushed away the fear growing at the edges of Maggie's mind.

"It would seem incredibly odd to have a ladder reaching down to something one could not stand upon," Bertrand continued. "If the brethren merely wanted access to the water beneath, I could only imagine two reasons why—to fetch water, in which case a bucket and rope would do just as well. Or to send a person permanently into the rushing abyss."

"And then who needs a ladder?" Maggie said. "Just toss them in and have it done."

"What a cheery pair we are."

"When the moment calls for it."

"Solid ground it is, Miss Trent. Be careful, the rock is uneven."

Maggie chanced a glance down. Bertrand waited below, patting the pockets of his coat.

"Missing something?" Maggie jumped the last rung to the ground.

"I'm not in the habit of packing spares."

Maggie peered into the darkness as Bertrand continued to search his pockets.

The rushing of water now came from behind them, where the map said the tunnel continued. The brethren hadn't smoothed out the stone ground. Cracks and bits of fallen rock marred the path into the darkness.

Shadows marked everything her light touched. Maggie stared at the shadows, waiting for them to swirl into a shape that would reach out to take her.

"Ah, here we are." Bertrand reached into his breast pocket, pulling out what seemed to be a wide, glowing string. When the string reached the length of his arm, he flicked his wrist. With a *pop,* the string thickened and grew ridged.

"For you, Miss Trent." He passed the glowing club to Maggie before reaching into his pants pockets and pulling out two fully-formed swords.

"Wow. And I thought just having pockets was cool."

"We can work on arranging hidden weaponry when we get out of here." Bertrand squinted into the darkness. "I think our arrival has been noticed."

The shadows behind a fallen rock churned, rising up to form a human shape.

With a nod, Bertrand started forward, both swords raised.

"Stay away from the fallen rocks, if you will," Bertrand said. "The fewer paths you give them to reach you, the safer you will be."

"Thanks." Maggie kept her knife high and her glowing club low, lending extra light to her feet as they followed the arcing path down toward the water.

Maggie glanced back at the ladder. A dim strip of feebly shimmering gold fought the darkness, and the hatch above glowed like a star leading them home.

"Ahh!" Maggie screamed before she knew she was falling. Her foot dropped below where the ground should have been as she stepped into a wide crack.

"Miss Trent." Bertrand dropped one sword, grabbing Maggie around the middle before she could hit the floor.

Shadows rushed forward, watching as Bertrand set her back on her feet.

"Thanks for that." Maggie tightened the band of her halo.

"Of course." Bertrand stared at his sword on the ground for a long moment before picking it up.

"Did anything get you?" Maggie asked as Bertrand examined his fingers.

"Not yet." Bertrand gave a small smile.

"Not funny." Maggie poked him forward with her club, carefully keeping her eyes on the path. "You know if something happens to you, this city is probably doomed, right?"

"That is a terrible weight to place on a person." Bertrand stopped, staring at a shadow that had appeared to their right.

The shadow raised its arm, fluttering its fingers in a terrifying wave.

"It's a weight you've taken on too many times to complain about it now," Maggie said.

The shadow tipped its head to the side.

"This is what you wanted." Maggie stomped down the panic in her chest. "Going to different worlds. Getting to be the hero."

"But at what cost? I have given what I had hoped to never lose. I can't stand to sacrifice anything more."

Pebbles clacked under his feet as he moved on.

"I have given too much toward the salvation of other worlds," Bertrand said. "If I give my life in Sarana as penance for my wrongs, so be it. But if I survive, I will live out my years here."

"And I'll be stuck?"

"I'll find a way to send you back to the Siren."

"And you'll stay and play house?" Maggie skirted a knee-high stone.

Shadows clawed at the edge of her light as she passed.

"I will endure my exile in peace," Bertrand said.

The cavern narrowed in front of them. The shadows crowded around the entrance to a tunnel.

"The Siren didn't exile you." Maggie forced herself to look at the crowd of shadows as they passed. "She wants you to come back."

"I wasn't speaking of the Siren's judgment. I was speaking of yours."

Maggie forgot to walk for a moment.

Bertrand's circle of light moved away from hers, leaving a gap of darkness between them.

Shadows peeled off the walls. A face pushed out at her, its mouth open in a silent scream.

Holding her breath, Maggie stepped forward, shoving the shadows aside. She ran the few steps to catch up to Bertrand.

Her light bathed the walls as they continued down the tunnel. But the cracks in the ceiling couldn't be reached by the glow of the halos. Shifting darkness stayed stuck between the stones.

Bertrand slowed as they reached the end of the tunnel and a wide space opened in front of them.

Stone slabs reached over the rushing underground river. Salt mixed in with the damp stench of the air, as though the sea itself had been bled to create the torrent.

"What is this place?" Maggie whispered.

The feeling of being somewhere worse than forbidden had stolen her voice.

"The primordial ooze where darkness begins."

Bertrand stood at the edge of the river, gazing down into its depths.

Maggie stepped up beside him, holding her club out over the rushing water.

Waves churned as water met stone.

Maggie watched the patterns twist and swirl. Forms appeared on top of the waves.

"It's not right." Maggie crouched, reaching her light farther out over the water.

"Careful, Miss Trent."

"The foam. It's black."

The murky foam latched onto the rocks. The bubbles dissolved, leaving black slime behind.

"Gross." Maggie shuddered.

"Indeed." Bertrand moved toward a bit of rock that reached farther out over the water.

"Do you really need to do that?" Maggie followed.

"There." Bertrand pointed to the center of a rock whose sides had been smoothed by years of fighting the current.

The black had pooled in a hollow in the rock. The darkness swirled and churned, shying away from the light of Bertrand's sword.

"This is where they come from?" Maggie said.

"The water gives the specters life."

"But if it's just the water, then the specters have always been here. The river didn't just spring into being in the last century. The specters shouldn't have randomly appeared either."

"There is always the potential for darkened death in every world," Bertrand said. "It only takes one person filled with enough malice to awaken what lies in wait."

Maggie's lungs relaxed as Bertrand stepped away from the edge.

"Miss Trent, I fear I must ask more of you now than I ever have before."

"If you want me to jump into that water, the answer is no."

"From this moment on, you must trust no one in this world

but me." Bertrand stared into Maggie's eyes. "The brethren and Barrister must know of the dark potential that lies here."

"Nilla—"

"Has been alive since the specters began," Bertrand said. "It would not be the first time someone was taken by their own creation. The only two people of whose innocence I am completely convinced are you and me."

Maggie gripped her knife and club.

"I know trusting me is the last thing you would ever choose to do," Bertrand said.

"But it's what I'm stuck with." Maggie stared at the dark water. "Fine, I'll trust you. But when we get rid of the demon goo, you come back to the Siren's Realm. You figure out what's going on with the Compère and the weapons and you save your own damn world for once."

"I…" Bertrand closed his eyes. "If you truly believe the Siren's Realm needs my assistance, I cannot turn my back on those I once called friends."

"Great to see you forgot us so fast." Maggie turned toward the tunnel.

A wall of shadows blocked their path.

"I didn't forget you, Miss Trent. In a thousand lifetimes, that would not be possible. I am the one in the wrong. I am the one who broke the incomparable pair we were. I placed too much weight on you in Histem. I let the end of an empire rest on your young shoulders. It's easy to forget that while I look so close to you in age, I have lived at least a hundred years more.

"I've run through it a thousand times." Pain etched the edges of Bertrand's words. "There was no way to save the magicians without destroying the pacel. No way to destroy the pacel while maintaining the peace. No way to save more lives while accomplishing our goal. No place for us on the council that would build a new world without usurping power from the magicians who had so long been oppressed. No way to stop the enslavement of a people but to crumble order and disappear to allow the magicians of that world take credit. I wouldn't be surprised if Alden isn't enshrined as a martyr for destroying the pacel."

"I hadn't thought of that," Maggie said. "A statue of Alden."

"Searching for a different path in that world is all that haunts my dreams. But there is nothing. No other route to their freedom and our survival I have ever found. But I could have been the one to do it, the one to make the crack that burned a world. It should have been me to carry that terrible burden."

A shadow grew up the wall, towering twenty feet overhead.

"What if you took our survival out of the equation?" Maggie asked.

The shadow spread its arms wide.

"Does that change how many people would have died in Histem?" She raised her knife.

"It only adds two more dead. And relieves us of the burden of guilt."

"Being right about helping the magicians doesn't change the fact that you took me away from my friends when they needed me." Maggie inched toward the tunnel.

Bertrand matched her movement. "There is nothing I will ever be able to do to make up for leading you from the Siren's Realm."

"As long as we're clear on that."

As they edged closer to the tunnel, the giant shadow grew, stretching to stand above the reach of their light.

"Are we really going to walk between the shadow monster's legs?" Maggie whispered.

"I don't believe the beast has left us a choice." Bertrand edged in front of Maggie, holding his sword high.

Maggie held her club behind her head, leaving a trail of light in her wake.

The rustling of shadows shifting came from the cavern up ahead.

Maggie glanced behind. The giant shadow had joined them, ducking into the tunnel.

"Bertrand," Maggie said. "Do specters often stalk the living?"

"Once they have their sights on prey, they rarely cease their hunt unless captured."

"Great. I've always wanted a few hundred shadows hunting me."

They stepped out into the cavern. A thin light carried from the ceiling high above, waiting for them.

Maggie kept close on Bertrand's heels, carefully leaping every crack and dodging the shadows cast by every large stone.

"Tell Nilla everything we found down here with absolute honesty," Bertrand said. "And make sure when you tell her I am watching to read her face."

"You're so romantic."

A shadow swirled in the corner of Maggie's vision.

The giant that had been following them seemed ill content with his enormous size. He breathed in, devouring all the shadows around him. His darkness deepened as his mass grew.

"A bit faster then." Bertrand ran toward the ladder.

Maggie sprinted behind him, narrowly avoiding stepping on his heels.

She dodged cracks and stones, fighting the urge to watch the specter grow. The rungs of the ladder came into view, hanging limp in the darkness.

A *crack* shook the air.

The ground under Maggie's feet crumbled. She leapt forward, her toes reaching for solid ground. The earth shook again.

Maggie toppled forward. Rocks pummeled the air from her lungs as her knife slipped from her grip and her halo flew from her head.

CHAPTER 18

"*M*iss Trent!" Bertrand let go of the ladder, lunging toward Maggie.

She scrambled forward, seizing her fallen halo and knife.

Ice wrapped around her right ankle.

"No." Maggie slashed down toward her feet with her glowing club.

The hand that had touched her vanished, leaving inky blackness crawling up her leg.

Bertrand leaned out of his own light, snatching up Maggie's halo and jamming it onto her head.

A tiny tendril of darkness whipped up, catching Maggie under her arm.

"We need to go." Bertrand dragged Maggie to her feet.

She gasped as she placed weight on her right leg. The cold had cut off feeling from her foot, leaving no sign the limb even existed anymore. Ice crept up Maggie's arm.

"Don't suppose you can do the suction thing down here?" Maggie asked.

The shadows surrounded them, blocking the ladder from view.

"I'm afraid this isn't the place for such a procedure." Bertrand slashed his sword at the nearest shadow. The beast recoiled with a *wail*.

"Perfect." Maggie swung her glowing club, knocking aside dark fingers that dared to graze the edge of her light.

Bertrand pressed his back to Maggie's.

"Stay right behind me, Miss Trent."

She matched his steps as he moved toward the ladder, swinging her club in front of her like a torch even as the cold swallowed her arm.

The giant shadow who had split the ground glided along the cavern wall, marking their steps.

"Do you really need to stare, you creepy bastard?" Maggie's foot fumbled on her dropped knife. She wedged her toe under the blade, kicking it up to catch the hilt with her good hand.

More shadows fluttered in and out of view. The massive beast shifted position constantly.

Maggie blinked, trying to find a pattern in the movement. Her fingers went numb.

Hold on to the light, you stupid hand.

She held the club steady, afraid too much movement would send her weapon flying off into the darkness.

"Bertrand, I don't know if I'm going to be able to climb the ladder." Maggie wobbled on a stone she couldn't feel. "I've got a numb foot and a numb arm."

"Of course you'll be able to climb, Miss Trent. You'll do it because you must."

The giant reached out from the wall, its fingers stretching for the rope ladder.

"Bertrand, on the wall."

Bertrand swiveled Maggie around, leaving her nose to the ladder.

"Climb!" he shouted.

Maggie tucked her club and knife into the back of her pants.

Gripping with her good hand, she hauled herself up onto the first rung.

Bertrand slashed his swords, cutting through the great shadow's wrists. But the beast's hand regrew, and it grabbed for the ladder again, high out of reach of Bertrand's blades.

Maggie looped her numb arm over the next rung for balance, and pulled herself up another step.

The giant shadow seized the rope, swinging the ladder as Maggie desperately clung on.

Even as she screamed, she looked down to Bertrand for help. The specters had surrounded him, making a dome around his light, blocking him entirely from view.

"Bertrand!" Maggie's mind raced—back to the house, the articles, the people who had been consumed, to the book sitting in her pocket. "*Melivious varax!*" Maggie's shout rang off the walls of the cavern.

Heat burst from her, sending light shooting out of her body. The shadows swirled away, fleeing from her spell as pain seared her arm and leg where the darkness had grown.

The light faltered as she screamed. Darkness born of pain edged into her mind.

"*Melivious varax!*" She shouted the spell again as the last of the shadows fled from Bertrand.

The agony of the light blurred her vision.

"Miss Trent!"

Her grip on the ladder faltered.

"*Iltsavor mortis.*" Dim lights fluttered away from Bertrand, dodging around the cavern. The shadows followed the lights.

"Like cats." Maggie swayed.

Bertrand leapt onto the ladder behind her, pressing her into the rungs.

"Nilla!" Bertrand shouted. "Nilla!"

The light pouring from Maggie faltered. The great shadow on the wall reached forward.

The world shook as the ladder lurched, hoisting them up toward the hatch above.

They moved faster than any one person could pull. Like a giant had seized a crank and was reeling them back into the realm of light. The square above them grew from a speck to the size of the trapdoor.

Bertrand wrapped his arms around Maggie, shielding her with his own body as they soared through the door and into the chamber above.

They hit the floor with a *thud*. Bertrand took the brunt of the blow. Maggie's head cracked into his shoulder, sending spots dancing in her vision as she rolled away.

"Nilla, my bag." Bertrand leapt to his feet.

The stars didn't leave Maggie's vision. Bright beaming spots moved around the room. But blackness tickled the edges, giving darkness to places where there should be only light.

"The shadows got out." Maggie fought to push herself to her feet. Her blackened ankle wouldn't hold her weight. The shadows crept up her leg and arm, reaching across her torso. "That's not good." She rolled onto her back.

The bright spots came back into view. They weren't dim dots of light as Bertrand had made in the caverns below. These lights had faces. Lips, noses, and eyes that seemed familiar.

"We must bathe her in light," the face spoke.

"Diven?" Maggie squinted at him. "This keeps getting worse."

"I will not have you bathe her." Bertrand knelt over Maggie, a glowing orb in each hand. "Miss Trent, I must ask you to trust me, and forgive me for the pain you are about to endure."

Shadows swirled over Maggie's eyes, stealing Bertrand's face.

No, not stealing.

Showing. Giving depth to the true nature of what he already was. Blackened bone with darkness taking the place of eyes.

Death and decay. An inevitable and unending darkness.

The specters weren't trying to turn her into anything other than what she was always meant to become.

White-hot pain ricocheted through Maggie's chest. She opened her mouth to scream, but no sound would come. A terrible ripping seized her side as someone tore her arm and leg from her body.

The shadows dove into her vision, begging her to join them, to give in and become one with the darkness where she would never again know pain.

No!

Maggie fought as black clawed at the edges of her mind.

The limbs that had been torn away reappeared, packed with burning coals.

This time her voice did work as she screamed.

The noise echoed off the walls.

The shadows vanished, replaced by an unmoving darkness. A soothing black that sought to lure her to sleep.

Maggie pushed against the pain, swimming up through the darkness to the front of her mind as she fought to stay conscious.

"Bertrand." The effort of forming the single word sent her tumbling down again.

She pushed harder, fighting to open her eyes.

"Lay still, Miss Trent." Bertrand's voice came from far above. "Let the pain recede and your mind clear."

"That was inhumane," Diven said. "We could have saved her."

"Saved her from something I was told the brethren didn't believe existed the hundreds of times I have come to the Sanctuary expounding the truth?" Bertrand said.

"The secrets of the darkness are not for the brethren to share beyond their ranks."

Serber.

Open your eyes, Maggie. Just open your eyes.

"As many times as you asked of the shadows, I offered you a place amongst the brethren," Serber said.

"How many have died because you have hidden the truth?" Bertrand spat.

"The truth is darker than the people of Sarana can survive," Serber said.

"That it not for you to decide!"

"It is more my decision than yours, Hunter Wayland," Serber said. "I have been battling against the darkness since I was a child. Sarana isn't your home to protect."

"Is it a battle if you don't fight?" Nilla said.

Eyelids.

They were keeping Maggie from the light. She forced her eyes to open.

"We do fight." Diven stood over Maggie. "We keep the shadows trapped beneath. We imprison the shadows who harm the people of the city."

"They should be destroyed!" Nilla said.

"We cannot risk the accidental destruction of an ancestor." Serber swept a hand toward the doors. "Would you send the spirit of your grandmother to the void?"

"Then you should stop more shadows from coming up from below." Maggie's words tore raggedly from her throat.

"Maggie!" A worried smile shone on Diven's sparkling face.

"Miss Trent." Bertrand knelt, wrapping an arm behind her shoulders and helping her to sit.

"The shadows are coming from the river," Maggie said. "But you must know that, you've got a nice little ladder to get down there."

"*Had* a ladder," Nilla said. "I might have destroyed it."

"There are thousands of them down there, waiting for a chance to climb up here," Maggie said.

"And we prevent that," Serber said. "We monitor the exit. We protect the city."

"Then how are they getting out? Because whatever you think

you're doing, it's not working." Maggie rubbed her eyes, sweeping away the last of the shadows.

"There are cracks," Serber said. "Tiny fissures we cannot fill. Every now and then, a malevolent shadow finds its way to the surface. We find them and bring them back."

"And lock them in with those who have been consumed," Nilla said. "You aren't saviors. You're monsters."

"No…" Diven shook his head, sending his sparkling hair fluttering. "We are trying to help, there is no other path to protection."

"How easy to say when you're coated in light," Nilla said.

"If you are not willing to find a way to protect this city, then we shall have to continue our work without you." Bertrand lifted Maggie to her feet.

"You cannot tell anyone what you've seen here," Serber said.

"They have a right to know what's living under their streets," Maggie said.

"The darkness below must always stay hidden," Serber said.

"Why?" Maggie said. "Afraid the kids won't be able to sleep at night? I'm a little more concerned about them being eaten by shadows."

"The black waters are the makings of the darkest sins of Sarana," Serber said. "Years of misusing the land, of ignoring the poor, and disrespecting our elders—"

"Disrespecting the elders who misused the land and ignored the poor?" Maggie said.

"The misdeeds of the past are not an excuse for the suffering of the present," Bertrand said. "That responsibility and burden lies with those who are here now, and fault falls on those who refuse to help."

The air went still, the only sound the rustling from the vaults.

"If you continue to refuse real action, the deaths of those who will be taken lie on your shoulders." Bertrand lifted his satchel. "I will continue to fight. I recommend you stay out of my way. Come, Nilla, Miss Trent—our battle has only begun."

Bertrand strode to the spiral staircase.

Nilla shot a glare at Serber before following.

"Maggie," Diven said. "Come back to the sanctuary. We can show you the good work we do. You can help us keep the shadows at bay."

"I'm not sticking my thumb in a dam," Maggie said. "I'd rather fight than wait. If you want to do something real, you can find me."

Maggie skirted the cauldron.

We'll find a way to set you free.

She hoped the shades would be able to hear her silent promise through the darkness.

Maggie froze as the *thump* of footsteps carried from above.

"I grow weary of this day, Bertrand," Nilla said as the Barrister stepped down the twisting stairs, his wide frame blocking their path.

"I'm afraid, Hunter Wayland"—the Barrister bowed—"you cannot be allowed to leave."

Maggie reached for the knife in the back of her pants.

"I told you I couldn't let you have the key." The Barrister raised both hands.

"Do not make me fight you," Bertrand said. "We are leaving, and I cannot allow you to stop us."

"I'm afraid it's a test of wills then," the Barrister said. "If people find out what we've hidden from them, I'll lose my position. I'll be voted out of office and driven from the city."

"There are more important things than politics, Barrister dear." A staff appeared in Nilla's hand. "I'm leaving and taking my compatriots with me. Please get out of my way before things become too heated for me to ever play cards with you again."

"No." The Barrister worked his hands as though pulling taffy. "I don't care if I have to lock you down here with the horde of shadows. I have spent my entire life building my career, and I will not allow three ruffian shadow stalkers to ruin everything."

A crackling ball of red appeared between the Barrister's hands.

"Please let me, Bertrand," Nilla said. "I've let him ogle my chest one time too many."

Bertrand stepped aside as spiraling shards of bright red metal shot toward Nilla's heart.

Nilla held her staff forward. *"Ezicham."* Light bowed around the staff. The scarlet shards bounced back toward the wide-eyed Barrister.

The ground shook beneath Maggie's feet as the air around the Barrister contracted and he soared into the chamber, smacking his head on the ceiling.

"Nilla, don't break the room," Maggie warned.

"I didn't shake the earth, pet." Nilla steered the Barrister over the cauldron.

A great *crack* sounded as the floor shook again. A line of gray split the ground as the trapdoor tumbled into the darkness below.

Tendrils of black kissed the edges of the light as the room trembled.

Nilla dropped the Barrister face first into the cauldron with a splash.

"What have you done?" Serber darted around Diven, sprinting for the stairs.

A *rumble* shook the walls. The vault doors cracked. Shadows peered through the gaps, searching for the freedom the brethren had stolen from them.

Serber screamed.

Maggie looked toward him just in time to see the floor beneath him crumble as he fell out of sight.

"Run!" Bertrand bellowed as the stone under the cauldron gave way.

CHAPTER 19

A rumbling *crack* shook the room again. Chunks of ceiling tumbled down, and the long table tipped into the ever-growing pit.

"Miss Trent." Bertrand had reached the wide crack that had swallowed Serber. "We must go!"

Maggie sprinted toward Bertrand, her mind barely having time to marvel as Nilla tossed her staff over the chasm. The pole widened, forming a glowing footbridge that reached up onto the stairs.

Nilla ran up the pole and out of sight.

"Go." Bertrand looked behind Maggie.

Toes at the bridge, she glanced back. Swirls of shadows dragged the table into the pit.

Diven stood frozen, his back plastered to the wall between two cells.

"Diven, come on," Maggie shouted.

Diven stared wide-eyed as stones flew up from below, cracking through the shimmering façade of the room, creating spider webs of darkness.

"Diven, we have to go." Maggie stepped toward him.

"Miss Trent, no!" Bertrand blocked her path.

One of the vault doors crashed to the floor, breaking through the stone and plummeting into the darkness.

Diven swayed and tipped, falling toward the abyss.

"No!"

"*Stratus!*" A violet cord shot out of Bertrand's palm.

The streak of purple wrapped around Diven, dragging him up from the pit. Shadows reached for his flesh but couldn't penetrate the glow of his skin.

"Go, Miss Trent!" Bertrand shouted.

Maggie ran across the bridge, ignoring the storm of shadows that brewed beneath its translucent surface.

"What's kept you?" Nilla waited on the spiral stairs.

"Diven." Maggie glanced back.

Diven ran just ahead of Bertrand.

A *crash* shook the steps. The doorway collapsed right behind Bertrand's heels.

"We should quicken our pace," Bertrand said.

"Fine then." Nilla sprinted forward.

Maggie kept her gaze fixed on Nilla's perfect braids as they wound up and into the tunnel.

"We have to save Serber," Diven said. "If you help me, I can go down and get him."

"Absolutely not." Nilla's voice bounced down the tunnel, carrying over the *rumble* of the walls collapsing behind them. "Chances of his surviving the fall, miniscule. Chances of us dying if we turn back, excellent. We're not going back."

"May the light forgive me," Diven said.

The tunnel shook, splitting the sheen on the golden floor.

"Damn." Nilla clapped her hands over her head.

Glowing silver armor blossomed around her body. Her hair twisted and shimmered, morphing into a shining helmet as a new staff appeared in her hand.

"How do you do that?" Maggie panted.

"Years of practice."

The gate to the street by the sea came into view.

"Malevolent shadows will take over the city," Diven said. "All hope for Sarana is lost."

"Hope is never lost until there is no one left who is willing to fight," Bertrand said.

Nilla slowed as she reached the gate.

"Bertrand dear." She stopped with her fingers on the glowing bars. "It seems all the shadows in Sarana are out tonight."

Maggie peered over Nilla's shoulder.

The street beyond teemed with dark figures.

Some drifted by, seeming to move without any hint of desire as to where the wind should lead them. Others roamed as though searching for something just beyond their reach.

But it was the third type that stole Maggie's breath away. A half-circle of shadows surrounded the gate, blocking their path to the street beyond.

"The specters have scented new blood." Bertrand stepped past Maggie and Nilla, tucking his satchel under his arm.

"They call for the payment of the sins of Sarana," Diven said.

"Superstitious nonsense," Nilla said. "They smell blood and fear."

"Miss Trent," Bertrand said, "do you feel well enough to move through the shadows?"

"Do I have a choice?" Maggie's skin stung at the mere mention of the freezing blackness.

"No," Bertrand said, "but I do wish that weren't the case."

"Let's just go." Maggie straightened the band of her halo and held tightly to her club and knife.

Nilla flicked her staff. A long blade appeared on the end.

"Ladies first." She stepped around Bertrand and shoved open the gate.

The specters inched back as the glowing metal bars swung toward them.

"Stay close," Bertrand said. "Do not let the shadows come between us."

Maggie stepped up next to Bertrand, letting Nilla take the lead, the blade of her spear sweeping the shadows aside.

The specters surrounded them but couldn't stop their light from moving forward.

"We need to get to the sanctuary," Diven said.

"We cannot hide and wait for Sarana to fall," Bertrand said.

"I have no intention of hiding," Diven said.

Maggie glanced back, wanting to see his glowing face to know if he really meant to fight with them.

Diven walked at the very edge of the light of her halo, his hands tucked behind his back even as he studied the shadows.

"Why do we need to go to the sanctuary?" Maggie asked.

"The sanctuary was built over the vaults," Diven said. "For our light to be the final blockade against the rising of the shadows."

"How noble," Nilla said. "Bertrand, shall we to the temple of light?"

"As the lady likes," Bertrand said.

"I'd like to kick in a glittery door," Nilla said. "It sounds like a bit of fun."

"The sanctuary door will not be closed to us," Diven said.

"I don't trust doors that should never be closed," Maggie said. "Feels too much like being lured into a trap."

"I think I might actually like your apprentice, Bertrand." Nilla turned down the side street that led to the seaside.

Shadows passed by as though they were nothing more than people strolling in the daylight. The street was more crowded with the dead than it had been with the living a few short hours before.

"I've never seen this many shadows in one place," Bertrand said.

"Neither have I," Nilla said. "Bertrand, remember your promise."

"I could never forget." Regret tightened Bertrand's voice.

Maggie raised an eyebrow at him.

Bertrand gave a tiny shake of his head. "Unto the breach."

Nilla started forward, leading them along the wharfs.

Shadows shifted on the ships moored in the darkness. The spirits of sailors climbed the rigging, their forms dark stains in the moonlight.

A flicker above her shoulder drew Maggie's focus back to the specters surrounding her.

The feeling of a thousand eyes searching her for weakness turned Maggie's lungs to lead.

How do you fight an army of shadows?

Every crack in the road held a darkness waiting to strike. Every corner they turned revealed more shadows come to take over the night.

The specters moved with them, their numbers growing as Nilla led them up the hill to the residential part of the city.

Lights glowed in the windows of every house as the owners fought to keep the shadows from the halls of their homes.

"We have to warn people," Maggie said as they passed a house that had dolls leaning against one of the bedroom windows. "They need to turn on every light they have and not come outside."

"We have no way of warning them," Bertrand said. "The brethren and the Barrister would never allow a warning system beyond the wail."

"Telling the people they need a warning system would only make them ask what they need to be warned of," Diven whispered.

"Did it ever occur to the brethren the truth might be the best thing to tell people?" Bertrand asked. "Beautiful lies are far more harmful than bitter truths."

"I…" Diven's voice faded away.

They passed a square filled with drooping trees. The shadow

of a little girl perched high in the branches, dangling as though she might fall at any moment.

She probably did.

"I am only an acolyte," Diven said. "I wanted to serve the brethren and be a part of the light that protects Sarana."

"A perfect son of the city." Nilla paused in the middle of a wave-laden road where two streets met.

In a moment, the specters surrounded them again.

"Uh, Nilla," Maggie said, "shouldn't we keep moving?"

"The Barrister fell, Serber fell," Nilla said.

"You can't save everyone," Maggie said. "The Barrister came to stop us, he threatened us."

"I feel no remorse for his death," Nilla said. "I can't pity either of them. I only wonder if they're here already. Staring at us through the eyes of a shadowy form I can't recognize."

Bertrand placed his hand on Nilla's back. "The only way to help anyone is to stop the specters."

A *rustle* of displeasure flitted through the shadows.

"May the light guide our steps," Diven murmured.

"To the light." Nilla slashed her spear at the specter nearest her.

The beast wailed as he split in two. The remnants of his form shifted and swirled, as though trying to find a way to rebond with itself.

Nilla stepped through the shadow, slicing into the next specter. "I'll not walk quietly through the dark. I will shout and scream of the horror the darkness has inflicted. *Veratus limofis!*"

Light sliced out from Nilla's spear, cutting through the shadows.

"No!" Diven shouted.

Maggie turned to him, raising her weapons, prepared to fight.

He kept his hands tucked behind his back even as pain filled his eyes. "Those could be ancestors."

"Child." Nilla stepped forward, still slicing her blade of bright light through the shadows.

Maggie stepped backward to follow Nilla, her eyes locked with Diven's.

"You see darkness and don't look beyond," Nilla growled.

The *shriek* of a dying specter pierced her words.

"It matters little that not everything lurking in the darkness wants to kill you," Nilla said. "I will not spare the dead who prowl. I will place the living above the dead, even to the point of my own demise. Clear a path, Bertrand."

"We're only trying to help." Maggie turned away from Diven, extending her club out into the shadows that crowded against the edge of her light.

Bertrand handed his satchel to Nilla. "*Marandus non sova. Ilarantus breanmore—*"

"Be ready to run," Nilla said.

"*Stavus morentar!*" Bertrand shot his hands out toward the shadows.

A wave of blinding light flew from Bertrand's palms, crashing through the street in front of them.

With a shout, Nilla charged into the clearing. Bertrand ran behind, drawing his swords.

"Come on," Maggie shouted.

She sprinted after Bertrand. The pounding of Diven's feet followed her.

The light had cut a straight path through the streets. Frightened faces appeared in the windows as they ran.

"The light behind is fading," Diven panted.

"So run faster." Pushing her legs as hard as they would go, Maggie stayed right on Bertrand's heels.

Nilla paused at a crossroad.

Bertrand's light had cut them a straight path, but the Sanctuary lay on a different road.

Shadows filled the street between them and the glowing sanctuary in the distance.

"Do the spell again, Bertrand," Maggie panted.

"He can't," Nilla said. "Another incantation like that could burn him out."

"You do it then," Maggie said.

Shadows peeled from the fronts of the homes, drifting down to the streets to join their fellows.

"I lived in the shadows for too long," Nilla said. "I'll never again be able to produce that sort of light."

"Then we fight our way there. *Veratus limofis*," Maggie said. A sharp edge of light blossomed from the tips of Maggie's weapons. "I really like that one."

She sliced at the fingers of a shadow.

Where the bright light met the darkness, the shadow gave thickness to the air, as though her blade had found something more than a void as its victim.

"Give me a weapon," Diven said. "I will beg forgiveness from the dead."

"Finally." Nilla sliced her blade through the chest of a specter.

Bertrand pocketed one sword, took his satchel from Nilla, and popped it open. A polished hilt waited for him. "How kind." He pulled out a gleaming long sword.

"Oh, hell no." Maggie held her club and knife out to Diven. He stared at the weapons in her hands. "We don't have time, just take them."

Diven took each weapon by its edge.

"I get the big kid sword." Maggie hoisted the blade from Bertrand's grip.

The street shook beneath her feet.

"They're almost here."

"Good," Nilla said.

"Behind me, if you will." Bertrand sliced through a specter's knees.

Where one fell, two more took his place.

Bertrand inched forward with each shadow that dissipated.

Maggie and Nilla stayed right behind him, each clearing their own side of the path.

The angry rustling of the shadows fluttered up and down the street.

The hiccups of Diven's tears came with every swipe of his blade.

Maggie felt nothing as she cut into the darkness. No remorse, no fear. Only blind purpose.

Get to the sanctuary.

With every slice.

Sanctuary. Sanctuary.

They moved from one block on to the next. The brick wall of a graveyard loomed in front of them.

A tiny form peered at Maggie as they passed the gate. A child taken by darkness.

The child's shadowy fingers wrapped around the metal of the gate, his arm lengthening to reach for the lock.

"No!" Maggie stepped forward, raising her sword to slice through the child's hand a moment too late.

A *wail* split the air, driving deep into Maggie's ears.

The shadows trembled at the sound, but didn't flee. The thousands had scented their prey. Nothing could stop them now.

"Who's out there?" a voice called from across the street.

Maggie's heart plummeted as the front door of every house in view swung open.

CHAPTER 20

"Get back inside!" Maggie's feet carried her toward the nearest house.

A man in his nightclothes stood on the stoop. He held a bright lantern in front of his face, which threw his expression of sheer terror into sharp relief.

"Miss Trent!" Bertrand shouted after her.

She didn't stop, couldn't even look away as shadows slipped under the protection of the man's light, wrapping around the backs of his ankles.

Maggie knew all too well the cold agony that pained the man as he dropped his lantern and fell to his knees. The light shattered, leaving him in darkness.

He was consumed before she reached the foot of his front steps.

"Maggie," Diven shouted from right behind her.

The newly coated shade tipped his face up, staring at Maggie as though blaming her for the horrible pain.

"I'm so sorry," Maggie whispered.

Specters blocked the man from view as they pressed in on the boundaries of Maggie's light.

Screams of fear and pain echoed down the street.

"Maggie!"

She spun around at Diven's shout.

He swung his knife toward Maggie, slicing through the specter that had squeezed between them.

Darkness packed the street, blocking their path to Bertrand and Nilla who fought back to back in the middle road. The piercing *wail* that had pulled people from their homes ate the deathly *howls* of the specters disintegrating.

But human screams carried over the bedlam.

"We have to get to the sanctuary." Maggie sliced her sword through the darkness and started toward the glowing building in the distance.

"What about the others?" Diven lashed out, bashing shadows with his club.

"I give it a sixty percent chance they beat us there."

The ground rumbled, shaking loose the bricks of the street.

"Dammit. We need to go faster." Maggie's arms screamed in protest as she swung her sword again and again.

By the time they reached the next house, the door had been ripped from its hinges and every light extinguished by shadows.

The shade of a stooping old woman shambled out onto the street.

"We'll lose the whole city." Diven gripped the metal of a lamp-post as the ground shook again.

A *crack* sounded behind them.

Maggie glanced back to see the brick walls of the cemetery crumble.

She screamed as she swung her sword again.

Like cutting through brush.

The specter of a giant man burst into nothing at a swipe of her sword.

Brush that could be people.

They reached the next doorway as a woman's face disappeared into shadow.

"Close the doors!" Maggie shouted toward the house, hoping someone might be left untouched inside. "Close the doors and stay in the light!"

The shade of the woman brushed past the specters, thrusting her chest on the tip of Maggie's sword.

"No!" Maggie screamed.

But the damage was done. With a faint cry, the shade vanished into nothing.

"Why?" The heat of tears trickled down Maggie's face.

"We have to keep going." Diven sliced through a specter, stepping up to stand by Maggie's side.

"Why did she do that?" Maggie lunged forward, striking again and again.

The windows burst out of a home in front of them. A man fell from the second floor, landing in the waiting arms of the shadows beneath.

"The darkness is too much for some." Diven quickened his pace, stabbing forward with every word. "Just as the light is too much for others."

A horrible *crack* rent the air. The bricks under Diven's feet crumbled away.

"Diven!" Maggie's sword fell to the ground as she reached out to grab Diven's hand.

He clenched his hands to his chest as he fell, keeping them out of Maggie's reach.

She waited for Diven to fall into the endless black, but he stopped six feet under the ground.

"Are you okay?" Maggie called down into the pit.

"Fine." Shaking, Diven pushed himself to his feet. Blood dripped from a wound on his chest. He dropped the club, clamping his hand over the dark spot of blood.

Bones surrounded his feet.

"May the dead forgive me for desecrating a grave." Diven stared down at the skull by his left foot.

"We need to get you out before the ground gives way."

A scream of terror echoed over the *wail*.

Don't let it be Bertrand and Nilla.

"Give me your hand, and I'll pull you out." Maggie reached for Diven, tipping her head forward, giving as much light to her arm as she could.

"I can't." Diven shook his head.

"Diven, we have to go." Maggie inched closer to the edge of the grave.

"I've been coated in light, Maggie." Fear creased Diven's forehead. "The touch of a person will wipe the light away. I cannot take your hand."

"You have got to be kidding me."

"*Melivious varax!*" At Nilla's cry, a bright light flashed from farther up the street.

"Keep fighting, Bertrand," Maggie whispered.

"Go with them, Maggie," Diven said. "The light will protect me."

"Great job it's done so far." Maggie reached into her pocket, fishing out the little blue book.

She flipped frantically through the pages.

The ground shook again. A split formed beside her. Fingers reached up, clawing the bottom of her brightness.

"Just go." Diven looked up at her, his face calm, his breathing steady.

"No." Maggie scanned the pages. "There's a way to get you out without touching you. I just have to…find it."

Reseum mellor.

Her finger hovered over the spell.

"Oh, this is a terrible idea." Maggie took a step back. The shadows around her swirled their rage. "I'm really sorry about this."

"About what?"

"*Reseum mellor!*"

The bones under Diven's feet rose, carrying him along with them.

Maggie focused on the crumbled ribcage.

Come to me. Come right over here to me.

A rib slipped from beneath Diven's foot. He wobbled for a moment as the bone flew up, catching him under the arm.

The air around him quivered as the bones lifted him out of the grave. He reached his toes for solid ground, tipping off of the skeleton and onto the street.

"You did it." He rolled onto his back, hand still covering the gash on his chest. "Thank you."

Blood seeped out from between his fingers.

"We need to go. *Reseum mellor.*" The club flew out of the pit. "Keep yourself lit."

Diven tucked the knife into his robe and snatched the club from the air, holding it close to the deep red that spread down his chest.

"I can't fight like this." Diven scanned the street.

Nilla and Bertrand had disappeared from view. The lights in all the houses around them had gone out.

"We'll be fine." Maggie tucked the notebook back into her pocket and tightened her grip on her sword. "Just stay close."

The shadows in front of her rustled tauntingly.

"I've got a halo." Maggie sliced deep into the shadows, surging a step forward. "And I've got a badass sword." She swung again. "I've been in worse jams than this."

The shadow in front of her vanished with a *shriek*.

"And I'm still standing." She swung the sword in a wide arc, cutting through four shadows at once. "But you know why we'll be fine?" Maggie charged forward, skewering shadows. "Because Bertrand Wayland is fighting." She tore her blade up, cutting through the shadows' heads. "And he isn't going to stop until this city is safe. And he will not abandon me to the darkness."

Her sword clanged against the metal railing of a stone porch. Sparks danced in the air.

"How wonderful to have such faith in someone." Diven kept right behind Maggie, coming close enough to be bathed in the light of her halo.

Seven shadows leapt from the windows of the home in front of her. Whether specter or newly-coated shade, Maggie didn't know.

"You don't happen to know a spell that might help us out?" Maggie grunted as she sliced through the knees of a towering specter.

"Not many," Diven said.

"I'm open to anything."

Diven gave a sharp exhale. His warm breath cut through the fabric of Maggie's sweater.

"*Lissam man au lish, marrim a en tempre.*"

Maggie fought on as Diven chanted behind her. His words gave rhythm to her swings, guiding her forward, giving her arms strength even as her hands begged her to drop the blade.

A trickle of light began in the distance, shimmering toward them from the front of the sanctuary two blocks away.

"*Adsuvum lish, canurvem lish.*"

The light drifted down through the shadows, who cowered away from its brightness.

A path formed in front of them, growing brighter every moment as more glittering light poured out of the sanctuary.

Maggie took off at a run, Diven keeping close behind her. The glowing path reached toward the door of the sanctuary.

"Almost there," Diven panted as the doorknob came into view.

Maggie reached for the handle, not bothering to knock.

An otherworldly roar carried from high in the sky.

Hand still on the glowing gold door, like a child claiming safety in tag, Maggie turned toward the sound.

The giant specter from the vaults had found its way to the street. His form towered above the houses, dwarfing Bertrand and Nilla who battled the shadows at the beast's feet.

"Dammit." Maggie let go of the door.

"We have to get inside," Diven said.

"You go," Maggie said. "Rally the brethren. Tell them the time for pretty lies is over. The darkness has risen. If they hide, the city dies. Tell them Serber is gone, and it's time for them to come out and fight."

"Come with me, Maggie." Longing filled Diven's eyes.

"I can't." Maggie stepped away from safety. "Go on."

Panicked voices carried from inside the sanctuary as Diven opened the door.

Maggie didn't turn around to look. She kept her gaze focused on the shadows waiting ten feet in front of her, all staring at her, waiting for her to stray back into the darkness.

Squaring her shoulders, Maggie ran onto the street.

The force of the shadows pushed against her. She tipped her chin down and gripped the headband of the halo to her head with one hand, hoisting the sword in front of her with the other.

The monstrous specter reached down toward the street, scooping up stones and bones and throwing them into the air.

Nilla screamed as bricks rained down on her.

"Nilla!" Bertrand ran toward her, slicing with both swords.

Maggie sprinted the last few feet.

Bertrand knelt beside Nilla, clasping her hand in his. She lay still on the street. Her helmet had vanished. Blackness covered her face.

"Oh no," Maggie whispered. "Bertrand, do the thing. Save her."

"I can't," Bertrand said. "I've lost my bag of tricks."

The blackness trickled down Nilla's neck.

"There's got to be something you can do." Maggie scanned the street for a sign of Bertrand's satchel. "We'll find your bag. Or is there something in the notebook?"

"It's too late." Bertrand let go of Nilla's hand as the shadows seeped down to her chest. "I'm sorry I couldn't keep my promise, sweet Nilla."

"You still can. We'll go to the brethren, and—"

"She wanted me to kill her before letting the blackness take her again, Miss Trent." Bertrand stood, backing away as Nilla's form swirled into shadow. "But I cannot give up on saving you so quickly, Nilla. You'll forgive me for your suffering when I bring you back into the light."

"Bertrand, we'll save her."

"We will." Bertrand bowed to Nilla's shade and turned his face up to the great beast.

"How do we destroy the big bad?" Maggie planted the tip of her sword on the ground.

"I must recommend you retreat," Bertrand said.

"Not gonna happen."

A hint of a smile creased the corners of Bertrand's eyes. "You stay low and strike at the beast's feet, I'll aim high."

"Aim high how?"

Bertrand ducked around Nilla's shade and between the monster's legs without replying.

"Great." Maggie looked to the shadow that had been Nilla. "Just stay out of the way, okay? I don't want to accidentally get you with the sword."

The shade didn't move.

"Okay, I'll just…" Maggie pressed through the shadows to the left of Nilla, stepping up to face the monster's feet.

The beast bent over and tore at the ground with his dark fingers. Bones and stone littered the street behind him.

Maggie hoisted her sword. Gritting her teeth against the ache in her arms, she slashed her way to the monster's ankles.

The beast showed no hint of pain as she sliced into him.

Light blossomed in the distance. Maggie blinked against the dazzling rays as wings unfolded on the far side of the street.

"*That* the monster will notice." Maggie raised her sword as the beast raised his head.

The wings flapped, sending their wearer soaring above the houses. Light shone off Bertrand's face.

The avenging angel.

Maggie shivered at the thought and brought her sword down on the monster's ankle.

The specter tipped his head up, shrieking in rage.

Bertrand pulled his swords from his pockets, slicing down as the beast reached up to grab him.

Maggie raised her own sword, chopping down into the beast's ankle again and again as though she were brandishing an axe.

Specters packed in around her.

One drifted in front of her sword, blocking her from reaching the monster.

She slashed through the sacrificial shadow, and moved closer to the monster so the light of her halo touched the beast's form.

The monster shrieked again, but Maggie didn't look up. She stabbed her sword into the shadow, screaming as she twisted the blade. Pain throbbed in her shoulders. She pulled the sword out, stabbing again.

The shadow began to dissolve, twisting and squirming as it fought to maintain its form.

Maggie stepped into the swirling black, swinging her sword at any form that seemed to solidify.

A *wail* sounded high above as a giant sphere of light burst through the beast.

The street quaked beneath Maggie's feet as she stabbed up into the leg of the shadow.

With a painful *shriek*, the beast dissolved. Clouds of black drifted to the ground as nothing more than dust.

CHAPTER 21

*B*ertrand folded his wings into his body as he floated to the ground, landing ten feet from Maggie.

"Why didn't you use the magic light wings when we were stuck in the cave?" Maggie slashed her way through the shadows toward Bertrand.

"To be quite frank, I'm not terribly good at steering."

Maggie swallowed her laugh. "I probably shouldn't be happy you're not perfect at something right now."

"Find joy when life allows." Bertrand's wings disappeared.

The shadows pressed in around them as the light faded.

"They aren't going to stop, are they?" Maggie looked out over the shadowy horde. "We can keep fighting, but they're always going to outnumber us. The specters have already taken more people tonight. They took Nilla."

Maggie searched the shadows for one she might recognize, but they all looked the same. Dark, drifting nothings that wanted to devour her.

How will I know which one is Nilla?

"Our only chance is to find out who is controlling the shadows." Bertrand decapitated two specters.

"And how do you suggest we do that?"

"There are two options I can see." Bertrand moved toward the sanctuary. "Either we allow me to be partially coated and hope I can gain insight to who the Master might be."

"I hope the other plan is a little less suicidal." Maggie leapt forward, thrusting her sword into a crowd of shadows.

"We come up with a daring plan and hope the Master of the shadows is fool enough to show himself," Bertrand said.

"Daring plan it is."

A wave of light glided out from the sanctuary door, reaching toward Maggie.

"Thank you, Diven." Maggie fought toward the yellow-coated road.

Bertrand reached the light before she did. He waited until she was behind him before sprinting for the open door of the sanctuary.

Diven and the weathered old woman waited just inside the door, Diven's face twisted in fear. The woman's sagging brow had moved beyond fear to sad resignation.

"If you'll excuse me." Bertrand slipped through the door, slamming it shut as soon as Maggie was inside.

Maggie blinked against the glow of the sanctuary.

"The end has come," the old woman said. "The sins of Sarana have become too great for even the brethren to combat."

"These specters are the result of no sin but allowing darkness to fester for so long," Bertrand said.

"Where is Nilla?" Diven asked.

"Taken." Maggie hoisted her sword up onto the table, laying it beside the shimmering flowers.

"May the light find her a path to return." Diven bowed his head.

"I need access to your records." Bertrand strode through the entryway and into the hall of light.

Maggie dragged her sword back off the table to follow him.

"Those records are only for the eyes of those who have been coated in light," the old woman said.

"Pity I don't have time for a bath," Bertrand said.

Dozens of brethren sat on the benches in the hall of light, their faces tipped up to the ceiling as though in silent prayer.

"I'm afraid we couldn't coat you anyway," Diven said. "The bath is empty."

"How?" Maggie asked.

"Dolt used the lish to paint the street," the woman said. "Our sacred protection used to mop the floor."

"I kept the only people who are truly fighting from being taken." Diven's hands clenched behind his back.

Bertrand didn't slow as he exited the hall of light and strode straight to the library.

"There has to be a common thread," Bertrand said. "If we know what the Master wants, we can lure him out."

"There is no master but sin." The old woman toddled behind Bertrand, shaking her head at his back.

"You may sit idly by telling yourself lies, but I haven't the time to listen to them." Bertrand stepped into the library and rounded on the woman. "Go pray with the others, arm yourself to fight, or make a cup of tea. Whichever you choose makes no difference to me, but if you care for any of the lives in danger tonight, you will stay well out of my way."

"Impudent youth," the woman said.

She stared at Bertrand for a long moment before turning away and shuffling back to the hall of light.

"Come, Miss Trent." Bertrand ran to the stacks of books.

"Are you going to help us?" Maggie asked as Diven hesitated in the doorway.

"I have already traveled too far down this path to turn back now." Diven shuddered as he stepped into the library. "What are we looking for?"

"Anything that might show intent." Bertrand pulled down a book whose shimmering spine read *The Atonements of Protection.*

"A prayer book?" Maggie searched the shelves for anything that might be useful. Passing up *A Practical Guide for Internment* and *The Patterns of the Long Lost.*

"I have survived long enough to have made several realizations about the mortal condition that carry from world to world," Bertrand said.

Maggie pulled *A History of the Brethren* from the shelf.

"Never underestimate the ill effect of hunger on an army," Bertrand said, "never discount the lengths to which a mother will go to protect her child, and always listen to the things people pray for."

"Prayers to the light are private." Diven slipped a giant black book from the shelf.

"Then why do so many insist on saying them loudly in public?" Bertrand flipped to the back of a book. "A family that prays for food fears hunger most. A society that prays for peace fears losing their world to unending war. A city that has more prayers written for the safety of its politicians—that is telling in a brilliant new way."

"What do you mean?" Maggie abandoned her book to read over Bertrand's shoulder.

"Prayers for light to bathe the Barrister, prayers for protecting the homes of all elected officials..." Bertrand thumbed through the pages.

"It is our duty as brethren to protect those who protect the city," Diven said.

"But why be so worried about the Barrister?" Maggie said. "I don't think he ever raised a pinky to help anyone but himself."

"Because someone planted a specter in his hallway," Bertrand said. "It wasn't the Barrister trying to test me or get rid of me. It was someone trying to get rid of the Barrister."

"Well, it worked," Maggie said. "I'm pretty sure he's dead."

"But it didn't start with that particular Barrister, did it?" Bertrand asked.

"The elected officials have always been in danger," Diven said. "It is part of the perils of leadership. The closer to the light, the more danger from the darkness."

"But the shadows themselves are indiscriminate," Bertrand said. "To the dead, there is only death and life. Our scent is all the same when they choose who to hunt."

"Unless the Master is setting elected people as a target," Maggie said.

"And there we have it." Bertrand slammed his book shut and ran back out into the hall.

"Have what?" Diven said.

"It's best not to ask," Maggie called over her shoulder as she ran after Bertrand.

She dodged through the door to the hall of light just before it swung shut.

"Brethren." Bertrand's voice rang around the room. "The city of Sarana has fallen into a time of great darkness. As I speak to you now, hundreds are being taken every moment. By sunrise, I doubt there will be any living left outside the walls of this sanctuary. So it falls upon us to save the city. We need to act as one, now, before it is too late. If we wait for the safety of dawn, our only choice will be to board ships, seek refuge across the sea, and hope the darkness cannot find a way to follow us."

A silent shudder waved around the room.

"We need a plan to fight," Bertrand continued, "and we need a leader to push the living forward. There are none of you who have fought as I have. None who have ever dared end specters who steal life. I hereby nominate myself as Supreme Leader of the living of Sarana until such a time as life can be restored to those who have been taken by the darkness."

"The city is falling, and you beg for power?" A man stood up.

"I do not beg. I demand," Bertrand said. "If any of you have a modicum of a plan that might hold a hope for saving the city, I urge you to speak now. If you have no strategy beyond hiding in your sanctuary, then elect me to fight for you. If I lose to the shadows, my reign will be short indeed."

"I vote for Hunter Wayland as Supreme Leader," Diven said.

"That isn't even a real position," the man said.

"I vote for Hunter Wayland to be Supreme Leader." Stilla stood, walking over to stand by Diven's side.

"I'll vote for you to lead if you leave my sanctuary," the old woman said.

"I will gladly leave." Bertrand bowed.

"I vote for the rogue to lead." The old woman bowed back.

One by one, the brethren stood and bowed to Bertrand.

"Excellent." Bertrand pinched the sides of his halo, drawing the light up in large swatches to form a crown. "Now, let us see who despises me."

He walked to the front door of the sanctuary.

"Is the crown really necessary?" Maggie asked.

"Every display of power will only enrage the Master." Bertrand turned to Maggie.

He tipped her halo back and winced as he tugged on the front of the ring.

"Now you've a tiara, and we can both be targets," Bertrand said.

"Thanks?" Maggie straightened her gleaming tiara and lifted her sword.

Bertrand opened the door and stepped out into the night. The terrible wailing had stopped. The quiet pressed on Maggie's ears, making each beat of her heart seem as loud as a drum.

"Dear shadows," Bertrand said, sweeping his arms toward the throng that filled the street, "I am Bertrand Wayland, Supreme Leader of all Sarana. I have been elected by the living of this city to rule as I destroy you. This is my land. Bow down to me."

A *rustle* of hatred fluttered through the dead.

"Did you really need to add that last bit?" Maggie whispered.

"Of course," Bertrand said. "Now I will find your master and destroy him. If you care for the one who raised you up from the darkness, warn him. Because tonight, I banish the specters for good."

Maggie scanned the shadows, waiting for one to flit away to tell of Bertrand's new position. Even as the specters constantly shifted, none of them left.

"I don't know if it worked," Maggie said softly.

"Of course it did." Bertrand stepped out onto the thin path of gold. "Keep close."

The door swung open behind Maggie.

Diven and Stilla stepped out with three other young acolytes behind them.

Diven had a bandage over his chest and Nilla's knife in his hand.

Stilla clutched the glowing club.

"We're coming with you," Diven said.

"We will not sit idly by as the city falls," Stilla said. "We fight with you."

Bertrand looked over his shoulder as the shadows reached for the edges of his light.

"I am always grateful when the younger generation has the will to fight," Bertrand said. "It gives me hope for a brighter future. However, I cannot guarantee you will live to see that future if you follow me tonight."

"I have parents and sisters out there," a girl with a shaved head said. "I'm fighting."

The other four acolytes nodded.

"Then onward we go," Bertrand said.

Maggie followed him, keeping her sword low.

Stay away, Nilla. If you've any sense of yourself in the shadows, stay away from us.

Bertrand kept walking until he reached the edge of the golden path.

The ground didn't quake beneath their feet as Bertrand searched the darkness.

The soft footsteps of the acolytes stopped behind Maggie. The last three didn't even have any weapons.

"Bertrand, do you happen to have anything left in those pockets of yours?" Maggie asked.

"Only a weapon with which I cannot part." Bertrand stepped off the path in the opposite direction from where they'd come.

The shadows piled thickly in front of him.

Maggie stepped behind him. Beads of sweat rolled down his neck as he pushed his way forward.

In ten steps, the path behind the acolytes had closed, cutting them off from the thin strand of light.

Bertrand held his swords in either hand, but rarely swung them, instead pushing forward through sheer force of will.

After a block, Bertrand's steps began to falter.

"Let me take a turn," Maggie said, resisting the urge to step forward and wrap her arm around his waist to keep him from falling.

"It's me they want," Bertrand said. "I am the Supreme Leader. They must place themselves between their Master and me. Even to the point of their own destruction, one order carries to them from the void."

Maggie rose up on her toes, squinting against the light of her own halo to see into the distance.

A pack of shadows ten deep moved behind them, keeping the acolytes pressed into the group.

The same thin layer moved on either side of them.

But in front of Bertrand, reaching down the street to their right, a thick layer of specters packed their path forward.

"Bertrand," Maggie said, trying to form the words to tell him what her eyes couldn't understand, "can buildings be taken into shadow?"

"I've never heard of such a thing," Bertrand said.

"I think it's just happened," Maggie said. "I think the shadows ate the Barrister's office."

CHAPTER 22

*S*hadows wrapped around the bricks, giving the building the look of having been dipped in ink. Starlight danced on the shining black, the surface beneath undulating as though trying to rid itself of even that faint light.

Specters surrounded the building, blocking the way forward through sheer numbers.

"Do you ever get tired of being right?" Maggie asked.

"More often than you will ever know." Bertrand studied the specters, sword tips to the ground.

"We have to fight our way through," Maggie said. "We can do it. Unless you think you can fly us over."

"I'm afraid flight for more than one is beyond my skill." Bertrand looked up to the roof of the building where a lone window peered out from the attic.

The shadow of a child drifted past the glass panes.

"How many innocents might we harm if we continue to fight?" Bertrand said.

"As a wise friend once pointed out, sometimes there isn't a choice," Maggie said. "We can't walk away, we can't let the city fall forever. The only option left is to push forward."

"We might be able to help." Stilla struck a shadow with her club as she stepped up to Maggie's side. The shadows hovered an inch above her skin, reflecting her every movement like a twisted mirror.

"What do you suggest?" Bertrand said.

"We still have a little light left to give," Stilla said. "It won't last long, but it should get you to the door."

"And you?" Bertrand asked.

"Our place is to protect Sarana from the shadows," Stilla said, "and yours is to save Sarana from the Master."

Stilla tucked her club inside her robe and stared down at her palms.

The other acolytes shifted through the shadows to stand beside Stilla. Each looked down at their hands as she did.

Diven glanced at Maggie, giving her a small smile before tucking his knife into his robe and bowing his head.

Stilla began to murmur, her voice too low for Maggie to hear.

"Thank you," Maggie whispered.

Pale light drifted from each of the acolytes, floating up into the air and falling to the street like snow made of pale gold.

The light sizzled on the shadows as it touched them. The specters twitched backward, leaving Bertrand and Maggie a clear path.

Maggie kept close to Bertrand's heels as the light fell more quickly. The flakes of brightness left texture on her shoulders, coating her with a thin layer of shimmer as though she herself had been bathed in light.

The golden path reached all the way to the front door of the Barrister's office.

Bertrand leaned his crown close to the door before twisting the handle.

The dim glow of candles bathed the hall inside.

Maggie looked back to beckon the others forward. Her gaze

followed the trail of light to where the five acolytes had worked their magic, but there were no glowing bodies to see.

"Bertrand, wait for—"

Diven's pale eyes looked up from the shadows that devoured him just as the black coated his face.

"Diven!"

Bertrand blocked Maggie's path with a sword.

"We have to help them." She knocked Bertrand's blade aside with her own.

"There's nothing to be done now," Bertrand said. "They've already been taken."

Diven's shade floated forward, closing the gap in the horde.

Maggie brushed the tears from her cheeks.

"We cannot let their sacrifice go to waste."

Maggie nodded. "Right." She turned toward the open door. "Right."

"Into the lair." Bertrand stepped over the threshold of the Barrister's office.

The desks waited just as Maggie had seen them before. Papers stacked high with work the clerks hadn't finished before the end of their day.

The bright lights had been replaced by candles, which sat on every surface. The flames did little to light the room. Their flickering glow left wide swatches of darkness for shadows to breed.

"Why haven't the specters followed us in?" Maggie said.

"No idea."

Something in the wood clicked as Bertrand pushed the center desk aside.

Maggie bit the inside of her lips, willing her hands to stay steady as she followed Bertrand down the hall.

Squeaks she hadn't noticed in the daylight carried from the floorboards under her feet. Every flickering shadow held the potential for death. Every time she passed their wavering, her heart leapt into her throat.

But there were no long fingers reaching for her, no giants growing to tear the walls apart.

Bertrand stopped in front of the door to the Barrister's office.

The Barrister's chair was empty. A crystal decanter sat unstoppered on his desk.

Bertrand studied the room for a long moment before moving down the hall.

They paused at each door, peeking into the ones that had been left ajar, quietly opening those that had been locked.

Chairs had been overturned around a large fireplace in a sitting room, as though the people who had been spending their evening in this place had somehow been surprised by the horde of shadows taking over Sarana.

A faint trickle of black oozed onto the floors and tinged the bright colors of the walls.

They reached the corner of the hall where they had turned when Bertrand had saved the office from a specter only a little while ago.

Maggie's heart pounded in her ears as they made their way down the short hall toward the closet.

Every patch of darkness they passed without incident made her more aware of how dangerous the next shadow might be.

Sweat slicked her palms. She switched her sword from hand to hand as she wiped her palms on her pants.

The closet door squealed as Bertrand wrenched it open.

Nothing but mops and broken chairs waited inside.

Can't the Master just jump out at us and scream?

It was a foolish thought, but waiting to find something terrible felt somehow worse than facing the terrible thing itself.

Don't worry, Diven. We'll find the Master. We'll save the city.

She couldn't bring herself to promise to save him, not even in the solitude of her own mind.

Bertrand doubled back, leading Maggie to the far side of the short hall. A door waited opposite where the closet stood.

Bertrand stared at the handle for a long moment. He tucked his left sword under his arm and turned the handle.

The door swung open with a whisper, as though the staircase beyond had given a sigh of relief at being discovered.

With a nod to Maggie, Bertrand started up the steps.

The walls packed in on either side of the stairs as they twisted up and out of sight, leaving barely enough room for Bertrand's shoulders as he climbed.

Maggie tested each step, carefully shifting her weight each time she heard a *squeak*.

There's no way the Master doesn't already know we're here.

But then why hasn't he shown himself?

Bertrand reached the top of the stairs. He waited for Maggie to be only a breath behind him before climbing into the room beyond.

The floor didn't *creak* under Maggie's feet as she stepped up into the attic.

Paintings of past barristers rested against the walls. Candles perched on the exposed brick of the chimney.

A shining desk of dark wood waited at the far end of the attic, behind which sat a man in a jet-black chair.

Maggie blinked at the man's face, trying to reconcile the benign smile and glasses with the knowledge of who the man must be.

The clerk gave both Maggie and Bertrand a nod before adjusting his glasses and rising to his feet.

"Hunter Wayland," the clerk said. "Miss Trent. I had hoped it wouldn't come to having to meet you here tonight."

"Did you believe your specters would stop us before we reached their master's door?" Bertrand strode across the attic.

The shadow of a little girl floated to the front of the Master's desk.

"It had been my hope." The Master gave a half-smile. "But plans do not always work out as one wishes."

"Indeed." Bertrand stopped in front of the little girl.

Her skirts swished through the darkness as she twirled back and forth.

"I would humbly suggest," the Master said, "you go back out the way you came. Remove that ridiculous crown and allow my army to accept you as one of their own. I assure you they will be most welcoming."

"Your army?" Maggie said. "Is that what you've taken everyone's lives away to create?"

"Indeed," the Master said. "They are the most beautiful army Sarana has ever seen."

"I do hope you'll forgive me," Bertrand said, "but as far as an army of the not-quite-dead goes, I've seen better. Your army is hardly effective."

"You had to sacrifice more than half your party to make it through my door." The Master pulled off his glasses and slipped a handkerchief from his pocket. "I think my shadows have done very well for their first true test." He cleaned his lenses.

The little girl twitched as he frantically polished the glass.

"Their first true test is taking the whole city?" Bertrand stepped closer to the front of the desk, the light of his halo forcing the girl from her post. "What would the next test be? Will you ship your shadows across the water to destroy other lands?"

"Don't be foolish." The Master shoved his glasses back onto his face. "Sarana should be for the people of Sarana, and Saranans should stay within her loving arms."

"If you love a city so much, why destroy it?" Maggie asked.

The little girl left the Master to circle Maggie.

"The city was destroyed long ago," the Master said. "Allowing the misplacement of our ancestors' bones. Giving weight to corrupt politicians who care more for stuffing their pockets than protecting the people of this city."

"And have you protected the people?" Bertrand asked.

"Yes." The Master nodded so hard his glasses slipped to the

end of his nose. "I knew as soon as I found the dark river. The shadows are the heart of our city. They are the home to which we are all called to return. If some return sooner than their natural time, so be it. There could be no kinder fate for the people of Sarana than to return to her loving bosom of darkness."

"You're stealing people's lives from them," Maggie said. "Have you ever even felt the specters taking you? It hurts like hell."

"Of course I haven't felt the touch of the darkness." The Master fluttered his hands through the air. "That is the great sacrifice I make to save all. I will never know the comfort of darkness, so I can bring everyone else into the fold."

"I see," Bertrand said.

"Wow. Just, wow." Maggie planted the tip of her sword on the wooden floor. "You know, I've heard some great justifications for murdering people before, but yours is...wow."

"Miss Trent," Bertrand warned.

"Look," Maggie pressed on, "Bertrand is the Supreme Leader, so why don't you hurry on into the blackness, and we'll make sure everyone stays nice and shadowy."

The little girl stopped in front of Maggie, tipping her chin up to stare at Maggie's face.

"The task can be trusted to no one but me," the Master said. "There have been too many false leaders who have done too much damage. I've removed them all. All who would sully this city. I've always admired you, Hunter Wayland. Even as you failed, I never doubted the purity of your intention to help."

Bertrand said nothing.

"But I'm afraid it's time for darkness to fall for all," the Master said. "And that must include both of you."

The ringlets around the little girl's head began to sway, moving with a breeze that touched nothing else in the room.

"And I'm afraid I must do my best to stop you," Bertrand said. "I will not allow you to doom this city to darkness."

"I expected no less. Naphalie"—the Master looked to the girl—"bring them into our fold."

CHAPTER 23

*I*f the child's face had had features, Maggie felt quite sure she would have been smiling.

"Miss Trent," Bertrand said, "I'm afraid I must leave you to defend us."

"What?" Maggie said.

"*Primurgo.*" A shield blossomed around Bertrand.

"I had thought better of you." The Master sat down behind his desk.

"Full of surprises, that one." Maggie lifted her sword.

The child watched Maggie move, her hair twisting and curling around her.

"I really don't want to hurt you," Maggie said. "Be a good little specter and go outside with the others, okay?"

The girl's hair grew, unfurling into tentacles that spanned the width of the room.

"Fine then." Maggie swung her sword.

The blade met the blackness and stopped with a *clang.*

Vibrations shot up Maggie's arm, numbing her hands.

"*Melivious varax.*" Light enveloped Maggie's blade.

She sliced at the curls again.

Guilt surged through Maggie as the child shrieked in pain.

"Just get out of the way," Maggie said.

The girl snaked her curls toward Maggie, surrounding her with darkness.

"Or not." Maggie sliced again and again, gritting her teeth against the child's wails.

Pain throttled the back of Maggie's head as something crashed into her from behind. Her halo slipped forward. She dropped her sword and clamped both hands to her headband.

A *creak* sounded behind her.

Maggie spun in time to watch a painting of a fallen Barrister tear itself from the wall and soar toward her head.

She dodged the painting, which flew through the child and crashed into Bertrand's shield.

"Call her off," Maggie said. "I don't want to hurt a little girl."

The Master blinked at her from behind the girl's curls.

The child stepped forward, blocking Maggie from her sword.

Maggie ducked as another painting soared toward her.

"*Melivious varax!*" Light burst from Maggie's skin as she shouted the spell.

The girl shrieked, backing away from the glow.

"*Reseum mellor.*" The blade flew into the air, slicing through the child's chest as it soared into Maggie's grip.

A faint *wail* escaped the girl as she swirled into nothing.

"Naphalie!" The Master stood, pushing his glasses farther up his nose. "I had not thought you so low as to damage a child."

"I'm not the one who made shadow children," Maggie said.

"I will not allow you to interfere with my plan." The Master carefully rolled up his sleeves as he walked to the front of his desk. "Will you dare to fight me on your own?"

Maggie glanced to Bertrand. He stood in the center of his shield, flipping through a red book.

"I guess so," Maggie said.

The Master worked his hands through the air, pulling shining black shards out of nothing.

"*Primurgo!*" Maggie's shield surrounded her.

The black shards bounced uselessly to the ground.

"Is this what the great shadow stalkers have come to?" the Master said. "Hiding in shields?"

"I'm working with a really limited vocabulary. *Stratus.*" She pressed her hand through her shield as a streak of purple burst from her palm. The violet cord wrapped around the Master's legs, knocking him to the floor.

"*Brantam,*" the Master said even as he struggled to his feet.

Maggie tensed, waiting for whatever the Master's spell was meant to do. Before she could blink, the floor collapsed beneath her.

Maggie's scream covered the sound of another shouted spell. She plummeted through the floor. And stopped.

Tightness seized her chest as she soared back through the hole and into the attic. She landed in a heap on the dusty wooden floor.

"Thank you, Miss Trent." Bertrand waved a hand and his shield disappeared. "I had hoped there would be a more refined way to end all of this."

He stepped toward the Master, raising both his swords.

"I have never understood why shadow stalkers favor such weapons." The Master flicked his wrist. A swirling void appeared in his palm.

Maggie inched closer to Bertrand as the void twisted and grew, sucking in all the air from the attic.

The Master threw the disk of nothing at Bertrand.

"*Ezicham.*" A sheet of light grew from Bertrand's sword, blocking the Master's spell.

The patch of darkness fed off the magic of Bertrand's spell for a moment before disappearing.

"Well done." The Master smiled. "Perhaps there is a bit of

worth to you after all. I had stopped expecting much from one so young."

"There are many foibles that come with great age." Bertrand stabbed his swords into the floor.

The wood beneath the Master's feet peeled up as though torn by a giant's hand.

The Master leapt into the air, landing on his desk.

"When one has seen so much and outlived so many, it is easy to forget the worth of others. *Garun thamus*," Bertrand said.

Light burst into being on the desk, stretching into long lines and rising up to form a cage around the Master.

The bright beams pressed in on their captive.

The Master covered his face with his arms. As the light drew closer, his skin changed. Wrinkles and spots appeared on his hands. His dark hair faded, leaving nothing but tufts of white.

"*Karitum.*" The cage shattered. The Master glared at Bertrand as the sagging wrinkles under his eyes disappeared. He pushed his glasses up his nose.

"You began the plight of the specters a long time ago," Bertrand said. "I'm amazed you hid your age and plan from so many for so long."

"*Tirano miluvisus.*" The Master grinned as shadows peeled themselves from the walls, knocking over portraits as they scrambled to do his will.

Maggie slashed through the shadowy tentacles that reached for her and Bertrand.

"I am still quite a bit your senior." Bertrand swung both his swords, slicing through the darkness as he moved closer to the desk. "I have seen more evil come and go than you can possibly imagine, and I've run from it only once."

The shadows reached up to the ceiling, tearing down the heavy beams that supported the roof.

"I can only hope my own ancestors will forgive me, for I know not another path to take. *Stratus.*" Purple flew from

Bertrand's chest, wrapping around the Master, binding him from ankle to neck. "*Inexuro.*" Bertrand whispered the spell.

The desk burst into flames.

The Master screamed. His specters dove toward him, trying to rip the fire away.

But darkness held no power against the light.

A *creak* sounded above.

Bertrand dropped one of his swords and grabbed Maggie's wrist, yanking her past the flames to the window beyond.

She didn't hear the window shatter as Bertrand launched both of them through the glass. The shrieking of thousands of specters overwhelmed the noise.

A bright sheet of light enveloped Maggie and Bertrand as they fell to the ground.

Pain shook Maggie's spine as her halo tumbled away. Gasping for air, she snatched up her ring of light.

A *crash* shook the street. Sparks flew through the air as the Barrister's office collapsed.

Maggie scrambled to her feet, hauling Bertrand up with her.

"We have to go." She dragged him away from the burning building. "We've got to move."

"Miss Trent." Bertrand raised a shaking finger, pointing to the specter who pressed in against her light.

The specter wailed and twisted. Bits of its blackness pulled away, falling to the ground as dust.

Behind it, more shadows twisted and dissolved, writhing until they finally fell to nothing.

The wailing stopped, leaving only the crackling of the fire to fill the street. Thousands of shadows still surrounded them. All of them turned to Maggie and Bertrand, reaching toward their light.

"Please." Bertrand tipped his face to the sky. "If only this once, please."

A drop of rain fell onto Maggie's face, tumbling down her

cheek as though the sky itself had decided to do the work of crying for her.

The sky didn't stop with a single drop. Rain pounded down from above, hissing as it met the flames.

The cold of it cut through Maggie's sweater, drenching her skin.

A shadow floated in front of Bertrand, reaching for the light.

The shadow's palm didn't hold perfect blackness. Streaks of pale skin cut through the dark.

"Please," Bertrand whispered.

Lightning shot through the sky, flashing over the street.

A streak of red hair unfurled from one shadow. Another wiped its face, leaving brown eyes to stare at Maggie.

The shade in front of them ran her hands over her hair, wiping away the shifting shadow to leave long, shimmering black hair behind.

"Bertrand?" Nilla asked.

Bertrand stepped out of Maggie's light, pulling Nilla to his chest.

"You're a horrible beast for breaking your promise." Nilla's voice shook.

"I am well aware," Bertrand said.

A shout of delight carried from the far side of the street as a little boy shook like a dog, splattering the darkness from his skin.

A woman cried and fell to her knees, washing her hands in a puddle on the street.

Warm tears cut through the rain on Maggie's face as more people freed themselves from the darkness.

Shadows drifted between a tall man with shining white hair and an old woman who glared at all those celebrating around her.

"Why didn't it save them?" Maggie asked.

"They're spirits," Nilla said. "The shadows of our ancestors. They belong here as much as we do."

194 | MEGAN O'RUSSELL

"Then we did it?" Maggie said. "We actually saved people?"

"Maggie!" Diven shouted, running toward her from down the street, the other four acolytes trailing behind him.

The shimmer had left the acolytes' skin and clothes, but still they beamed with radiant joy.

"Thank you, Hunter Wayland. Thank you, Maggie." Diven bowed. "I never dreamed such a night would exist in Sarana."

He reached for Maggie's hand.

A tingle raced up Maggie's arm as his fingers grazed her palm.

"The light granted us greatness when it returned you from the shadows." Diven pressed his lips to the back of her hand.

"Mama." A tiny child toddled past. "Mama!" She stopped in front of Bertrand. "Where's my mama? I want to go home."

Nilla knelt beside the child. "Sweetling, do you know what year it is?"

"Year of the Red Tide." The girl rubbed her tear-filled eyes.

"All right." Nilla's smile didn't reach her eyes. "Come with me, and we'll find you a nice place to get dry."

"They can come to the sanctuary," Stilla said. "It's our place to care for those who have returned."

"It's going to take more than a little bit of care." Nilla lifted the girl and carried her down the street.

"We should bring the rest." Pain creased Diven's brow.

"What's wrong?" Maggie said. "We saved everyone. Isn't that a good thing?"

"The Year of the Red Tide was sixty-seven years ago," Diven said. "Unless her parents were taken—"

"She doesn't have a family anymore."

CHAPTER 24

*P*ounding fatigue radiated through Maggie's skull.

Sleep. Nothing in any world the Siren had ever heard of could possibly be as wonderful as sleep.

Maggie swayed on her feet as she made another trip from the front room of the sanctuary to the library. A boy only a few years younger than her walked two steps behind, his feet scuffing against the floor.

Ask him his name.

But after name came family name, and then came the horrible question—were there any relatives left alive?

The sun had climbed high in the sky, but still they had more waiting on the streets. Standing in line to have their lineage checked. Those with no family would be assigned a bed. Those with relatives would be escorted to their family's home.

"Right in here." Maggie ushered the boy into the library.

The old woman sat behind the desk, her skin still gleaming with the light of the brethren, giant volumes open in front of her.

The boy hesitated in the doorway.

"You're okay," Maggie said. "No matter what happens, you aren't alone. You're going to be taken care of."

The boy nodded and, trembling, walked forward to sit in front of the woman's desk.

Maggie leaned against the wall in the hall, closing her eyes and letting the world around her swim for a moment.

"Miss Trent?"

Maggie yelped at Bertrand's voice.

"Are you quite well?" Bertrand examined her.

"Fine." Maggie brushed her hair out of her face. "Overthrew an evil master, brought tons of people back from the shadows, saved a city. I'm doing great."

"I'm afraid our work isn't done." Bertrand beckoned Maggie to follow him.

"We had a deal," Maggie said.

She held her tongue as they walked through the hall of light where those seeking lost relatives waited on the benches.

"You said you would come back to the Siren's Realm with me and take care of the Compère." Maggie grabbed Bertrand's arm as he weaved through the crowd on the street. "You don't get to back out of our deal."

"I'm not attempting to." Bertrand lifted Maggie's hand from his sleeve. "But our work here is not yet done."

"What happened to *leave after the fighting because rebuilding is for those who will stay behind?*"

Bertrand stopped in the center of the street. He turned to face Maggie, his brows knit tightly together. "I had no idea you listened so closely."

"Well, when you're not really wrong about something, you have an annoying habit of being really right."

Bertrand raised one black eyebrow. "There is one more thing we must do." He stopped at the edge of a gaping pit in the ground.

The claw marks of the giant shadow had ripped through the earth, toppling an entire house into the chasm.

The rushing of water came from far below where the light couldn't reach.

"The darkness lay beneath Sarana long before the Master discovered the waters and the first specter walked the street," Bertrand said.

"So the question becomes how to get rid of the horrible darkness forever," Nilla said.

She'd changed into a long, flowing purple dress that hugged her waist.

Diven, Stilla, and the other acolytes walked behind her. None of them had been rebathed in lish.

"The brethren have contained the dark waters for years," Diven said. "No one has ever found a way to destroy it."

"But we have something the brethren did not." Bertrand spread his arms toward the sun.

"Use what we have and burn it away?" Maggie said.

"Like cauterizing a wound," Bertrand said.

"I was going to go for a creepy kid with a magnifying glass, but yours is good too." Maggie shrugged.

"How?" Nilla said. "I'm afraid I don't have a mirror quite large enough for this in my magical stores."

"There's a reason I wanted all of you here," Bertrand said. "One reflection large enough to light the darkness might well be impossible, yet many small reflections will be bright enough to cut through even the deepest black."

"You are rather brilliant, aren't you?" Nilla cooed.

"Don't encourage him." Maggie didn't bother to bite back her smile.

Bertrand reached toward the pit. "*Travasio.*"

A faint shimmer drifted from his palm, growing and solidifying into a shining disk five-feet wide before settling at the bottom edge of where the sun stretched into the chasm. The light hit the surface, creating a ray that reached farther down into the blackness.

"*Travasio*." Nilla's gleaming spell drifted down to join Bertrand's, piggybacking the light farther down.

"*Travasio*." The spell buzzed as it soared from Maggie's hand. She had expected the magic to be difficult. Expected it to be hard to know where to place the disk. But the disk drifted down, settling into the perfect place as though the spell itself wanted nothing more than to amplify the light.

Stilla added her spell, and the rocks at the bottom of the chasm came into view.

The next acolyte's spell gave light to the water, burning away the black.

The next added her spell, and the next his.

Every rock and surface was bathed in brilliant sunlight.

"It seems the light has won without my help," Diven said.

"A little more light never goes amiss," Bertrand said.

"*Travasio*." Diven's spell drifted down into the pit, stopping just above the water.

Bright light shone from the chasm, giving a perfect view of the sparkling, clear water far below.

"Not a bad way to end a battle," Maggie said.

"Indeed, Miss Trent."

They all stared down into the chasm for a long moment. A bird flew overhead, chittering away in the midday sun.

"Now, we are done," Bertrand said. "It's time we return."

"Return?" Nilla said. "To the land across the water? Why would you want to do that?"

Biting her lips together, Maggie backed away, heading toward the shade of a drooping tree that arched over the street.

"What do you mean you *slipped* into our world?" Nilla shouted.

"Now, Nilla…"

Maggie didn't hear the rest of Bertrand's hushed reply. She ran her fingers along the bark of the tree, searching for the marks of magic, though she had no idea what they might feel like.

"Are you really going to leave?" Diven ducked into the shelter of the tree.

"We have to get back home," Maggie said. "The people there need us."

"Is that what you do, run from place to place, saving those in need?" Diven said.

"Sometimes," Maggie said. "It doesn't always feel like it, but walking away would be worse."

Diven reached for Maggie's hand. "Sarana will need people to help restore order—so much has been destroyed."

Diven's touch warmed Maggie's skin as she slipped her hand into his.

"You'll be great at helping them," Maggie said. "The city will be fine without Hunter Wayland and his apprentice."

"I will always be grateful for the help you gave," Diven said.

"Maybe set up a plaque for us, but make sure I'm listed above Bertrand. You can feel free to tell the world he was failing at stopping the shadows until I showed up."

"I will make sure all remember." Diven squeezed Maggie's hand.

"You are utterly insane!" Nilla shouted.

"Should I go help him?" Maggie asked.

"Is it any more than he deserves?" Diven said.

"Probably not." Maggie leaned into the branches of the tree, gazing up through the leaves.

"Is where you come from really so wonderful?" Diven asked.

"No better than most places, not when you really get to know it." Maggie trailed her fingers through the leaves. There was something in their texture that felt familiar. Like the leaves and Maggie herself were spun from the same thread.

Magic.

"Miss Trent," Bertrand called from the middle of the street.

"Goodbye, Diven," Maggie said. "I hope you have a wonderful life."

"Goodbye, Maggie, savior of the shadow stalkers."

Maggie laughed as she walked to Bertrand.

Nilla stood, glaring at Bertrand, who rubbed a pink mark on his cheek.

"I am offering you one last time," Bertrand said. "Come with us."

"I have lost too much saving this city to simply walk away," Nilla said. "There are children who need families. Families whose homes have been destroyed."

"And you will be a great grace to helping them." Bertrand bowed. "Try to remember me fondly, should you ever feel the urge to forgive."

Nilla swiped the tears from her cheeks. "Run away to your mythical realm, and go save someone else."

"I will never forget you, my wonderful Nilla." Bertrand strode down the street back toward the West Worth Graveyard.

"Bye, and thank you for taking care of him," Maggie said.

Nilla gave a stiff nod and looked away.

Bertrand had turned the corner onto the next street before Maggie caught up to him.

"You couldn't convince her to come with you?" Maggie asked.

"I don't think anything I could have said would have worked, and it would have been cruel to truly try."

"Maybe you can get rid of the Compère really fast and—"

"Once I leave this place, I cannot come back. I would be too tempted to stay forever."

"I'm sorry. I wish I didn't have to make you leave."

"It's not your doing, Miss Trent. It's many, many years' worth of mine. I have invested more of my life in the Siren's Realm than I have in any other place. I do not think I could ever redeem myself if I were to ignore the plight of the people I have come to care for in her world."

"Life is about more than redemption," Maggie said.

"I hope you will always see the many worlds you visit in such a wonderful light."

They stopped in front of the wrought iron gate of the graveyard. The brick wall surrounding the cemetery had been torn apart.

Still, Bertrand swung the gate open, bowing Maggie through before closing it.

His hand lingered on the metal.

"Are you okay?" Maggie asked.

"There is a very good reason I never stay in any world for too long. I'm afraid I don't have the strength for it."

"I'm sorry."

"As am I." Bertrand looked into Maggie's eyes, holding her gaze for a long moment before starting toward the divot in the far corner of the cemetery.

The grass at the bottom of the dent swayed with a breeze that touched nothing else as Maggie and Bertrand approached. The air held a scent of something beyond the damp sea air of Sarana.

Spices, salt, and magic filled Maggie's lungs as she walked to the bottom of the basin.

The ground beneath her feet stayed solid.

"She's not going to take me without you," Maggie said.

Bertrand stepped into the base of the divot.

Maggie took a deep breath, preparing for the pressure of the void. She looked to Bertrand as her lungs began to burn and the ground beneath their feet stayed solid.

I've gotten what you sent me for. Now let us in.

A whisper of wind tickled Maggie's ankles. The grass around her feet swayed and shone a brilliant green.

Maggie gasped another breath as the ground beneath her disappeared and she plunged into darkness.

The void pressed in on her, leaving her with nothing but the rushing of the black around her.

But there were no shadows reaching for her. No specters come to steal her away. Only pure darkness.

Seconds ticked past. Maggie's lungs ached as instinct told her she needed air.

A bright flash of brilliant green light enveloped her.

The gurgling of water filled the air as she landed in the middle of the creek.

CHAPTER 25

Beep, whirr!

Maggie coughed out the silty water. "Nic?"

"Maggie!"

Hands gripped Maggie under the arms, hauling her backward out of the creek.

"Maggie, are you hurt?" Alden set her down on the edge of the bank.

"I'm fine." She wiped her sopping hair from her eyes. "Where's Bertrand?"

"Here." Bertrand stood twenty feet downstream, examining the sunset.

"We did it." Maggie pushed herself to her feet. "We made it back. How long have we been gone?"

"Oh, well"—Alden blushed to the roots of his dark hair—"not long, I think. I was sitting here feeling rather sorry for myself, and then I noticed the sun was setting and you wanted me to see Lena. So I got up to leave, and you fell into the creek."

Maggie threw her arms around Alden's neck, soaking him with Nilla's sweater.

"I'm so glad you're safe." She pressed her cheek to his.

"I'm glad you're home," Alden whispered.

Nic beeped indignantly.

"Thanks for watching out for him." Maggie patted Nic's head.

Nic whirred.

"It was a very trying time," Alden said.

"We need to head to the Textile Town," Bertrand said. "If the Siren wanted me back here badly enough to send Miss Trent after me, there must be a reason. For four years I lived in Sarana and she sent no one after me. There is something she wants that has to do with time here. Come, we've a mystery to solve."

He turned away from the sunset to face Maggie and Alden. The lines on his face from his time in Sarana had disappeared. The Siren had returned him to the Bertrand Maggie had always known him to be.

With a twinkle in his eye, Bertrand clapped his hands. His Saranan clothes swirled away. A billowing white shirt and long tailed coat appeared.

"Shall we?" Bertrand straightened his collar.

"Where to?" Maggie ran the few steps to be at Bertrand's side. Her shoes sloshed with water.

She felt for the well of magic that filled her. There were no gaps. Her time in Sarana had refilled her stores.

I wish for my clothes to be dry.

A faint tingle touched her skin as the Siren took her price. In a moment, Maggie's clothes had dried. She pulled off her sweater, knotting it around her waist.

"Was it cold where you went?" Alden asked as they cut through the woods back to the edge of the tent city.

"Cold and wet," Maggie said. "And dark. It's a long story, but I think you'll like it."

"Perhaps you can tell me during our picnic by the Endless Sea," Alden said.

"I'd like that."

The long row of tents came into view. Maggie balled her

hands into fists, waiting for the Siren to steer them off of their path.

Bertrand slipped between the tents.

Maggie stayed close on his heels, resisting the urge to cling to Bertrand's and Alden's sleeves to make sure they weren't separated again.

Beyond the narrow gap between canvases, a lane lined with tents waited for them.

"Oh, thank you." Maggie beamed at the tents.

Bertrand raised an eyebrow at her.

"I wasn't completely convinced the Siren hadn't decided to strand us in the woods forever." Maggie shrugged.

Bertrand led them through the Textile Town at a brisk pace, heading straight toward the palace.

"Tell me everything you know of the Compère," Bertrand said.

"He runs the circus, he likes to hide his face in red mist, and whether he made it happen or not, weapons were allowed in the brawl at the opening night of his spectacle," Maggie said.

"He also hired those with no magic of their own, or very little magic left, to work for him in the tent," Alden said. "From what I understand, he offered them a fair cut on all the goods they sold."

"We can therefore surmise he is first and foremost a businessman," Bertrand said.

They turned down a wide road lined with bright orange flowers as tall as the tents they shielded.

"If the Compère only wanted to wreak havoc, there would be no need to create an employee base for continuing commerce," Bertrand said. "It would be simpler and more cost effective to lure people in and cause a fight while employing as little outside help as possible."

"He wanted the evening to be nice so people would come back again," Maggie said.

"What could be gained from such an endeavor?" Bertrand asked.

"Magic," Maggie said. "He must have acquired a massive amount in one night. Enough to last for years."

"Importance," Alden said. "That much pomp and circumstance. Everyone in the realm now knows of the Compère."

Bertrand stopped suddenly in the middle of the street. "And that is the true question."

"What is the true question?" Maggie asked.

Bertrand didn't answer as he turned down a narrow alley with tents so close together the fabric brushed against Maggie's shoulders.

"Bertrand, what is the true question?" Maggie stepped out onto a wide lane and dodged around a woman carrying wine.

"The Siren, in her wisdom, has never shown any anger toward commerce," Bertrand said. "As long as one doesn't hoard the riches that perpetuate life in the Siren's Realm, one may be as industrious as one chooses. She would have no need to bring me back to the Siren's Realm because the Compère has found an ingenious way to gain magic."

Bertrand cut between two tents, leading them onto the road that held the palace.

"However, if she finds the Compère's rise to infamy to be distressing but cannot break her own decree, then outside help would be needed." Bertrand stopped next to the emerald green tent.

"Might I suggest," Alden said, "there may be a third option you haven't considered? Perhaps the Siren wanted you to come back because she wanted *you* in her realm."

"I've been gone for ages," Bertrand said. "The Compère is the only change in circumstances that would have driven her to force Maggie to bring me back."

"Unless she was waiting for Maggie to—"

Maggie elbowed Alden in the stomach. "If the Siren wanted

me to take a wrong turn into those woods, she could have twisted my path through the Textile Town whenever she wanted."

"The Siren sees time and life very differently than we do," Bertrand said. "The issue of the Compère bothers her enough to desire a speedy resolution."

"Absolutely." Maggie shot a glare at Alden.

"That is the clear answer." Alden widened his eyes at Maggie as Bertrand turned away.

Maggie grabbed Alden's hand, dragging him after Bertrand.

The minotaur waited on the far side of the tent, guarding the entrance against the line of patrons who waited to indulge in the pleasures of the palace.

Alden tried to stop at the end of the line, but Maggie dragged him forward to stand right in front of the minotaur.

"Good evening," Bertrand said. "I'd like to see Lena."

The minotaur stared down at Bertrand, glaring with his beetle black eyes.

"It's rather important I see her immediately," Bertrand said.

"I'm not sure if she's available," the minotaur said.

Maggie tried not to stare as the minotaur spoke through his bull's lips.

"We'll wait inside then." Bertrand gave a nod and stepped around the minotaur.

"He should wait at the back of the line," a man tall enough to reach the minotaur's chin said.

Alden turned to the man. "I'm very sorry."

"If you're sorry, then get to the back." The man crossed his bulging arms.

"I should have been clearer." Alden picked at the sleeve of his shirt. "I meant I'm sorry not to have warned you before you spoke. This is Bertrand Wayland. If he says he'll wait inside, it's best to agree and stand aside."

"Why you little—" the big man shoved Alden.

"Out of line with you." The minotaur grabbed the man by his

throat, tossing him onto the street. "You were on warning, Cristof, and now you're out."

"I am quite sorry," Alden said.

"This way." Bertrand held open the emerald tent flap.

Maggie shoved Alden through the flap before her, getting him away from Cristof's glare.

The shade of the tent made the chandeliers sparkling from above shine all the brighter. Unnaturally soft grass covered the ground, lending the earth extra give through Maggie's boots.

Fainting couches, comfy chairs, and tables loaded with wine, cheese, and chocolates lay scattered around the room. Curtains portioned off sections of the grand tent, allowing privacy for the patrons.

Maggie scanned the faces of those she passed, though she wasn't entirely sure what she was searching for.

Bertrand stopped at a red velvet sofa flanked by two sapphire chairs. He paused, studying the upholstery before sitting down.

"You all right?" Maggie asked.

"It's strange," Bertrand said, "how things once so familiar fade to something from a different life."

Alden looked to Maggie.

She shook her head.

Bertrand settled himself on the sofa.

"Do you think Lena will know anything?" Maggie asked.

"I know more than you could ever dream of." Lena sauntered out from behind a scarlet curtain. "The real question is, are you ready for the type of knowledge I have?"

She sank down onto the sofa next to Bertrand, brushing imagined lint off his collar.

"The Compère," Bertrand said. "Who is he?"

"Right to it then." Lena poured herself a glass of wine. "You smell different. Where have you been?"

"I went for a walk in the woods," Bertrand said.

"And missed the spectacle?" Lena pushed her long platinum

hair behind her shoulders. "I thought you would have wanted to join me in my box."

"It was a very long walk in the woods." Bertrand lifted Lena's hand, pressing her fingers to his lips. "I'm afraid I've never seen the Compère and must rely on your wisdom."

"Your flattery is quite brilliant," Lena said. "I've never seen the face behind the Compère's shroud. Whoever he is, he keeps his real identity a secret."

"But?" Maggie sank into a sapphire chair.

"The spectacle may have made the Compère a very wealthy man," Lena said. "But all magic comes through the palace eventually."

"Who has brought you more magic?" Bertrand asked.

"Not one person in particular," Lena said. "The ones who live on the outskirts."

"How do you mean?" Alden asked.

"Those who choose not to dwell amongst others either do a great deal of trade before retreating to their homes or choose to live off of very little to avoid society," Lena said. "Those who have long shunned the bustle of the Textile Town are coming in with great stores of magic to spend."

"And how have they been earning their magic?" Bertrand lifted Lena's glass from her hand, taking a sip of her wine.

"No idea," Lena said. "But it all feels the same flowing through me. It's filtering down from the same source."

"Then we need to find the source," Bertrand said.

"How fun." Lena took her wine back. "Going on a hunt?"

"I don't suppose I could entice you to come with us?" Bertrand said. "So many are more likely to speak to you than to me."

Lena raised her glass to Maggie. "She'll do just fine. But remember, dear. Smile when you ask for information, purr when they really don't want to talk, and keep the twinkle in your eyes if you have to hurt them."

"Oh dear," Alden said.

"I'll keep that in mind," Maggie said.

"Lena, darling!" A woman with dark curls pressed her lips to Lena's cheeks. "I've been waiting outside for ages."

"If you'll excuse me." Lena stood, twining her fingers through the woman's. "Some people have real reasons for visiting the palace."

Bertrand stood, bowing to both women before beckoning Maggie and Alden to follow him.

"Thank you, Lena," Maggie said.

"Any friend of Bertrand's." Lena winked.

Maggie jogged to catch up to Bertrand and Alden.

"So we go to the outskirts and find what waits there," Bertrand said. "With any luck, we'll find the Compère before dawn and begin a new day in the Siren's Realm with all put to right."

"Can't we just asked the Siren to send us to the Compère?" Alden said.

"Ah." Bertrand weaved between tents, leading them toward the fountain square. "The Siren simply leading us to the Compère would go against her decree, which rules us all."

They stepped out into the square. The last rays of sun glinted off the platinum statue of a woman draped in thin fabric standing at the center of a fountain flowing with golden liquid.

Bertrand pointed to the inscription that ran around the base of the pool.

> *In the Siren's Realm a wish need only be made.*
> *Her desire to please shall never be swayed.*
> *But should those around you wish you ill,*
> *the Siren's love shall protect you still.*
> *No two blessings shall contradict,*
> *so be sure your requests are carefully picked.*
> *Wish for joyful pleasure to be shared by all*

of the good and the brave who have risked the fall.
But a warning to you once the wish is made,
the Siren's price must always be paid.

"Asking for the identity of the Compère would go against his wish for anonymity in masking his face," Maggie said. "We have to do the work on our own."

"To the outskirts we go," Bertrand said.

The fountain swayed in front of Maggie, twisting the statue of the woman.

"Bertrand," Maggie said, "I haven't slept in more than a day, neither have you. If we go after the Compère now and it comes down to a fight, I don't know if we would win."

Bertrand tented his fingers under his chin.

"Don't say we're just going to wish to feel like we had slept," Maggie said.

"We'll go to the Fortress," Bertrand said. "Sleep and find the Compère first thing in the morning."

"You know, I think that may be the most reasonable thing you've ever said." Maggie led the way, moving as quickly as her leaden legs would carry her.

Nic trundled along beside her, humming encouragingly whenever her pace slowed.

People roamed the streets without any trace of fear remaining from the battle in the square the night before.

Stars took over the sky as they reached the stone streets of the Fortress. Clouds crept in, shrouding their brightness.

"Bertrand"—Maggie blinked up at the sky—"do those look like storm clouds?"

Bertrand tipped his head back, squinting into the darkness.

"We need to reach my home." Bertrand seized Maggie's arm, dragging her forward as the first drops of rain fell from the sky.

CHAPTER 26

"*I* have to get to my rock." Maggie's arms shook as she pushed against Bertrand's grip. "I have to make sure my house is safe."

"There is nothing you can do to protect your home from the storm," Bertrand said. "We need to get inside."

"I have time to make it to the sea," Maggie said.

Lightning streaked across the sky as though the Siren herself laughed at Maggie.

Maggie's toe caught on the uneven street.

Alden wrapped his arm around her waist, holding her steady as the rain slicked the stone.

"Why?" Maggie asked. "Why is she doing this?"

The door to Bertrand's house swung open as they stepped under the overhang.

Thunder shook the street as Alden slammed the door shut behind them.

"Is the storm a bad thing?" Alden leaned against the door.

"Yes." Maggie marched up the steps into the house, heading straight for the couch in front of the fireplace.

"The Siren brings storms to cleanse her realm," Bertrand said.

"When the Derelict who have no magic left to give wander up onto the streets, she brings a storm to wash them away."

"It was her big way of dealing with people she didn't want around." Maggie sagged onto the couch. "No one could ever die here, so the Siren would just wash them away into nothing."

Alden sat beside Maggie, unraveling the threads he'd pulled loose from his sleeve.

"But then the blackness came," Bertrand said, "and with it death. The Siren rid herself of those known to hoard magic."

"Have there been Derelict running around?" Maggie asked Alden.

"I've not seen anyone who seems out of place or poor," Alden said.

"Then what is she doing?" Maggie pressed her knuckles to her temples, fighting to think past the throbbing in her head. "She wouldn't send a storm just because."

"She has a reason." Bertrand lifted the teapot from the mantle, pouring three cups before handing one to Maggie. "For every line in her decree, for every wish not granted, for every storm she has raised, she has a reason."

The sweet steam of the tea relaxed Maggie's lungs. "Is there anything we can do about it?"

"I hate to say it"—Bertrand pursed his lips—"but I am afraid we are quite powerless until the storm passes."

Maggie watched the rain lashing against the window. Sometime before her cup was empty, she drifted into sleep.

~

A clap of thunder shook the house, dragging Maggie from her slumber. She moved her hand to balance her teacup only to find it had disappeared, replaced by a blanket someone had tucked around her. Someone had also laid her down across the sofa.

She kicked her legs over the side.

Nic rolled up from the corner, giving a soft *hum*, and pressed her back to lying down with one of his spindly arms.

Lightning lit the room.

Alden slept soundly in the high-backed chair, his blanket pulled up around his chin.

Nic pressed on Maggie's blanket, tucking her in.

Before she could murmur a thank you, sleep had taken her again.

~

The breeze kissed her shoulders as she ran through the trees. She tipped her head back and laughed. Even as the bright joyous sound escaped her, she saw the great stone buried in the mountainside. A dark opening cut into the boulder, leading to the tunnels beyond.

Her feet carried her toward the tunnel even as her heart raced, telling her to run away.

"Come on." The boy reached for her hand. "Just come a little closer."

"No." Maggie batted his hand away, fleeing for the safety of the trees.

"It'll be fine," the boy called. "You just have to come a little closer."

The boy didn't scream as the ground beneath him cracked and crumbled. He smiled at her as he tumbled away into the chasm below.

"This is a dream," Maggie said. "This isn't how it happened."

Green light shone from the bottom of the pit.

"There was no light!" Maggie shouted. "It was mist. Green mist. You showed me his face, and I was trying to save him."

The light grew brighter.

"What's the point in having a nightmare if you're not even getting it right?"

Maggie stalked to the edge of the pit.

"You want to take me? Fine. I'm already here."

She blinked against the dazzling light that filled the chasm.

Something moved. Altering the brightness. Giving form and shape to the light.

A face both terrifying and beautiful gazed up at her.

"Who are you?" Maggie said.

The chasm stole her voice, whisking it away as though she spoke into the wind.

Tendrils of mist crept up from the light, snaking toward Maggie.

She tried to run, but the earth had grown up around her feet, rooting her in place.

"Wake up."

The green mist reached her, wrapping around her legs.

"Wake up, Maggie. Just wake up."

The mist touched her face, caressing her cheek.

"Wake up!"

~

*M*aggie gasped, fighting to free herself.

"Maggie."

She kicked out, breaking free from her blanket.

"Ouch." Alden jumped back, clutching his shin.

"Sorry." Maggie tossed the blanket aside. "I'm sorry."

"It's fine." Alden limped to sit next to her. "Are you all right?"

"I'm fine." Maggie waved a hand in the air, resisting the urge to wipe the sweat from her forehead. "Just a little nightmare."

"I heard." Alden took her hand. "I'm sorry."

"For what?"

"For whatever the universe won't apologize for that gives you such awful dreams," Alden said.

A fresh wave of thunder shook the windows.

"How long have I been sleeping?" Maggie asked.

"No idea, but it still seems to be the middle of the night."

Nic whistled sleepily.

"She can make the night last as long as she wants." Maggie blinked, trying to brush away the horrible fatigue that pressed on her eyes.

"You should go back to sleep." Alden squeezed her hand.

"And have more nightmares?" The room blurred as Maggie shook her head. "I'd rather stay awake."

"Here." Alden leaned back into the corner of the sofa, propping his arm up to leave a place for Maggie. "I may not be the most experienced with practical magic, but I am very good at defending against nightmares."

Maggie laughed.

Thunder rumbled its reply.

"I'll be fine, really," Maggie said.

"You're allowed to be more than *fine*." Alden picked up the blanket from the floor. "Come sleep. We'll wait out the storm together."

"*Fine*."

She curled up next to Alden, laying her head on his shoulder. He pulled the blanket up, covering them both.

"Sleep well, Maggie."

She drifted away before she'd taken a breath.

~

"The storm has passed." Bertrand's voice dragged her out of the blissful nothing.

"Huh?" Maggie yawned, blinking at the bright sunlight that filled the sitting room.

"At last," Alden said.

His chest rumbled under Maggie's arm.

Heat flooded her cheeks as she looked from Bertrand to Alden.

"Let's go stop the Compère." She wriggled away from Alden and kicked free of the blankets.

Needles stung the arm she'd been sleeping on as blood rushed back into her fingers.

Bertrand lifted a tray of rolls from the mantle. "Never go into battle hungry."

"Thanks." Maggie grabbed a roll and headed for the door.

"I do wish we could bring your swords," Alden said. "It feels rather foolish to be venturing after the Compère empty handed."

"Well," Maggie said, "either he won't be able to have weapons either, or we'll wish ourselves up something really great to fight with."

She waited in the small hall that led to the outside door, holding onto her warm roll with both hands.

"What if the Siren washed away the Compère with her storm?" Alden asked.

"Then our task will be simple." Bertrand unfastened the lock.

"What if the Siren washed away most of her realm?" Maggie asked.

Bertrand froze, his hand on the door. "Then it is best to see what troubles lie ahead as quickly as possible. One cannot act wisely without knowledge."

"Right." Maggie bit into her roll as Bertrand swung open the door.

Bright sunlight filled the street outside. The rain-kissed air held the scent of a new morning.

"A promising start," Alden said.

The stone sidewalks along the canal had been scrubbed clean by the rain. The glass of the barred windows looked to have been carefully polished by a meticulous hand.

"Maybe she just wanted everything to be super clean to welcome you home?" Maggie whispered.

"Perhaps." Bertrand stopped, staring up and down the canal.

The soft melody of distant music, so often heard drifting by, had been silenced. The streets were abandoned and windows shut tight.

"We should head to the market square before moving on to the outskirts," Bertrand said.

"Make sure there are other people left here?" Maggie said. "Sounds like a great idea."

As she turned to follow Bertrand on the path to the Textile Town, a flicker of movement caught the corner of Maggie's eye.

A black bird with a bright orange feather on his shoulders landed on the stones at the edge of the canal, his gaze locked on Maggie.

The bird cocked his head to the side, jumped two feet farther down the walkway, and looked back at Maggie.

"Damn. Bertrand, you're going the wrong way." She shoved the rest of her breakfast into her mouth.

"What do you mean, Miss Trent?" Bertrand stopped far down a different branch of the canal, heading toward town.

"The Siren doesn't want us going toward the market square," Maggie said. "She wants us going toward the Endless Sea."

"How do you know?" Alden jogged back, Nic rolling at his heels.

Maggie pointed to the bird, which took off, flying to the farthest point down the water Maggie could see, before landing and turning back to Maggie.

"As the Siren wills it," Bertrand said.

Maggie kept her pace slow as she led the others toward the bird.

Maybe it's just a mistake. Maybe the bird only wanted some of my food.

They reached a bend in the water and a new path of the canals came into view. The bird took off, flying low over the water and alighting on a stone bridge.

The bird turned to Maggie, giving her an angry *tweet*.

"Okay, we'll hurry up." She jogged toward the bird.

The bird chirped and flew to the far side of the bridge.

The sun sparkled off the water as they ran over the bridge and down a broader portion of the canal.

"I had no idea the Fortress reached out this far," Alden said.

"Neither did I." Maggie paused as the bird soared up in a spiral before leading them farther down the canal. Here, the waves lapped the stone walls in earnest.

Beyond the last gray stone house, the canal widened, opening up into the Endless Sea.

The bird landed on the last stone in the walkway before the canal gave way to open water.

"What do you want us to see?" Maggie stopped three feet away from the bird.

He stared down into the canal, chirping madly.

Beneath the sparkling surface, something pale drifted in the dark water. Swirling fabric surrounding hands that reached toward the sky.

"Miss Trent, wait!"

The water closed around Maggie's ears before the end of Bertrand's protest.

She dove down toward the person, kicking against the pull of the canal. The cold water stung her skin, but she swam deeper, pushing away the fabric of the billowing skirt and grabbing the woman's waist.

Pulling with her free arm, she fought for the surface. Panic pushed precious air from her lungs as the current held her down, as though determined to keep the prize it had captured.

Kicking as hard as her legs could manage, she dragged the woman free of the canal floor.

Arms reached down from above.

Maggie shoved the woman into the waiting hands and broke through to the surface, gasping for air.

"She's not breathing." Alden dragged the woman onto the stone and pressed his ear to her chest.

"Miss Trent"—Bertrand seized her hands, lifting her from the water—"did it not occur to you diving into that water could kill you?"

"She needed help." Maggie wrung out her hair. "The Siren wanted us to find her."

Alden placed his mouth on the woman's, forcing air into her lungs.

"The Siren sometimes demands sacrifices," Bertrand said. "I would prefer you not be the price we pay."

The woman coughed, her black hair covering her face as Alden rolled her onto her side.

"Breathe gently now," Alden said. "You're going to be fine."

She shoved her hair away from her face as she coughed out more water.

"Nilla?" Her name fell from Bertrand's lips.

Nilla looked up at him, fear and loathing in her eyes.

CHAPTER 27

"*W*hat have you done?" Nilla shoved Alden away from her.

"How did you get here?" Bertrand reached for Nilla's hand.

"Don't you dare play games with me, you vile, horrible scum." Nilla pushed herself to her feet, swaying dangerously over the water.

"Careful." Maggie grabbed Nilla's arm.

"I told you to leave me alone," Nilla said. "I told you I was happy staying in Sarana. Where am I? In your little fairy land?"

"You're in the Siren's Realm," Maggie said.

"I knew it." Nilla gripped Maggie's arm. "You're a monster, Bertrand Wayland."

"Nilla, whatever you think of me can be discussed later," Bertrand said. "The much more pressing subject is how you came to be in the Siren's Realm."

"You dragged me here, you evil—"

"I did no such thing," Bertrand said.

"Look at me." Maggie stepped in front of Nilla. "Don't pay attention to Bertrand, just look at me."

Nilla gave Bertrand one more glare before giving her focus to

Maggie.

"Good," Maggie said. "Now, tell me how you got here."

"He dragged me here," Nilla said through gritted teeth.

"How?" Maggie said. "What happened? Did you go to the West Worth Graveyard? Did you just wish yourself out of a dark place?"

"No, I was walking by the docks." Nilla shook beneath Maggie's fingers. "There was a new batch of ships coming in. The day was bright and beautiful."

"But something went wrong," Maggie said.

"A storm kicked up," Nilla said. "I'd never seen anything like it. The sky just turned to black, and the waves crashed in. I knew something was wrong, but I couldn't run. Couldn't make myself move. A wave came up over the seawall and dragged me out into the ocean. I tried to swim, but green light filled the water, pulling me down. I should have drowned. Have I drowned, am I dead?"

"You're very much alive," Bertrand said.

"No thanks to you." Nilla shook free from Maggie's grip. "Did you want me to die? Have I disappointed you?"

"It wasn't him," Maggie said. "Bertrand didn't drag you here. Even if he had wanted to, he couldn't have managed it."

"Then why am I here?" Nilla asked. "Did you really always come from across the water and I just floated here by chance?"

"The Siren pulled you in," Maggie said. "She wanted you here, so she took you."

"This has got to be some awful joke," Nilla said. "Getting dragged into a faraway pretend world by a mythical creator? It's not possible."

"It is very much possible," Bertrand said.

"And consider yourself lucky," Maggie said. "You got a better welcome than she gave me when she yanked me out of my world."

"I have to get back." Nilla clapped her hands. Her sopping wet dress stayed firmly in place. She clapped again.

"That won't work here," Bertrand said. "All magic comes through the Siren. If you want your clothes dry, you'll have to ask her."

"If I'm going to ask this *Siren* anything it will be to send me home," Nilla said. "I have a life in Sarana. I have people who are counting on me. I need to get back there, Bertrand. Whether you had a hand in dragging me here or not, you most certainly have an obligation to send me home."

"Can you ask the Siren to send her home?" Alden said.

"Asking the Siren to return a person to a particular world takes more magic than any of us can provide," Bertrand said.

"I cannot stay here," Nilla said.

"Fortunately for you," Bertrand said, "Miss Trent and I are very familiar with the link between this world and yours."

"I hate to interrupt," Alden said, "but what of the Compère? Weren't we to—"

"The Compère will have to wait," Bertrand said. "We cannot afford to keep Nilla here while we try and find him. If time continues to move as it did during my absence, a day here will be more than a month there."

"What do you mean a month will have passed?" Nilla said. "I have people who need me, Bertrand. I can't just leave them alone for a month."

Nic tinked one of his metal arms against his chest.

"What in all the light is that?" Nilla stepped back.

"He's fine." Maggie took Nilla's arm, drawing her away from the edge. "Siren, will you please dry Nilla's clothes and mine?"

Her feeling of foolishness at speaking aloud to the Siren lasted only a second. As Maggie felt the magic siphon from her body, Nilla squeaked at having her clothes instantly dried.

"This is a mad world filled with mad people," Nilla whispered.

"I told you for years, I am not crazy," Bertrand said. "I simply exist in a world of insanity and have gained insight into its workings. Now, if you would like to be returned to Sarana in a reasonable time, we had best hurry. Even a few hours here could mean weeks in Saranan time."

Nilla turned to Maggie.

"He's right." Maggie shrugged.

"Fine. Lead the way home." Nilla poked Bertrand in the chest. "But know I will never forgive you for whatever part you played in this misery."

"I would never expect you to." With a nod, Bertrand started back the way they'd come, leading them through the Fortress to the Textile Town.

Maggie walked next to Alden behind Nilla and Bertrand.

Alden turned to Maggie, opening his mouth as though to ask a question.

Maggie shook her head.

Better to figure out the why once we've gotten her home.

An ache of fear stayed knotted in Maggie's chest as they reached the gray tents that bordered the stone houses.

The tents were just as they should have been, with no hint of damage from the night before.

Tired murmurs came from within the canvas.

How long did the Siren keep us asleep?

Maggie leaned in to Alden's ear to whisper the question.

Nilla screamed as they turned onto a wide lane. Centaurs moved between their tents, tending the large patches of flowers that bordered the walkway.

"This is a dream." Nilla covered her eyes. "I'm in a nightmare filled with terrible creatures."

One by one, the centaurs rounded on Nilla, drawing themselves up to their full and terrifying height.

"I hope you'll forgive her." Bertrand dragged Nilla forward. "She's rather new."

The centaurs moved into a line, blocking Bertrand's path.

"Shit." Maggie darted in front of Bertrand and Nilla. "By *new* he means she got here about fifteen minutes ago. Her world is filled with shadows and has nothing as majestic as centaurs. Imagine only ever having lived with puny humans and then seeing the might that is multiple centaurs right after arriving in the Siren's Realm. Poor thing barely has her head on straight."

The centaurs continued to glare.

"She thought Nic was going to kill her, and he's barely three feet tall," Maggie added.

Nic rolled forward, whistling his assent.

"If she insults us again," a dappled mare said, "we'll destroy her and throw her to the Derelict."

"And I won't fight you on it." Maggie bowed. "Thank you for your mercy."

The centaurs parted ways.

"Move." Maggie beckoned the others forward.

"We really aren't in the same world as Sarana," Nilla said. "You weren't just lying and sailing across the sea when you left?"

"I wasn't," Bertrand said. "The Siren's Realm is a beautiful place that links countless magical worlds. Miss Trent and I travel to different worlds together, finding adventure and helping where we can."

A wind blew up, kissing the back of Maggie's neck, giving her the whole-hearted desire to run as fast as her legs could carry her until a marvelous adventure blocked her path.

They turned onto a narrow lane of tents whose pale fabric rippled in the breeze.

"They came to my world and saved magicians from years of oppression," Alden said. "Magic where I come from would have gone extinct without them."

"And you hop into Sarana and save us from the shadows," Nilla said. "Perhaps I'll stop protesting the statue they want to build for you by the edge of the chasm."

"A statue?" Maggie shook her head. "How many statues of Bertrand Wayland do magical worlds need?"

"It's to be a statue of you both," Nilla said. "Diven's the one who's been planning the memorial park."

"You'll have to thank him for me," Maggie said.

The lines of tents ended. Grass overtook the edges of the dirt road as the forest rose up before them.

"The outskirts. So many trees with so few people." Bertrand walked to the edge of the well-traveled path, his hands tented under his chin.

"Is the great shadow stalker suddenly afraid of a few trees?" Nilla said. "If you'll tell me where to go, I would be happy to finish this journey without you."

"You'd never find it," Bertrand said. "And I have no fear of the woods, only trepidation in the presence of coincidence."

"Do coincidences happen in the Siren's Realm?" Maggie asked.

"No," Bertrand said. "But for the moment, we shall simply be grateful both of this morning's tasks have led us to the same place."

"I'm so glad not to have inconvenienced you." Nilla strode into the woods. "If we could hurry, I would rather not miss out on any more of my life while stuck in this awful place."

Bertrand stayed still, scanning the woods. "We should proceed with caution."

"We will." Maggie ran to catch up to Nilla. "Look, I get it." She directed Nilla sideways, closer to the stream. "I didn't want to come to the Siren's Realm, either. I got sucked out of a battle and ended up here."

"And just decided to stay with the horse men?" Nilla said. "Have a life of adventure with daring Bertrand?"

"I wanted to go back," Maggie said. "But we don't know where the entrance to my world is. There was no way for me to get home."

"I'm sorry." Nilla slowed her pace, letting Maggie walk by her side.

The wind whispered gently through the trees. Their leaves

full and alive, showing no signs of damage from the storm the night before.

"What kind of a power pulls people out of their homes?" Nilla asked.

"The Siren." Maggie laughed. "I used to dream of asking her why she dragged me here."

"And now?" Nilla raised an eyebrow.

"I hope I don't have dreams at all," Maggie said.

The stream gurgled in front of them.

Nic whirred.

"Further up and further in," Alden said.

Bertrand walked far behind the group, stopping every few feet to lean over the crystal water or stare up into the trees.

Maggie slowed her pace to keep from losing Bertrand in the woods.

A giant rock split the stream up ahead.

Maggie's heart flipped in her chest, remembering the feeling of the void pressing in around her.

"We're here." Maggie stopped next to the boulder. "Climb on up and jump in on the downstream side. It'll be dark, and you won't be able to breathe. Just stay calm, and you'll end up in the West Worth Graveyard."

"You are all stark raving mad." Nilla slogged out toward the boulder.

"Probably." Maggie untied the sweater from around her waist. "I forgot to give this back."

"Keep it."

"Thanks," Maggie said. "For what it's worth, it was nice to see you again."

"I'll pretend it was a strange dream." Nilla climbed up onto the rock, staring down into the swirling water at the base. "Maybe it is just a dream."

She took a breath to jump.

"It won't work," Bertrand said. "Jump if you like, but it won't lead you home."

"This is the place." Maggie pointed to the water. "This is where we slipped through to Sarana."

"Most definitely," Bertrand said, "but the stitch is gone. The passage has been erased."

"How?" Maggie waded into the stream.

"No, I have to go home." Nilla leapt off the rock.

Maggie held her breath as Nilla's feet hit the surface of the creek.

For a split second, it looked as though she might sink away and out of sight. But she landed in waist-deep water.

"No." Nilla smacked the surface. "No, no, no. I have to get home. Bertrand Wayland, you send me home."

"He can't." Maggie trailed her fingers through the creek, searching for a tingle of magic and finding nothing but cold. "The stitch is gone. There's nothing he can do."

A cough caught in Nilla's chest as she began to sob. "I have to get back. I have to go home."

Maggie wrapped her arms around Nilla, holding her as she shook.

"I'm sorry, Nilla. I'm so sorry," Maggie whispered. "It'll be okay. You're going to be just fine."

The lie stung Maggie's tongue.

Nic tapped his chest.

"The Compère will have to wait," Bertrand said.

Nic turned his eye to Bertrand, giving a high whistle.

"If the Siren chose to wash away this stitch, will she have left any other path out of her realm?"

The weight of the realm crushed Maggie's chest. "We have to find another way out of here."

Maggie's adventures will continue. Stay up to date by joining Megan O'Russell's Readers' Community: https://www.meganorussell.com/book-signup

ESCAPE INTO ADVENTURE

Thank you for reading *The Girl Cloaked in Shadow.* If you enjoyed the book, please consider leaving a review to help other readers find Maggie's story.

As always, thanks for reading,

Megan O'Russell

Never miss a moment of the magic and romance.

Join the Megan O'Russell mailing list to stay up to date on all the action by visiting https://www.meganorussell.com/book-signup.

MAGGIE LIVED IN A WORLD OF MAGIC
BEFORE SHE ENTERED THE SIREN'S
REALM.

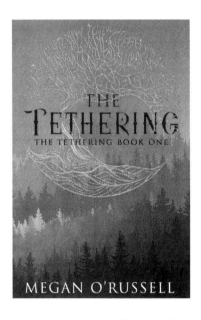

Discover the witches and wizards of our world in *The Tethering*.

Read on for a sneak peek.

WINDOWS

*J*acob rolled over, unwilling to let the sound of his alarm tear him from his dream. He tried to hold on to the image of her, but it was already drifting away into memory. He reached out and turned off the alarm.

He hadn't dreamt about her in months. Not that he hadn't thought about Emilia. He did that every day. The memory of the day he had first met Emilia Gray, seven years ago now, was one of the best he had.

He rolled out of bed and stumbled to his dresser. He had changed a lot from the little boy hiding under a tree. Now sixteen, Jacob was one of the tallest boys in his class, though he still had the thin look of someone who had grown quickly in a short time. His hair was as blond and shaggy as ever, and he had developed a golden tan from working outside all spring.

"She's gone," he told himself. "Get used to it."

He dressed quickly, throwing on whatever smelled clean, and stopped on his way out the door to check in his father's room. Jim had been gone for a few months now, and since the bed was still made, Jacob assumed he hadn't come home last night.

"Great," he muttered, slamming the front door behind him on his way to another day at Fairfield High.

Fairfield, New York was a nice place. At least in Jacob's opinion. Of course, he had never actually been anywhere else. The town was small and picturesque, and the streets were always clean. With summer's approach, the only scent in town came from the iris blossoms that coated the town square. Planted in color-coordinated beds, they surrounded the gazebo that was regularly used to host town events. Signs rising above the blooms proudly stated the irises were a gift of the Ladies' Library League, the group of women who kept the town pristine and perfect.

The schools were excellent, the stores locally owned, and the houses well painted. Except for Jacob's house, which hadn't been painted in his lifetime. He tried to keep up the house as much as he could, but Jim didn't care enough to help. The Ladies' Library League always noticed, but what was Jacob supposed to do?

Jim had drifted from job to job ever since Jacob was two. That was the year his mother died. When Jacob was eight, Jim had started taking work away from Fairfield. He was hardly ever in town anymore. It was normal for him to disappear for months at a time, working…somewhere. He usually left some cash behind, but Jacob didn't care about Jim's money so much anymore. He'd been doing odd jobs for years, and now that he was older, people around town were willing to give him larger jobs with better paychecks. Thanks to a profitable spring, he'd had enough money not only to eat since the last time Jim had skipped town, but to keep the electricity and water on, too. Jacob laughed to himself. That had been a feat.

No one greeted him when he walked into Fairfield High, but he didn't mind. Anonymity suited him. School was a means to an end, and Jacob wanted out. Out of Jim's house, out of Fairfield. But most of all, he wanted to be good enough for her.

Jacob had made up his mind freshman year that he was going to be the best in the whole school. He was going to get a scholarship, go to college, and make something worthwhile of himself. Days at school flew by. Teachers loved him. Students ignored him. It was perfect.

Jacob sat in chemistry class, allowing his mind to wander. He had already read through the entire book, and the lectures were useless since his teacher insisted on reading from the book verbatim every day.

There was a cough at the door.

Jacob looked over with the rest of his classmates, hoping something would break the monotony.

Principal McManis stood in the doorway, his hands flitting between his watch and glasses. He seemed like a decent guy, and Jacob liked him, so he gave an encouraging smile.

The principal did not smile back. "Jacob Evans, I need to see you in my office."

Sweat beaded on Jacob's palms. He could feel the eyes of his classmates burning holes into his face. He got up to follow the principal.

"Bring your bag."

That wasn't a good sign. Bring your bag meant he was in so much trouble he wouldn't be returning to class, or maybe even to school, for quite a while. But Jacob was always very careful to stay out of trouble. If the school wanted to talk to his father about his behavior, they would find out how often Jim was gone. Then Social Services would be all over him.

Jacob picked up his bag and carefully repacked his chemistry book before starting toward the door. Every time he passed a desk, its occupant started to whisper. By the time he reached the principal, the room sounded like a balloon slowly letting out its air.

Jacob's worn sneakers squeaked as he walked down the hall, and McManis's loafers clacked like they were made of the same worn tile as the floor. The sound of their shoes echoed through the corridor like a siren, telling every room they passed that someone was being led to the principal's office. Not once did McManis look over at Jacob.

McManis ushered Jacob into his office and shut the door. Windows surrounded the room, looking out at the secretary's office and the locker-lined hallways. The secretary kept glancing through the window at Jacob. When he caught her eye, she quickly began shuffling papers on her desk.

"Please sit down." Principal McManis took a seat behind his desk, still avoiding Jacob's eyes. He took a drink from his *#1 Educator* mug, set it down, and rubbed his thumb along the rim, wiping away something Jacob couldn't see.

Was McManis waiting for him to speak or just buying himself time?

"Look," Jacob said, "whatever you think I did, it must have been someone else. You know I would never—"

"This isn't…" McManis paused. "I'm—there was an accident."

Jacob stared at his principal. If there was an accident, why was he in trouble?

"I'm afraid I have some bad news," the principal said, studying his hands. "Your father was found in a hotel room. They aren't sure yet how it happened." He finally met Jacob's eyes. "I'm afraid he's gone."

Jacob's heart stopped. His brain started to scream. All of the bones in his body burned. McManis was still talking, but Jacob couldn't make out the words over the screaming in his head.

A sharp *snap* slammed into his ears right before the windows in the office exploded, sending shards of glass everywhere. The shrieking in his mind was punctured by more glass breaking, more windows flying apart. He stared down at the bits of glass shimmering on the floor.

He gasped as the principal knocked him to the ground, covering Jacob with his own body. Other screams echoed in the distance. It took Jacob a moment to figure out the panicked screaming wasn't in his head. As the fire alarms started wailing,

Jacob tried to push himself up to see what was happening, but Principal McManis forced him back down.

Voices cut through the mayhem as teachers tried to calm their students. Students shouted for help, not knowing what to do.

The principal cursed. "Stay here, Jacob. Do not leave this room until a fireman or I tell you to. Got it?" McManis didn't wait for an answer as he shoved Jacob under the desk.

The shattered pieces of the *#1 Educator* mug cut into Jacob's palms, and the smell of spilled coffee filled the air. The coffee puddle was warm, and he watched with fascination as his red blood mixed with the brown liquid.

Jacob listened to Principal McManis order a school lockdown. The *thud* of doors slamming shut echoed down the hall. A few moments later, McManis's voice came back over the speakers, saying to evacuate as quickly as possible. A school with broken windows couldn't be locked down.

Jacob waited in the office for McManis. A few minutes passed before the principal returned for Jacob and led him outside to the rest of his class. Jacob was almost grateful for the confusion when the fire trucks arrived. No one stopped him or asked if he was all right. He blended perfectly into the chaos.

The emergency workers set up triage sites for the injured, but no one had been badly hurt. A few students needed stitches, and some were so panicked they had to be sedated, but there were no real injuries.

The police bomb squad swept through the building but found nothing. They checked for a gas leak, but the lines all seemed to be in good working order. The rumblings in the crowd said the police were at a loss to explain how every piece of glass in the building had shattered. No one was allowed to leave.

At what should have been dinnertime, all of the students' parents who had rushed to the school brought them food. But Jacob had no one who cared that his school had apparently been *attacked by terrorists*. At least that's what the news reporter nearest him told her viewers at home. A woman from a church group gave Jacob water, food, and a blanket at about nine o'clock in the evening, and he was too tired to refuse.

Finally, the police said they'd gathered all the information they needed, which was none at all, and that they would be in touch with updates.

Jacob started to walk home. Principal McManis's booming voice carried over the crowd, calling Jacob back, but he kept walking. Social Services would come for him soon enough.

The lights were off in the house, but Jacob was used to that. He was used to being alone. He opened the creaky door and sat down on the couch. This may not have been a happy home, but it was the only one he knew. He looked around the living room. The dingy wallpaper peeled away at the corners. A faint scent of dust and damp hung in the air. Jacob kept the house clean, but Jim never gave him the money to fix anything. The couch he sat on was older than he was. The stained fabric glistened in places where the springs were beginning to wear through.

He should be doing something. Like planning a funeral. But he didn't even know where Jim's body was. Not that he had the money to pay for a funeral anyway. Sleep. He needed sleep. Everything else could be handled tomorrow.

Jacob climbed the stairs to his room. Out of habit, he looked into Jim's room. It was the same as it had been that morning with the bed still untouched. For some reason, Jacob had expected it to look different, as though permanent absence would leave a visible mark. He pulled Jim's door closed and went to his own bed.

He didn't even remember closing his eyes, but a steady tapping that echoed through the empty house pulled him back out of sleep. He dragged the blanket the woman from the church group had given him over his head. He wanted sleep, not social workers.

But the tapping continued. It sounded closer than the front door. Maybe it was hail. No, the sound was too regular for hail.

Jacob sat up and looked blearily around his room. The sound came from the window. A figure crouched outside, tapping lightly to wake him up.

THE MANSION HOUSE

*J*acob tossed off the blanket, ran to the window, and
threw it open.

And there she was. Emilia Gray.

She pushed herself through the window and threw her arms
around Jacob's neck. "Jacob," she said, her voice full of pain and
concern. "I'm so sorry."

Jacob froze for a moment, unsure if he was actually awake,
until the cool night air whispered through Emilia's hair, carrying
with it the soft scent of lilacs. "Emi?" he whispered, wrapping his
arms around her. She felt warm and incredibly real.

She pulled away to look him in the eye. "I came as soon as I
heard everything that happened. Are you all right?"

"I'm—" Jacob reached up and touched Emilia's face, brushing
a strand of long black hair from her forehead. "You're here?" His
voice sounded raw. "Are you really here?"

"I'm really here," Emilia said. "I came back for you. I promised
I would. Jacob, I'm sorry."

He pulled her into his arms and buried his face in her hair,
trying hard to remember how to breathe. She hadn't changed

that much. Her hair was long and black, and her eyes were misty grey. She was taller now but still her. Still perfect.

"Are you okay?" Emilia whispered.

"I'm fine." Jacob pulled away and ran a hand through his hair, trying to stop his head from spinning. "I think I might be in shock or something. I'm so used to Jim being gone. I guess I just don't understand that he isn't coming back. Is that weird?"

"I don't think so."

"How did you know?" Jacob asked. "How did you know about Jim so fast? I mean, I only found out this morning."

"I know, and I know this is an awful time. But I had to come now before it was too late."

"He's dead. I don't think there's really a time crunch," Jacob said with a hoarse laugh. The laugh caught in his throat and turned unexpectedly into a sob. He tried to breathe, but it only made the sobs louder.

Emilia pulled him over to the bed and curled up in the corner, putting Jacob's head on her shoulder.

Jacob didn't know how long he had cried, but he hurt everywhere. He hurt like he had run a marathon. His throat was dry, and his eyes stung. He stayed sitting next to Emilia on the bed. She had held him as he cried for losing the father who was never there. As Emilia reached up to wipe a tear from his cheek, he vowed he would never cry for Jim again. It was over. Jim was gone.

Jacob took a deep breath. "Thank you." He looked down at Emilia's hand holding his.

"I'm so sorry, but we can't stay here." She silenced Jacob's protest. "I didn't come here because of your father. I came to get you. Just like I promised I would. It's time now," she said slowly. "I am so sorry about Jim, but I need you to come with me."

Something wasn't right. Emilia was here in his room. They were together, but she looked worried. Almost frightened.

"I came because of what happened at your school. What you did to your school."

Jacob shook his head as her words sank in. "Is that what the police are saying? I was with Principal McManis when it happened. It wasn't me." Panic crept into his chest. He looked around his bedroom, sure the police were going to break in at any moment to arrest him.

"The police think it was some sort of terrorist attack. I love how they can invent logical explanations for just about anything." Emilia pulled Jacob back when he started toward the window to look for police cars. "They don't suspect you at all."

Jacob searched Emilia's eyes, unsure if he should be relieved or more afraid. Who else but the police would come for him?

"But we know you did it," Emilia said. "You broke all those windows. Well, every piece of glass in the building actually."

"What do you mean I broke the windows?"

"Jacob. You are special. Different, like me. You have abilities you don't understand, but when you're upset—"

"What are you talking about?"

"Magic, Jacob. Wizardry, sorcery, *maleficium*, whatever you want to call it. I'm a witch, you're a wizard, and we need to get out of here."

Jacob stared at Emilia. He ran his hand over her cheek.

She grabbed his hand. "Jacob, I'm real. And this is real. There is a whole world out there. A magical world. But you have to decide right now if you want to be a part of it. There are things in my world that are beyond your imagination, but if you come with me, you can never go back to being normal. You can never come back here."

"Emi." Jacob shook his head. "This is crazy."

She brought his hand between them. It was covered in small cuts from shards of McManis's mug. His hand warmed in her grasp. Not unpleasantly so, but as though it were submerged in warm water. Then his skin tingled and stung. The places where the skin had been broken became almost iridescent. Finally, the glow subsided, and the cuts started to fade. After a few seconds, his hand had completely healed.

"It is real." Emilia stared into Jacob's eyes. "Will you come with me?"

Get your copy of The Tethering *to continue Jacob and Emilia's story.*

ABOUT THE AUTHOR

Megan O'Russell is the author of several Young Adult series that invite readers to escape into worlds of adventure. From *Girl of Glass*, which blends dystopian darkness with the heart-pounding danger of vampires, to *Ena of Ilbrea*, which draws readers into an epic world of magic and assassins.

With the *Girl of Glass* series, *The Tethering* series, *The Chronicles of Maggie Trent*, *The Tale of Bryant Adams*, the *Ena of Ilbrea* series, and several more projects planned for 2020, there are always exciting new books on the horizon. To be the first to hear about new releases, free short stories, and giveaways, sign up for Megan's newsletter by visiting the following:

https://www.meganorussell.com/book-signup.

Originally from Upstate New York, Megan is a professional musical theatre performer whose work has taken her across North America. Her chronic wanderlust has led her from Alaska to Thailand and many places in between. Wanting to travel has fostered Megan's love of books that allow her to visit countless new worlds from her favorite reading nook. Megan is also a lyricist and playwright. Information on her theatrical works can be found at RussellCompositions.com.

She would be thrilled to chat with you on Facebook or

Twitter @MeganORussell, elated if you'd visit her website MeganORussell.com, and over the moon if you'd like the pictures of her adventures on Instagram @ORussellMegan.

ALSO BY MEGAN O'RUSSELL

The Girl of Glass Series
Girl of Glass
Boy of Blood
Night of Never
Son of Sun

The Tale of Bryant Adams
How I Magically Messed Up My Life in Four Freakin' Days
Seven Things Not to Do When Everyone's Trying to Kill You
Three Simple Steps to Wizarding Domination

The Tethering Series
The Tethering
The Siren's Realm
The Dragon Unbound
The Blood Heir

The Chronicles of Maggie Trent
The Girl Without Magic
The Girl Locked With Gold
The Girl Cloaked in Shadow

Ena of Ilbrea
Wrath and Wing
Ember and Stone
Mountain and Ash

Ice and Sky

Feather and Flame

<u>Guilds of Ilbrea</u>

Inker and Crown

Manufactured by Amazon.ca
Bolton, ON

25926811R00150